GRAND SLAM

Also by Heidi McLaughlin

Third Base
Home Run

GRAND SLAM

HEIDI McLAUGHLIN

FOREVER

New York   Boston

Forever
Hachette Book Group
1290 Avenue of the Americas
New York, NY 10104
forever-romance.com
twitter.com/foreverromance

Originally published in ebook by Forever in May 2017.
First Trade Edition: August 2017

Forever is an imprint of Grand Central Publishing.
The Forever name and logo are trademarks of Hachette Book Group, Inc.
The publisher is not responsible for websites (or their content) that are not owned by the publisher.

The Hachette Speakers Bureau provides a wide range of authors for speaking events. To find out more, go to www.hachettespeakersbureau.com or call (866) 376-6591.

Library of Congress Cataloging-in-Publication Data
Names: McLaughlin, Heidi (Romance fiction writer) author.
Title: Grand slam / Heidi McLaughlin.
Description: First Trade Edition. | New York ; Boston : Forever, 2017. |
Series: The boys of summer ; 3
Identifiers: LCCN 2017008726| ISBN 9781455598311 (paperback) | ISBN 9781455598304 (ebook) | ISBN 9781478975274 (audio download)
Subjects: LCSH: Man-woman relationships--Fiction. | Baseball players--Fiction. | BISAC: FICTION / Romance / Contemporary. | FICTION / Contemporary Women. | GSAFD: Love stories.
Classification: LCC PS3613.C57535 G73 2017 | DDC 813/.6--dc23
LC record available at https://lccn.loc.gov/2017008726

ISBN: 978-1-4555-9831-1 (trade pbk.), 978-1-4555-9830-4 (ebook)

Printed in the United States of America

LSC-C

10 9 8 7 6 5 4 3 2 1

Happy Birthday, Grandma

ACKNOWLEDGMENTS

I want to thank the Chicago Cubs for giving me one of the most exciting World Series ever! The late nights were so worth it.

Thanks to my dad for giving me the tools to love and understand the game of baseball.

Thank you to Yvette and Amy for being my sounding board with Travis and for laughing hysterically each time I dropped one of his one-liners.

Thank you to my agent, Marisa. I appreciate everything that you do for me on a daily basis. The Boys of Summer wouldn't be possible without you.

Alex, thank you for everything. You guide me through frustration, teach me how to be a better writer, and understand when I have a meltdown on one particular day. I am forever grateful to have you in my life.

Madison and Kassidy, you both are my light. Being your mom is the best job I could ever have.

Thank you to all the readers and bloggers who have supported the

Renegades from day one! I hope that the journey was worth it.

My dedication is to my grandma, who would've celebrated her birthday on release day. I can't imagine a sweeter gift to her. I only wish she were here to receive it.

GRAND SLAM

ONE

Travis

The one I'm eyeing for the night bends at her waist and lines her pool stick up with the cue ball. She slowly pulls the wooden rod through her fingers until the felt top finally connects. The hard, white plastic ball rolls toward her target, hitting it perfectly and stalling as the blue-striped ball rolls into the pocket. I let out a massive sigh and lean on my stick, waiting my turn. I should've known better when she approached me, asking if I wanted to play a game or two of billiards with her. I know better than to let a good-looking woman hustle me out of money, but I wasn't thinking with my right head. I never am, and once again I'm getting my balls busted, no pun intended, by a pool shark.

"Sweetheart, are you going to let me play? My balls are getting lonely." If she thinks I'm crude, she doesn't say anything. In fact, she looks at me from over her shoulder and winks before shimmying her ass toward my crotch. My internal groan is epic. For almost an hour, she's been leaning over, licking her lips, showing her ample cleavage, and shaking her ass. Not to mention, she brushes against me each time she passes me. And the touching isn't subtle. I can read her loud and clear, all the way from her tight-as-sin jeans to her plunging neckline.

"I can't help it if you suck."

"Do you?" I ask, stepping in behind her. My crotch is lined up perfectly with her backside, earning me another hair-tossing look over her shoulder.

She stands and turns to face me, sitting her ass on the edge of the table. "What do you have in mind?" Her finger trails down the front of my shirt until she reaches the buckle of my belt. The tug is slight, but definitely felt. Message received loud and clear.

"What's your name?"

"Are names important?"

"Of course. When I demand that you come for me, I need to know what to call you."

"Demand?" she questions.

"I'm greedy like that," I tell her, placing my cue stick against the table as I step closer to her. I lean in and try to get a whiff of her perfume, but a mix between the stale air from the bar and the beer on her breath makes it hard to tell what she's wearing. I do love a woman who takes the time to add the perfect scent on her skin, though.

"Blue."

"My balls aren't blue, darling, and haven't been in years."

"No, my name is Blue."

"That's a very unique name," I say as my hand rests on her hip.

"What can I say? I'm a unique woman, Travis."

Ah, she knows my name. That's usually how things go for me. Rarely am I given the opportunity to introduce myself. Everyone knows who I am, and while I enjoy the fruits of my labor, sometimes anonymity would be nice. One day, I'd like to talk to a woman who doesn't know that I'm Travis Kidd, left fielder for the Boston Renegades and one of the town's most eligible bachelors. "You know who I am?"

"Doesn't everyone? I'm a Boston girl; I know my Renegades."

I nod and reach for my beer. It's the off-season, and technically I shouldn't be here. I usually head south for the winter but opted to stay home this time. After a long season, one that saw my former manager die and one of my closest friends on the team become a dad to twins, I thought I'd stay around and see what the winter had to offer. Aside from the cold, I haven't found much, except Bruins hockey and Celtics basketball. Those games have been the highlight of my time off.

The pickings for women have been slim. Without trying to bag on the female population, it's evident that they're seasonal as well. Right now, the puck bunnies, gridiron groupies, and court whores are in full effect, and the cleat-chasers are resting like the rest of the baseball world. Maybe I should've been a dual-sport athlete. That way I would've had the best of both worlds.

"Travis?"

"What?" I ask, mentally shaking the cobwebs out.

"Where'd you go? It's your turn." Blue nods toward the table, and I look over her shoulder to see the cue ball sitting there.

"Why don't you help me?" I know how to play the game of pool, but since she seems to be a pro, why shouldn't she show me? I would've happily slid up behind her and taught her how to handle her stick, but she took the fun out of it.

Instead, she's off to my side and leaning into me, giving me a perfect sideways glance down her shirt. I smirk, ignoring everything she tells me, and watch as her mounds of flesh move each time her hand does. They're real, that's for sure. None of that fake silicone shit on this chick.

"And that's how it's done," she says, righting herself. She contin-ues to slightly lean over the table, though, jutting her chest out for me to ogle. I cock my head to the side and wink before taking aim at the cue on the table.

My first shot goes in, and the second quickly follows. I line up the third and fire, and that is when I see a raven-haired beauty nursing a drink at the bar.

Saylor Blackwell is off-limits to anyone her agency represents. That includes me. Although I wish it didn't. I would have switched man-agers to be with her if she asked me to, but I fucked that up. When she needed me, I wasn't there. And I haven't spoken to her since.

It's my dumb luck that she's sitting at the bar with her long, slen-der legs crossed. She's dressed like she recently got off work, and her eyes are set on the television, ignoring the gaggle of men staring at her. I remember that she was a hard nut to crack back when I wanted to know her better. I can't imagine what she's like now that she's even more successful.

My last shot is sunk into the corner pocket. "Eight ball, right side," I say, nodding in the same direction I plan to send the black ball in order to finish this game. I'm in a rush now, eager to speak with Say-lor. I know I shouldn't but I can't help myself.

"Where ya going?" Blue calls out.

"To the bar. Rack 'em," I tell her. It's not a lie. I am going to the bar, but with the intention of speaking to another woman. I'm smooth, though, and I can easily play it off while I order another round of drinks.

"Two, please." I put up two fingers as I motion toward the barten-der. Leaning in, I know I'm blocking Saylor's view of the television, which is all in my game plan. "Hey, Saylor."

"Travis," she says coldly. I often remember the night we spent together and the regret that was on her face when we were done. Even though we were at my house, I wanted to leave. I had never felt so uncomfortable after getting laid. Everything was awkward, from the way she spoke to how fast she dressed and ran out of my place. Rarely do I bring women home, opting for theirs so I can bail, but Saylor was different. I still can't get that night out of my mind, and it's been almost two years. With Saylor, everything was backward. It's like she used me to scratch an itch, and once I took care of that, she didn't need me anymore. "What brings you in?"

She looks everywhere but at me. "I'm meeting a client."

"And nursing your what?" I take her drink from her hand and sniff. "Scotch? When did you start drinking the hard shit?"

That gets her to look at me. Her glare is deadly as it penetrates mine. "As if you know anything about me."

"I know enough."

"You don't know shit, Travis Kidd. Go back to your booty call. She's looking at me like she's ready for a catfight, and I assure you, you're not worth fighting for."

Saylor turns, giving me the cold shoulder. If I weren't so stunned by her outburst, which I did not deserve, I'd tease her. But there's obviously something bothering her, and I'm the last person she needs making shit worse.

With the bottles of beer dangling between my fingers, I go back to the pool table where Blue is indeed throwing daggers at Saylor's back.

"Down, kitty. She works for my manager." I run my hand down her arm, trying to defuse the situation. Jealous women usually turn me off, and this should be my sign to hit the road, except I'm an idiot and want to stay mostly so I can watch Saylor.

Taking Blue by her hand, I lead us over to the stools, and I sit down, pulling her between my legs. My hand is planted firmly on her leg right under her butt cheek. It's a risky move, given all the nosey Renegades fans who are always around, but I don't care right now. It's the off-season. I'm allowed to have a little bit of fun.

"You have nothing to be jealous over," I tell her.

"Okay."

"We good? Wanna go back to kicking my ass at pool?"

She looks over at the table and nods. "You rack, and I'll break." Blue saunters away, giving me space to watch Saylor, who turns and makes eye contact with me. I wish I could tell what she's thinking. Is she second-guessing her harsh words? I am. I want to go back over and offer to pick up her tab. Or ask how she's getting home. It's late, and the roads are shit. If she's driving, she shouldn't be drinking. She has a kid that depends on her.

"I'm ready," Blue says seductively. The tone of her words catches me off guard. It's hard to decipher if she's ready to play another game or two of pool. I hope that's what she means because I have no intention of leaving as long as Saylor is at the bar. Or is Blue ready for me to fuck her and never ask for her number? Because that is bound to happen as well.

I break, sending the balls off in every direction. Four drop. Two of each, giving me the choice of what I want to be. Blue is yammering in my ear about the setup and which would be the best. Her angles only work for her, though, and I see that I can run the table on her if I line up correctly.

"We should've bet," I tell her as I walk around the table.

"I'd hate to hustle you out of your money, Travis."

I laugh off her comment and proceed to clear the table. She huffs when the eight ball falls into the designated pocket.

"Well, would you look at that," I say, taking a bow. Blue pushes me lightly and falls into my arms. Her lips are on mine before I can push her away, and doing so now would be embarrassing for her, so I kiss her back and find myself opening my eyes to watch Saylor watch me.

As soon as I pull away, Saylor is sliding off the bar stool and heading toward the door.

"Be right back. I need some fresh air." A true gentleman would've invited his lady friend outside, but that is not who I am.

"Do you need a ride home?" I ask as soon as I see Saylor standing near the curb. "And what happened to your client?"

"He canceled."

It didn't strike me as odd earlier when she said she was meeting a client, but it does now. I've never met anyone from the agency at a bar, let alone this late at night.

"How about that ride home?"

"Travis." She draws out my name and then drops her head into her hands. Without thinking, I pull her into my side. "Come on, Saylor. It's a ride. Nothing else."

"What the hell is going on? I thought you were taking me home." Blue speaks loud enough for everyone on the block to hear.

My arm drops, and Saylor steps away from me. I turn at the sound of Blue's voice behind me.

"I'll be in. Give me a minute." I smile, hoping to placate Blue, but it doesn't work.

"I see some things never change," Saylor says as she steps off the curb and waves at a cab, only to be passed by.

Shaking my head, I push my hands into my pockets for a bit of warmth. If I knew Saylor would be out here when I returned, I'd run in and grab my jacket. "It's not like that."

"What, do you like her or something?" The sound of Blue's voice grates on my nerves.

Saylor looks over my shoulder and rolls her eyes.

"Or something," I say, without taking my eyes off Saylor.

As soon as a taxi pulls up to the curb, Saylor is sliding in.

I make a split-second decision to get in with her, but not before Blue yells at me. "Where the fuck are you going?"

I answer her by slamming the door shut. I have Blue on the outside screaming and Saylor looking at me like she's going to kill me. Saylor opens the door, and I hear Blue say, "Fuck you, Travis Kidd. You'll pay for this." And before I realize what's happening, Saylor is standing outside the cab. When we drive off, my tongue is tied, and I watch through the back window as Saylor disappears the farther I get down the road.

TWO

Saylor

My phone vibrates repeatedly on my kitchen counter, causing it to move as if there were an army of ants underneath it. I glance at the clock on my microwave before picking it up. The motto at work is that it's never too early to start working. Unfortunately, being a single mom, that isn't how I can function. My daughter comes first, and my employer is very aware of this fact.

Except this morning seems to be different. A quick swipe and his text message, along with numerous others from my co-workers, appears on my screen. The message is simple: Get to work ASAP. That's code for something, and likely something has happened to one of our clients. It could be anything from a Good Samaritan deed, the birth of a child, a divorce, or the type of publicity I don't like to deal with, accusations for rape, murder, and the like.

Being a public relations specialist has its perks. If I want to attend a sporting event, I call my client. If I need to woo the pants off a prospective client, I set them up with a luxury suite at whatever game they want to attend. And as with any job, it also has a downside. My hours are long, the job is never ending, and sometimes I feel like a babysitter. But I wouldn't trade what I do for anything. My clients and co-workers have become my family.

Lucy, my five-year-old daughter, comes sashaying into the room, dressed as her favorite princess for her school's character festival today. Her blue Cinderella dress is one that we bought last year from Disneyland, along with her matching tiara.

"Well, don't you look like a pretty princess?" Crouching down so we're eye level, I push a lock of hair back up into the bun she attempted to do on her own.

"Cinderella doesn't have brown hair," Lucy tells me.

"No, I suppose she doesn't, but that's the best part about make-believe. You can make her look like anything you want."

The smile she gives me feels like I've won Mother of the Year, even though I feel far from it. I struggle emotionally when it comes to Lucy. Her father, my ex, has wanted nothing to do with her until yesterday. I haven't heard a peep from him since the day I told him I was pregnant, and now he's asking to see her. It would be easy to say yes and give Lucy the answers to all her questions. Hell, I want answers, too. I'm like her. I want to know why her father hasn't wanted to see her. But I don't trust him. If he could so easily dismiss her before she was born, what's to say he won't do the same after he meets her?

Deep down, I feel it has to do with his wife and the family they've started. Some of my clients are in constant battles with their exes, and it's never pretty. Most importantly, I want to know why now, after all this time, he's interested in Lucy.

"Have you brushed your teeth?" Lucy nods. "Okay, let's get ready to go." I kiss her on her nose before she runs off. I can hear her singing "Bibbidi-Bobbidi-Boo" and getting only a few of the words right.

Slipping my phone into my messenger bag, my hand brushes against the envelope that brought me to my knees yesterday. I intercepted the handwritten letter about Lucy that has the power to ruin everything I've built. I thought I could go to the bar and seek comfort in an old friend, but I was mistaken. Holding the glass with two fingers of Scotch only reminded me of the hell I've been through. I purposely ordered liquor that I can't stomach, hoping that it'd curb my desire to drink. It didn't. A man in the bar did.

Once I saw Travis Kidd standing next to me, I knew I had to get out of there. He's trouble—he knows it, and I know it. I've been down this road with him before, and I've determined that he's not worth my career. One mistake with him led to a long line of legal troubles for me. My employment agreement states that I will stay away from the athletes, despite how appealing they can be, and the indiscretion with Travis nearly cost me everything.

Lucy comes out of her room, ready to go. Her tiara has been replaced with a knit cap to keep her head warm, and her fingers are covered in mittens. It's chilly, but not overly cold at the moment. Although the cold weather is right around the corner, and that isn't something I'm looking forward to. Winters in Boston can be brutal.

Walking hand in hand, Lucy and I make our way to her school. It's only a few blocks from our apartment and close to the subway, which makes it easy for me to get to work, because my office is only two stops away. I remind Lucy that her grandmother will pick her up from school today and tell her to be good before I make sure she's in the hands of her teacher.

Now that she's in school, my mode switches to work. With my phone in hand, I've quickly become one of those people who walk and text at the same time. I look up periodically to make sure I'm not about to be run over or, better yet, crash into someone while I answer what feels like a hundred messages.

As soon as I step into the office, the assistant I share with my boss takes my coat and bag and tells me that my boss is waiting. Stepping into Jeffrey Tay's office is like walking into a sports museum. His walls are covered with pictures of him and most of his clients. Jeffrey motions for me to sit down as he continues his phone call. He pinches the bridge of his nose while pacing back and forth, agreeing to whatever is being said on the other line.

"Fuck," he roars, throwing his headset across the room. The somewhat flimsy product lands with a loud thump against the wall, causing me to jump. Jeffrey faces the large window that overlooks the Boston Harbor and laces his fingers behind his head. By the shudder in his shoulders, I can tell he's let out a sigh or maybe even two. "Travis Kidd needs our help."

The mere mention of Travis's name has me feeling uneasy and uncrossing and crossing my legs to find a bit of comfort. While Jeffrey continues to stare out the window, last night's encounter runs through my mind. Nothing I said last night, or any actions on my part, could be construed as a violation of my employment contract. Only my actions years earlier, but I've kept those under wraps.

Then I remember what Jeffrey said, and that Travis Kidd needs *our* help, and that seems to quell a bit of the building anxiety. He's done something that has Jeff visibly upset, which means it's going to be a lot of work for me. But it means that my secret is still safe.

I'm afraid to ask what he's done. The list running through my mind right now is a mile long. It could be drinking and driving, although I saw him get into the cab last night and watched it leave. Assault is always a possibility. Or maybe he was drunker than I thought and he wound up walking into the wrong house. It's bound to happen and, unfortunately, is an action we, in the business of sports management, have had to deal with, especially in the off-season.

Regardless of the situation or how I feel about this particular client, I have a job, and I take immense pride in it.

"What's he done?" I almost add "this time" to the end of my question but that would be unfair to Travis. Yes, he's wild and a publicity nightmare but he's rarely in trouble. I can usually put a positive spin on his actions, and while some may be questionable, I make him look like a saint. I was able to turn one of his dumbest ideas—of opening a kissing booth outside of Faneuil Hall and charging five dollars—into a massive fund-raiser for the children's hospital. Even though he gave me little warning, one phone call to the local radio station had women lining up for hours. The donations poured in, and at the end of the night, he was the town's hero again.

Jeffrey turns, and the turmoil on his face tells me that it's something bad. Reaching for the pad of paper and a pen that I see on his desk, I prepare to take notes.

"That was Irvin Abbott on the phone."

"Travis's lawyer?" I ask, interrupting Jeffrey.

Jeffrey makes eye contact quickly, telling me that he doesn't appreciate the interruption. "He called to let me know that Kidd voluntarily went to the police station after being visited this morning. It seems that he's being accused of rape."

I swallow hard as I listen to Jeffrey's words. That means that Travis went somewhere else last night. The woman he was with at the bar seemed rather put off that he was speaking to me. I can't imagine she would have given him the time of day after the way he brushed her off.

Jeffrey sighs, running his hand through his hair before sitting down and resting his face in his hands.

"This isn't our first accusation of rape," I remind him, although it's the first for Travis.

"No, it's not, but this is Travis Kidd. His antics alone, his habits and the lifestyle he leads, have made him a prime suspect, and according to Abbott, the district attorney is ready to throw the book at him. You can bet that the media will be all over this. The DA is always looking to have his face in front of the cameras."

"Was he arrested?"

Jeffrey shakes his head. "Not yet, according to Abbott. He got the call from Kidd and went right there. He called me on the way, telling me what he knew. Kidd is saying he's innocent and has an alibi who can testify that he left the bar by himself."

My throat swells, and my palms begin to sweat. "Did he say who?" I croak through my question. Relief washes over me as Jeffrey shakes his head. I may have been in the cab with Travis but didn't stay, and the woman at the bar got into a car before I walked off. That doesn't mean he didn't circle back, though. And that doesn't mean I'm his alibi.

"Abbott indicated that Kidd wants to speak to this person before he gives the police their name."

"And I gather the police aren't that easily swayed?"

Jeffrey's lips go into a fine line as he shakes his head. "Unfortunately no." He stands and moves to the far wall, looking at the framed images. "I need you to go down there for the press conferences. The DA is hungry. It's an election year, and Kidd handed him the case of the decade. Abbott is planning his own press conference to plead Kidd's case to the public. The people of Boston

love him, and we need the fan support. Stand with Abbott and protect Kidd."

As much as I want to tell Jeffrey no, I can't, it's my job, despite
how I feel about this particular client. What Travis and I shared was
a mistake, and I vowed to never let anything like that happen again.
I've made good on my promise, and I refuse to let anything come between my job and me.

I'm excused from Jeffrey's office and head to my own. I don't have
much time to do anything except ask my assistant to clear my schedule for the day. A quick glance at my calendar tells me that it's five
meetings that she'll have to move, three of which are new clients. I
ask her to reschedule them for tomorrow and make the necessary
travel arrangements for those who aren't local.

Jeffrey was right. By the time I reach the police station, the media
is lingering around, waiting for someone to come out and talk to
them. My name is called out, asking for a comment as I pass by, and
I ignore each and every reporter. They know better than to ask, but
they wouldn't be doing their job if they didn't. I run smack into Paul
Boyd from ESPN, falling off-balance until he catches me.

"Thanks, Paul," I say, straightening my clothes. I offer him a soft
smile and sidestep to go by him.

"Hold up, Saylor." I shake my head and take another step toward
the entrance, only to be halted.

"What do you know?"

This is where the sports business is tricky. If I need something to
be leaked, I make a few phone calls, and any one of my clients is
front-page news. The media wants something in return, so they expect the same from me. I can't work like that. The privacy of my
clients is first and foremost for me.

"You know I can't say anything, Paul."

"Did he do it?"

I look away, fearful that my eyes will tell him something when my mind and heart mean something else. "Wait for Abbott's press conference."

"Wait—we were told only the DA is making a statement."

I look over Paul's shoulder and frown. It seems as if the state is already trying to manipulate the news with only one sports outlet being on-site.

"Abbott's having one. Spread the word for me, okay?"

"What's in it for me?"

This is the nature of the beast in this business. You scratch my back, and I'll scratch yours. Pushing my hands deep into my jacket pockets, I shrug. "You can have the first public interview that Kidd gives."

I don't wait for Paul to agree before making my way up the last few stairs to enter the police station. The desk sergeant knows why I'm here and motions for me to walk down the hall after telling me they're in room five. I knock and enter. Both Travis and Abbott's eyes are on me.

"Travis is in trouble," Abbott says. Those are the last words I expected to hear when I walked in.

THREE

Travis

If there is one thing I've learned from my former coaches, it's to always be honorable. To show respect, even in situations where it may not be shown toward me in return. I may not always be this way, especially when it comes to women, but you can bet your ass I am when it comes to Boston's finest. So when I answered someone knocking on my front door and the man dressed in a suit introduces himself as Detective Hook and asks for a minute of my time, I let him in.

Maybe if I had known what he wanted when he was standing on my stoop, I wouldn't be here right now. Here, being the Boston precinct, where people who were in the drunk tank are calling my name out, and the officers I pass are asking what my predictions will be for next season.

Detective Hook leads me down the hall and into a box-shaped room. Now, in the off-season, I watch a lot of television, with crime shows being my favorite, and I can tell you that this interrogation room looks nothing like the ones in Hollywood. It's dark, drab, and doesn't even have a small window. Also missing is the two-way glass I'd really like to see.

Hook motions for me to sit down and pulls out his chair. I cringe at the sound of the metal legs scraping against the flooring. As I sit in the metal chair with a ripped seat cushion that is missing half the foam insert, the errant pieces of vinyl dig into my legs through my track pants. In hindsight, I probably should've changed my clothes or grabbed something to eat before coming here.

"Mr. Kidd, I want to first thank you for coming down here."

"Please, call me Travis."

Hook nods, opens his folder, and silently reads over a sheet of paper before closing the folder. He pushes it aside, and then he slides a yellow legal pad in front of him, folding his hands, while smiling at me. It's all very mechanical, and if I didn't know better, I'd think this is a speed-dating course. I did that once for the hell of it. Some guy taught us how to pick up chicks in under three minutes. I don't know if it was successful or not. Most of the women figured out who I was and rang their bell.

"Travis, I'm going to ask you a few questions, and please remember that you can leave at any time. Can you tell me where you were last night around eleven thirty?"

I scratch my head, not out of confusion, but habit. "I think I was home."

"You think?" Hook picks up the pen that is sitting next to the folder and leans back in his chair. He depresses the button repeatedly, filling the room with that annoying clicking noise.

As if it's an automatic response, my shoulders shrug, and I nod.

"But you're not sure?" Hook sets his pen down and folds his hands together.

By the way he's looking at me, something in the back of my mind is telling me that I really shouldn't be here, that volunteering to come down to the station to chat was a mistake.

"Am I in some sort of trouble?"

"Travis, do you know Rachel Ward?" Hook asks. As I shake my head, he opens the folder and pulls out an image, sliding it over to me with his finger pinning it to the table.

"I met her last night, but uh…she introduced herself as Blue."

"Blue?"

"Yeah, we shot a few games of pool. Had some beer."

"Anything else?"

This is where you keep your mouth shut, Kidd. "We kissed a little."

"And where did you take Ms. Ward when you left the bar?"

I shake my head. "Nowhere."

"Are you sure about that?"

"Yeah, I am. Did she say she was with me? Did she do something wrong?"

Hook takes the photo and places it back into his folder. "No, Travis. Ms. Ward went to the emergency room last night and informed the nurse that she had been raped…" Hook lets that sink in for a minute before he goes in for the kill. "By you."

My back pushes into my chair as if a bucket of bricks has been thrown at my chest. The imaginary force causes my breathing to labor and my fists to clench. I shake my head as I try to regain my composure. I didn't touch that woman once I left the bar. In fact, we never left the general bar area together, so how can she say something like this?

"Nah, man. She's lying. It wasn't me."

"Travis—"

I put my hand up to stop him. It's disrespectful, I know, but I'm not answering any more of his questions. "I think I need to wait for my lawyer." With his cold, dark eyes focusing on me, Hook picks up the folder and taps it a few times on the table before pushing his chair back. The nerve-grating sound of the legs pushing into the floor from his body weight sends a warning signal to me: *He's pissed and thinks I'm guilty of rape.*

———————◆———————

"Travis?"

My head pops up when I hear my name. Irvin walks in. Our eye contact is brief, and I can see it in his eyes. I know his question before he even has to say it, and I hate that I've put the doubt in his mind. "No, I didn't. I left by myself, but someone saw me leave."

Irvin sighs and sets his briefcase and jacket onto the table. "I already called Jeffrey. He's sending someone over."

"Why?" I ask. I don't see why my public relations manager needs to be involved. I didn't do anything wrong, so Irvin should be able to get everything taken care of, and I can be on my way.

"Because you're Travis Kidd and you're sitting in a police station. Whether you committed a crime or not, you're newsworthy, and the district attorney will use the media to his advantage to get them on his side."

"But I didn't *do* anything!" I say rather loudly with my hands in the air.

"They don't seem to think that's the case, Travis. I've already met with Detective Hook, and he's certain that the case he's building is going to be solid. He wants to talk."

I let my head fall forward, already feeling defeated. "So now what?"

Irvin sits down and pulls out his legal pad, much like the detective. "We're going to get your story, speak with Hook, and let Jeffrey's team take care of the media."

The door opens suddenly, and my eyes open wide as I take in Saylor, dressed similarly to the way I saw her last night, except now she's in work mode. I groan internally, wishing that Jeffrey would've come himself and not sent her.

"The media is preparing for something big. Jeffrey said you plan to speak on Travis's behalf after the DA gives his press conference?" Saylor states.

Saylor all but ignores me and focuses on Irvin. This is how things should be, right? The people I pay to protect me, doing their job?

"Of course. I'm not going to allow the DA to railroad my client," Irvin says, and she nods, finally looking at me, although it's brief.

There's a quick knock on the door, and Hook walks back in and takes a seat across from me and next to Saylor. There's a tinge of jealousy coursing through me that he gets to be next to her and I can't.

"Travis, now that you're in the company of your lawyer and—"

"My public relations team," I say, interrupting him.

"Right," he says, sighing. I'm sure he doesn't like dealing with athletes, but I have to protect every side of my life here, and the last thing I need is a scandal. Saylor can, and will, prevent that. "Tell me about last night."

Instantly, I look at Saylor, who peers down at the table, avoiding eye contact with me. I shake my head and start. "I met Blue while I was in the bar. We shot a few games of pool. I let her think she was hustling me, so she won a few games. We kissed a few times, but I ran into a friend, and when she left, I did as well."

"And Ms. Ward?"

I shrug. "I left her standing on the side of the road. I was more interested in my friend."

"And who is this friend?"

Once again I seek out Saylor. She shakes her head slightly, confusing me. "Um…"

"Do you know her name?" Hook asks as he slides the yellow legal pad over to me with a pen resting on top.

I can feel everyone's eyes on me, and I'm afraid to look back at Saylor out of fear that I'll give her away before we have a chance to talk about last night. "I need to talk to her first. I, uh…I can't do this to her without some warning."

"Do what, exactly?" Hook asks.

I wave my hand dismissively. "The attention that is sure to come with being tied to something like this."

"Travis, it'll help if you give them her name. We can protect her. Besides, she's not the one facing this accusation. You are, and let's face it, your reputation isn't going to help you here," Irvin says.

I process his words, knowing he's right. Another glance at Saylor, though, and I can see torment written all over her face. Something isn't right with her, and I want to know what it is.

"Was a rape kit done?" Irvin asks, steering the question away from me.

"Yes; we're waiting for the results."

"Great. Let us know when it comes in. Until then, we're done talking." Irvin and Saylor stand and motion for me to do as well. I follow them out and right into a media shit storm. The second the doors are opened, microphones are thrust into my face. The DA looks smug and pretentious as he glares at me.

Questions are thrown at me right and left, most of which I can't even comprehend. Every time I hear the word *rape*, I die a little on the inside. I don't have to force myself onto anyone, and I definitely know what *no* means.

Two police officers appear out of nowhere and try to put some distance between the crowd and us. Irvin holds his hand up, and microphones are pointed in his direction.

"We know you have questions, and while it seems that the state's attorney feels like he has an open-and-shut case, I assure you no charges have been filed. My client was here to answer questions and came in willingly. He was not, and has not been, arrested."

Irvin motions for us to leave. One of the officers leads us down the stairs while the other follows behind us. A black town car is waiting at the bottom of the steps for us to climb into. Once the door shuts, we speed off. While Saylor and Irvin talk about what happens next, my life, my career, and everything that I know flash before my eyes, and I don't like what I'm seeing.

FOUR

Saylor

While I'm busy with the sports media angle for Travis, I assume Abbott is doing the same, only on the legal side. Abbott and I have one common interest, and that is Travis. I'll work to keep his endorsement deals intact and make sure he's still given the same opportunities he would've been given days prior to the news breaking. Abbott should be working to prove that Travis is innocent, which I do believe he is.

Travis Kidd is a lot of things. He's a womanizer, a player, the quintessential bad boy, but never in a million years would I peg him for a rapist or a man who doesn't take no for an answer. In the years that I have known him, seen him in action so to speak, I've never witnessed him be forceful with anyone.

We pull up to the law office, and the media melee continues. Cameras are flashing before we even step out of the car. Abbott leads, with me following behind Travis. I remind him to keep his head down and mouth shut. The last thing I want is a sound bite of him spouting off with one of his one-liners. On a normal day, I welcome the media taking his comments and making memes and YouTube videos. Fans have a habit of keeping Travis, and my other clients, in their newsfeed, and today will definitely be one of those days. He will be a trending topic, and it won't be in a good way.

Abbott ushers Travis and me into a conference room, leaving us in here alone. I busy myself by making a cup of coffee. "Do you want a cup?" I ask with my back facing him.

"No."

I jump slightly at his tone, spilling some coffee not only on my hand but the cart as well. His demeanor shouldn't shock me. All it takes is one accusation to destroy a life. I can't let that happen. My next call will be to Ryan Stone, the general manager of the Boston Renegades. It's important that the organization stand behind their star left fielder.

"We need to talk, Saylor," he says, letting out a long sigh.

"I know." I turn and find him sitting at the end of the table with his head down and his hoodie pulled over his brown hair. "I don't want you to worry about the BoRes. I'll speak to Stone today. I promised Paul Boyd from ESPN that he would have your first interview. Once the rape kit comes back and you're cleared, we'll schedule that interview to take place in your home. We want the viewers to have sympathy for what you've gone through by the time this is all over."

"I don't care about any stupid interviews," he says. His voice is strained and laced with anger.

"Travis, I know things look grim right now, but—"

He lifts his head, and from across the room, I can feel his blue eyes, eyes that have seen every part of me, boring into mine and making me feel about two feet tall. My hand shakes as I set down my cup of coffee, afraid that I'm going to spill the hot liquid again if I don't.

"You know I didn't leave with that woman last night, Saylor."

"Travis, I—" He stands, effectively cutting my words off. I cover my face, shaking my head in the process. I know what I saw when I got out of that taxi, and I know that I could give him a witness, but it may not be enough. What if he doubled back?

"Listen to me, Saylor. I didn't rape that woman. I kissed her and may have touched her ass. But once I went outside with you, I never gave her a second thought. I got in that cab with you, and I know you watched me drive away, because I was watching you until I couldn't see anymore."

"What if you came back for her?"

Travis walks over to me. He's within arm's reach, causing me to step back. The more space between us, the better off I am. I made a mistake with him once. I will never do it again.

"If I did, why would I leave my car sitting at the bar?"

"Because you had been drinking."

He shakes his head. "Not enough to impair my driving abilities."

I used to think the same thing until I wrapped my car around a telephone pole and had to be cut out of it. I was lucky. I escaped with no major injuries, my life still intact, and a huge blemish on my driving record. Not to mention probation and the loss of my license and car, but at least I was still alive.

"Saylor, I need you to tell them that you were in that cab with me. Tell them the truth. Tell them what you saw and how she acted when I tried to leave with you."

Tears begin to form, blurring my vision. "I can't, Travis."

"Why not?" he asks, his arms flailing about in frustration.

"Because I'll lose everything."

He stares me down, making me feel like I'm the worst person in the world. Here he is, on the cusp of a crisis, feeling as if I'm the answer when I'm not. When I can't be. I have too much at stake, and while I know he does as well, he has lawyers at his disposal that can help him. I only have me.

Before Travis can say anything else, Irvin and his team come in. Each associate is poised and ready for action as they gather around the conference table, taking their respective seats. A plate of bagels, assorted cream cheeses, and bowls of fresh fruit are set in the middle, making my mouth water. My stomach growls, catching Travis's attention, and I watch while he reaches for some fruit. When he hands me the bowl, he does so with a smile. I know he's genuine, but at the end of the day, he's Travis Kidd, and that's not enough for me to jeopardize everything I've worked for.

"All right," Irvin says as he sits down, effectively breaking the trance that Travis has me under. "Travis, we need to go over your story."

He sits down and sighs. I'm tempted to fix him a bagel or get him a cup of coffee but I take my seat instead. The bowl of fruit mocks me, though. Travis did something nice for me, and I could easily return the favor. Except when I stand to do so, a young woman, who I would guess is an intern, is handing him everything he needs. She leans into him, brushing her breasts along his arm, and when he looks at what she's offering, a little piece of me dies on the inside. Not because I like him, but because he'll never learn. The man is facing a rape charge and he's gawking at this young woman's breasts.

"Tell me about last night," Irvin says, breaking Travis's concentration on the intern.

"I was bored and decided to hit the bar. I thought I'd play some darts, shoot a little pool, and wait for the hockey game to be let out."

"And Rachel Ward?"

Travis picks at his bagel, taking small bites. "She approached me, asked me if I wanted to play a few games with her. I bought a few rounds and let her hustle me for a game or two before I showed her I actually knew how to play pool."

"Did you kiss her? Take her to the bathroom for sex? What about touching?"

Travis frowns and holds his head in his hands before looking back at Irvin. "Lots of touching, but nothing close to having sex. She'd brush up against me or bend over to give me a view of her cleavage. I touched her butt. We kissed, once or twice. I don't really remember."

"You *need* to remember, Travis."

"I know," he says. "My mind last night—it was elsewhere. On someone else." He looks up and straight into my eyes. I deviate and take a sudden interest in what everyone else is doing. As I look around the table, everyone has their pens moving fluidly along their legal pads. A few scribble faster than others, flipping pages, drawing arrows, and adding sticky notes to the sides.

"On who? Is this the person you left with?" Irvin asks. He leans forward, knowing that this could break their case. I find myself doing the same, wondering if he's going to out me. Knowing that if he does, I could face jail time and lose my job.

"I need to speak with her before I can give anyone her name."

Irvin throws down his pen in frustration. "Travis, I need her name. I can subpoena her to testify."

Travis pushes his bagel away from him and folds his hands. "It's complicated. I'll talk to her. Besides, I didn't do this. Shouldn't the rape kit be enough to prove that?"

"Some rape kits come back inconclusive," an associate says. "We want a strong case moving forward, which is why we're getting all of this down now. It's fresh in your mind. When the DA submits their fact finding, we want to be prepared."

"Fine, so you left the bar with who?" Irvin sighs at the end of his question.

"The other woman, sort of."

"What do you mean, 'sort of'?" Irvin asks, his frustration level growing, which is evident by the veins in his forehead.

I have to bite my tongue to keep from speaking out. I hate knowing that I could have a say in this, but at what cost? Travis leans back in his chair and pushes his hoodie off. His hair is wild, crazy, and the exact reason the phrase *sex hair* was invented. I've seen this look on him before. I put it there.

"We both got in a cab together, leaving Rachel on the sidewalk. She yelled something about how I'm going to pay for this. My friend got out of the cab, though, before it could pull away."

"Where'd you go from there?"

"Home."

"Anyone witness you entering your house?" Irvin asks, while Travis shakes his head.

"Okay, how'd you get to the bar?"

"I drove."

"And where's your car now?"

"I'm hoping at the bar, along with my jacket. I was in a hurry to speak to my friend and left my coat inside."

More scribbling is done, and this time I pull out my cell and send a message to Jeffrey about Travis's car. I think we need to get it picked up before the police do. He's not under arrest, so they can't impound it, but the bar could have it towed.

"How'd you get to the police station?"

"Uber," he says. "I need to use the restroom." Travis exits, leaving us all a bit dumbfounded.

"This woman sounds like she's been scorned," one associate says.

"You can't say that. She was raped last night," another says.

"That's what she's claiming. Doesn't mean it was by our client."

"Are you calling her a liar?"

"No, I'm simply stating it wasn't *our* client who did it."

This ping-pong match goes back and forth until Travis walks back in. He's run some water through his hair, taming it slightly. When he returns to his seat, he picks at his food a bit more.

"Saylor, does Travis have any charity events coming up?"

I already know that he doesn't but pick up my phone anyway and go through his calendar. "No, but I can get him on the list for some. Jeffrey will think it's a good idea. We don't want Travis hiding from the public."

"Or answering questions. Right, Travis?" Irvin's voice is stern. Travis nods in agreement and hopefully he'll obey his attorney.

"I think, until the rape kit comes back and the DA moves forward, we have everything." The associates gather their things and start to exit the room, but Irvin stays behind. "I don't have to remind you that cooperating is in your best interest, but you will do so only if I'm by your side. Do not talk to or engage the media, fans, or anyone else regarding this matter. In fact, it's best that you ignore everyone except the people who are paid to protect you." Irvin stands and moves toward the door, only to look back at Travis. "And don't think about leaving town. Doing so would only raise suspicion that you're guilty."

"I'm not, though. I didn't touch her."

"I know, Travis."

Irvin walks out, shutting the door once more. There's awkwardness between us. It's personal and not work related.

"I should get back to the office. I'll call you with your schedule."

"Saylor, wait." He reaches for my arm, keeping me stationary. "Can I come over tonight? After Lucy has gone to bed. We need to talk."

I pull my arm away. "There's nothing to talk about."

BOSTON RENEGADES

We take a break from our off-season vacation to bring you some important news regarding left fielder Travis Kidd.

Earlier this morning, Kidd was spotted entering the police station. At the time, there wasn't any word as to why he was there. However, outlets are reporting that Kidd voluntarily went in for questioning in connection with a reported rape.

Attempts to reach Kidd have been futile, and the Renegades organization is refusing to comment.

Irvin Abbott, private counsel for Kidd, had this to say: "The truth will come out in due time. Right now, my client is upset and is asking for privacy. We feel that the state's attorney is being presumptive, and his press conference earlier this morning is nothing more than a witch hunt against my client. We will hold our own very shortly."

We will keep you updated!

The BoRe Blogger

FIVE

Travis

Irvin has his car service bring me home, after I was informed that Jeffrey was having my car picked up from the bar, if it hadn't already been towed away. As soon as the driver opens my door, the occupants of the numerous cars, vans, and whatever else is parked on my street do the same. I'm a sitting duck, out in the open, without any security. The media come at me with their microphones pointed in my direction, yelling questions that I can't answer. When one calls me a rapist, my steps falter. I hear someone laugh. Maybe it was the one who asked the question. I can't be sure. I want to turn around and square off with the person, and hate that I can't. They get to say whatever they want about me, and I have to take it. I have to ignore it and pretend that everything is okay, when it's anything but.

Standing on my stoop with my back facing the crowd, I hear words like *coward*, *piece of shit*, *loser*, and again *rapist*. Each one tears at my psyche, making me feel weaker than I already am. What happened to innocent until proven guilty? Are they like this because of who I am? And what if they're wrong? Will they apologize? I already know the answers. I've seen countless friends and peers be destroyed by the media, and once they're done with you, they move on to the next unsuspecting target.

My house is cold and dark, and for the first time in my life, I feel like I'm alone. Normally, I'd go out and find a female companion for the evening. Someone I can show a good time to and who can help warm my bed. But that is out of the question, and with very few of my teammates in town, including my best friend, Ethan Davenport, who is three thousand miles away visiting his family for the winter, I'm stuck in this solitude.

A light flashes in my eyes. It's someone with a camera, taking pictures of the inside of my house. I move swiftly to shut the blinds, and while that may keep them from peering inside, it doesn't keep their voices from being heard. Turning on the television to drown them out, my face is all over the screen. The only saving grace is that the photos are random and not a mug shot—although they have video of me leaving the police station, and the caption reads, "Renegades star brought in for questioning."

"They didn't bring me," I say to the TV. Why can't they get their story straight? I mute the volume and sit back on my couch and try to relax. The effort is futile, though, because my mind is racing a million miles a minute as I try to remember every little detail from last night. Aside from being crude, I don't think I did anything unwarranted. She never asked me to stop or shied away from me. And she became angry when I was speaking to Saylor. That is all this is, revenge, and in the worst possible way. She's going to ruin my life all because I decided not to go home with her.

My cell phone juts out of the pocket of my track pants. I turned it off earlier so I wouldn't be distracted. I turn it back on, watching the Apple symbol come to life. The messages start appearing, each one chiming as loud as the next. Everyone wants to know what's going on, and I don't have any answers. The last message to come in is from Ethan. Instead of texting him back, I call.

"Kidd, what the fuck is going on?" Ethan doesn't say hello or ask me how I'm doing. He cuts right to the core.

"I don't know."

"What does that mean?"

I lean back and set my feet on the coffee table. My picture is being shown again, and I have a feeling it's on every channel on cable and the local networks.

"I didn't do it," I tell Ethan. I think that if I keep saying it, everyone will start believing me and not what is being said in the media.

"I didn't say you did, but c'mon, man. This is some serious shit."

"I know. I can't really say anything else."

"Do you need me to come home?" This is one of the reasons Ethan is my best friend. He's willing to drop whatever he's doing to come to my aid. As much as I want to say yes, it would be selfish of me. Christmas is drawing near, and the last thing I want to do is interrupt his family time.

"Nah, I'll be okay."

"All right. Have you spoken to Stone or Wilson?"

"No, my manager's office was going to take care of that." I sigh, wishing that I could go back to yesterday when I made the decision to head to the bar. I don't even know why I chose that particular place. It's not like it's my favorite bar, and I don't go there a lot.

There's so much about yesterday that I'd like to change. Hindsight is a bitch.

After a long pause, I finally say, "Do you think I'm going to get suspended?"

There is a ruffling on the other end of the phone, as if he's moving around or leafing through a stack of papers. Faintly I hear someone in the background talking but can't make out who it is.

"Is there even a remote possibility that your hookup said no?"

"Nope," I say, shaking my head even though he can't see me. "We never even talked about leaving the bar."

"Well, let's hope that comes out sooner rather than later. You don't want this hanging over your head when we get to spring training."

He's right. But in all reality, the tests should come back clearing me of any wrongdoing. I hope to hell that it doesn't take months for that to happen. I'm not sure I can live my life under the scrutiny of others until then.

"I'm going to let you go, E. I need to grab some food, and you're on vacation. You shouldn't be coddling me because I met the wrong chick last night."

"Call me if you need anything, and, Travis…?"

"Yeah?"

"Don't feed into the bullshit. Seriously, keep your mouth shut, head down, and pretend they don't exist."

"Right. Tell Daisy I say hi. Bye." I hang up before he has a chance to respond. He means well—I know this. It's hard to hear, though. Never in a million years did I think I'd be in a situation like this. I thought, if anything, it'd be a pregnancy to throw my life into a tail-spin, not an accusation of rape.

I go into my kitchen and open the refrigerator; it mocks me while I stare into its empty confines. It should be stocked, but my house-keeper took a week off with the assumption that I could care for myself. I don't know how I survived college, let alone adulthood. Slamming the door shut, I lean against the counter with my fingers clenching the edge of the marble countertop.

I want to scream out loud at how fucked up everything is, but I have no one to blame but myself. The urge to punch and destroy everything in sight boils deep within my veins as my fingers grip the marble even tighter in an effort to control my anger. What gives her the right to accuse me of something so heinous because I chose not to go home with her? And why am I being punished for her lies?

Rushing back into the living room, I grab my phone and do the unthinkable. I type her name into the search bar of my web browser, and social media links pop up. Her face, the one I remember so vividly from last night, stares back at me. I hover over the link that will take me to her Facebook page. I shouldn't click. I don't want to see her happy while I'm sitting here in misery, afraid to leave my home because of the reporters that are camped outside.

But I click anyway because I have to know who she is. Her recent status is public, and she's feeling heartbroken. I thought I could love him. I want to comment and tell her that lying to get someone's attention isn't how the dating world works. She needs to know that just because a man rejects you, doesn't mean you can falsely accuse him. Part of me wants to tag her in a post, let-ting the world know that she's a liar. But what would that do? How would that be fair to her? I'm not the type of man who seeks re-venge, at least not in this form. I'm going to have enough trouble saving face with my peers over the accusations I'm confronting. If I were to say her name publicly, I have no doubt in my mind that I would end up looking even worse than I do now.

As I scroll through her pictures, I see that she's alone in most of them. There are a few with some other women, and I study those, looking to see if I know any of them. Maybe this was a setup—a scorned lover has Rachel doing her bidding. It's far-fetched but not unheard of. I'm not the only athlete to be accused of rape, and I admit I use my star status to pick up women, but never have I had to force myself on them. And I tend to never say no to them until last night.

Leaving her page, I type in Saylor's name. She's been on my mind since I saw her at the bar, more so, knowing that she can give me some sort of alibi for last night. It's not concrete, but she had to have heard what that woman was saying and how she was acting. Saylor is the one I wanted to leave with. She's the one that I haven't been able to get off my mind after we hooked up a couple years back.

I hated when she distanced herself from me, asking to be reassigned. I rejoiced when Jeffrey balked, making sure she stayed on my team, and since then I've done the stupidest things I could think of to get her attention. All so I could see her. Every move I've made on her, rebuffed. And it's frustrating. Saylor is the type of woman that I can see myself settling down with, joining my teammates in the ranks of matrimony and maybe even kids. Hell, she already has a daughter, who in my opinion needs a father, and that is a role I can see myself playing.

Her profile picture is of her and her daughter, Lucy. My thumb hovers over them both, wondering what they're doing tonight. I asked to go over there so we could talk, but she shot me down, leaving me no choice but to go see her at work tomorrow. I have to find a way to convince her to help me. She mentioned she could lose everything, but what?

Like a stalker, I screen cap a few of her pictures, and some with Lucy, to save on my phone. I know Saylor was in that bar last night for a reason—it's fate or kismet, or whatever the fuck that shit is called. When I saw her last night, I was reminded that she's who I want to be with. Now I have to convince her. Of course, a rape charge looming over my head is probably scaring her away.

"Fuck!" I yell as loud as possible, hoping the bastards outside can hear me. They need to know that I'm angry and hurt. I don't deserve this shit. I'm an upstanding citizen who volunteers and raises money for organizations in need. So what if I like women? Show me one warm-blooded hetero male that doesn't. It's in our nature. It's how we were created.

"Screw it," I say as I head to my front door. As soon as it opens, the voice levels rise and the people standing outside rush toward me. I stand on my stoop with my hands in my pockets and my hoodie covering my hair.

"I'd like to make a statement."

Those words alone have everyone moving fast toward me. Cameras click with each picture being taken, and bright lights from video cameras shine on me.

"My name is Travis Kidd, and I…" I pause for dramatic effect. "I'm hungry." I sigh and shake my head. "If someone could go get me some Chinese takeout from the place on the corner, I would greatly appreciate it. I have a tab there, and they'll know my order. Thanks." I wave and walk back into my house, hoping that someone will be kind enough to go get me some food. Unless of course, they want to follow me everywhere I go. Maybe next time I go outside, I'll tell them that I'm about to take a shit, and they can ask me questions about how I feel after the fact.

SIX

Saylor

From the moment I turned my phone on this morning, it's been going off nonstop. Every sports media outlet wants an interview. Most outlets want an exclusive, but that has already been promised to my local ESPN contact, and I refuse to go back on my word. They want to hear Travis's side of the story, and I know he wants to tell it, but we have to wait.

I believe Travis when he says he didn't do it, and it seems logical that we should put his story out there, but since the DA has already named him as prime suspect, anything we do now falls on deaf ears. Sure, some of his fans will believe him, but most will rally against him because of his ways, and that is the last thing we want.

As soon as I walk into the office, my assistant looks at me grimly. Taking a deep breath and squaring my shoulders, I walk into Jeffrey's office, prepared to handle whatever it is that he's going to throw at me.

"I love my job. I love my job. I love my job," he says repeatedly as he paces the floor. I know for a fact that he does, until a crisis hits, and then we all end up questioning why we chose this field.

"Do I want to know?" I ask, sitting down. He shakes his head as he pulls out his desk chair and plops into it. His exasperated sigh is loud and slightly obnoxious.

"Kidd should've never gone in for questioning yesterday."

"I agree. But we both know Kidd. He's a stand-up guy despite his reputation." I have no problem going to bat for Travis.

"Irvin and I spent a good chunk of the morning on the phone, going over what Kidd told them yesterday. You were there, right?"

"I was," I say, looking at my phone to verify the time. "What time did you get into the office?"

"Five. Kidd decided to speak to the press last night."

If I were looking in the mirror, I would have seen my face drain of all its color. How my skin turned clammy, and my heart began racing even though I was cold to the touch. I swallow hard, only to feel like something has lodged in my throat. Covering my mouth, I cough into my hands until my airway is clear.

"What did he say?" My words are hoarse, and my throat is in need of some water.

Jeffrey leans back in his chair and lets out another long sigh. I swear this man needs yoga or a meditation technique because of his stress levels. "He went outside and told them he was going to make a statement."

"Oh God."

He nods. "Yeah, and that statement was asking for someone to go get him some takeout from the corner restaurant, saying to put it on his tab."

I can't help but laugh, because that is something Travis would do, regardless of the situation. Jeffrey gives me a dirty look, but I don't care. After the day Travis had yesterday, he needs a little bit of comic relief in his life.

"It's really not that funny."

"It is, Jeffrey," I counter. "Travis is laid-back, and a practical joker. I imagine his house was covered with press last night, and he probably felt like he couldn't leave. It's brilliant, really, and a great marketing scheme. Unfortunately, he also has an issue keeping it in his pants, and that has come back to bite him in his proverbial ass."

"You need to meet with him today, go over his appearances, and remind him what is acceptable and what isn't. If he needs something at home, tell him to call you or call for delivery. No more press conferences unless you and I are with him."

I nod and keep my comments to myself. Jeffrey should be the one at Travis's side, not me. Instead, he's in his office, stressing out, and for the life of me, I can't figure out why. We deal with this type of negative press all the time. It's part of our job to fix what the athletes did and make them look good again.

Back at my desk, I turn on my computer and watch the e-mails come in one at a time. Hundreds sit unread, and the majority of them are regarding Travis. Picking up my phone, I press the button for my assistant's line. "Wanda, can you come in here when you get a chance?"

"Sure thing," she says, and within seconds, she's standing in front of my desk.

"I have a feeling I'll be working outside of the office until things with Travis Kidd get resolved. Jeffrey wants me to 'babysit' him. Can you start going through my e-mail and flagging the important ones? Anyone asking for an interview, tell them that we'll be in touch. With those e-mails, make a list of who they are and what outlet. Right now, Paul Boyd has the first exclusive."

"No problem, Saylor. Oh, *People* called. They want an exclusive as well."

"Right," I say. "I'll call them back today."

Once she leaves, I call Travis. His phone rings until it goes to voice mail. I contemplate leaving him a message but decide to call again instead.

"Personal or business?" Travis asks as he answers the phone.

"Always business. Where are you? We need to meet."

"At the clubhouse, in the gym."

"I'll be there soon," I tell him, and hang up.

Jeffrey wishes me good luck when I tell him I'm off to meet with Travis, and Wanda assures me that every e-mail will be taken care of. The train ride over to the stadium has me on edge. What I failed to do this morning was check the local paper, and now the image of Travis leaving the police station is plastered on the front page with a headline that reads, "Caught with His Pants Down." My stomach twists in knots. I can't imagine how he's feeling, seeing his face like this, in the city that he loves so much.

I eavesdrop on a conversation a few seats behind me, taking mental notes from two women who act like they know what happened. When one says she's been with Travis, that is something I have no doubt about. But what bothers me is that the woman is acting as if she's a victim herself and is telling her friend that she's going to call and file a similar claim, and *that* is something I have a problem with. I let them know that I'm onto their game when I turn and glare at her. The woman doesn't seem to care that I'm staring and continues to go on and on.

As soon as the train rolls into the station, I'm up and out of my seat, tapping my toe until the doors slide open. I walk while texting

Irvin, letting him know what I heard and praying that hopefully he can do something before this gets out of hand.

She's not the only one.

When I see Irvin's reply, my steps falter, and I crash into an un-suspecting man. Unable to take my eyes off my phone, I mumble an apology and keep walking. By the time I reach the bridge, I'm trying to run without killing myself. I'm praying that Travis hasn't heard this news yet. Not that I want to be the one to tell him, but someone has to.

I show my identification at the clubhouse door and head to the gym. The music is so loud that I can barely hear the clanking of weights. Walking through, I peer around the corner to find Travis standing in the mirror and holding a bar. He stands there with a wide stance, clad only in shorts. The tattoo on his left arm is the only ink he has unless he's gotten something new since we've been together. Seeing him like this brings back a memory that I rarely dredge up. Everything was perfect. The way he spoke to me, ca-ressed me, and showed me more passion in one night than any of my previous lovers. I was drunk on him, and booze. A bad and almost deadly combination.

But I wanted him. And he made sure I knew that he wanted me. I tried to play it off as a crush, but the longer we worked together, the harder it became to deny him. We went to a fund-raiser, not to-gether, but neither of us had dates. We danced, drank, and danced some more. That night, I felt like a princess. Travis introduced me to everyone as Saylor, and not as his PR rep. He made me feel like I was someone outside of my job title. I felt wanted, and I let lust control my decisions.

I went home with him that night, only to have Jeffrey text me. I made a mistake looking at my phone and left Travis there confused and begging me not to leave. I was drunk and upset, and wrapped my car around a telephone pole.

My life changed that night, but not in the way I thought. I lost my license, was put on probation, and reprimanded at work. One condition of my probation is that I'm not allowed in bars, which is why I can't tell the police that I saw Travis that night. I can't afford to lose my job or be sent to jail. No one is worth that.

"Are you going to stare at me all day?" he asks as he watches me in the mirror.

"No, I was uh—"

"Thinking about the last time you saw me without a shirt on?"

I nod but end up saying, "No." He laughs, finding humor in the fact that he's embarrassed me.

I'm rooted in my spot as he walks over to me. We're the only ones in the gym and that frightens me a bit. I'm not afraid of him, but of myself. He's sexy and enticing. He walks with a purpose and holds my attention by the way he's looking at me, like he wants to devour me, and I find that I want that, too.

When his hand reaches out, I lean forward and allow him to stroke my cheek. I find myself pushing into the softness of his fingers until he's cupping my face. My skin tingles while my heart picks up speed. I step forward, placing my hand on his wrist where I can feel his pulse beating rapidly.

Behind us, the door slams, and we jump apart. The voice mumbles an apology before disappearing.

"Saylor."

I hold my hand up and shake my head. "Don't. That was a mistake."

"Don't say that."

"But it was." Wasn't it? I don't know, because I can't look him in the eye and say those words. I don't want him to see right through me, to see that I'd give anything to not need this job, and give into the longing that I feel for him.

"I don't know why you always shut me out."

"Because I could lose my job, Travis, and I have a daughter to take care of."

"So quit," he says, as if it's that easy.

"And do what? Another night with you isn't worth quitting my job. I'm sorry, but someone has to be the responsible one, and that's me."

"We'd be good together," he tells me as he steps forward and places his hand on my hip. We *were* good together, but sadly, as much as I want to, I don't see a future with us.

I step away, adding some much needed distance between us. "Is there a place we can sit down and talk before we meet with Stone and Wilson? I want to go over your schedule and make sure you're in agreement with the events I've chosen. Plus, there are a few things we need to discuss."

"Discuss what, exactly?"

I swallow hard and ready myself for the explosive temper that I know is going to rear its ugly head. "More women are coming forward, claiming you raped them, too." I say the words so fast that they seem jumbled, but he catches every single one. I take another step back, and his baby blues turn almost black, his jaw clenches, and his fist flies into the wall.

SEVEN

Travis

Saylor steps in front of me as my arm cocks back in preparation to pummel the wall again with my fist. She looks at me with fear in her eyes, scared that I'm going to hit her, which is something that I'd never do. My clenched hand hangs suspended in the air, my pulse beating rapidly and my breathing out of control. My chest heaves, and my heart races as her fingers ghost over my skin, her hand wrapping around my bloodied knuckles. The tension eases slightly, but the anger still lingers. I don't think that will ever go away. It's one thing to be accused of something that I've done. Being an asshole in the batter's box, a prick in the clubhouse, the prankster with the team, but to have these inflammatory accusations being spread about me is ridiculous, and more importantly, they're hurtful. Not only to my self-esteem, but also to my career.

"Please stop. You're going to hurt yourself." Her voice is demanding, authoritative. She wants me to stop because it's her job, not because she cares. When that's all I want her to do, care about *me*.

"All I am is a paycheck to you. Move out of my way, Saylor."

"Travis, please. You're scaring me." Gone is the boss, and in her place is the soft, sensitive woman who hasn't given me the time of day since she left me at my house, pleading with her not to leave. To stay the night, in my arms, and have breakfast with me the next morning. That wasn't the first time I've been rejected, but it was the first time I had longed for a woman so deeply that my heart hurt when she left.

The grip of her hand on mine tightens, and even though it's not enough to stop the force of my arm, *she* is. The fact that she's standing in front of me, in the path of my fury, is enough for me to drop my arm. Saylor doesn't let go of my hand, but her grip lessens.

"We'll get through this."

I want to ask her how, because I don't see a way out. My reputation is tarnished, whether I committed the act or not. Everyone will remember that Travis Kidd was accused of rape, and my credibility with my teammates and the organization will be nil. It's not going to matter what my performance is like next season, because this will always loom over my head and will be at the forefront of management's mind when my contract comes up for renewal. No, it doesn't matter what happens—I'm done, while the victim that I didn't hurt gets to go on with her life.

I step forward, placing my body within inches of Saylor's. She breathes in, her chest rising and almost brushing against mine. When she lets go of my hand, I keep it at my side while my other hand finds a comfortable resting spot on her hip. I expect her to move, to push me away, but she doesn't. She gazes up at me, and her tongue gently grazes her lips.

In one swift motion, I pull her to me. Our bodies crash together as my lips press against hers. My heart tells me to go slow, to savor the moment, but my body is telling me to kiss her with reckless abandon, to show her how I feel. She whimpers and opens her mouth to me, giving me the access I so desperately need in order to kiss her the way I want, with urgency and determination. To show her that we belong together, despite everything that stands between us. Memories of the night we shared come rushing back, showing me how perfect and amazing we were together, taunting me, reminding me that I can't have her, that she feels like I'm not worth the risk. But I am, and I want to show her that I'd be everything she needs in a man, and more.

Stepping forward until she's flat against the wall, I bend slightly to lift her up, never breaking away from her sweet mouth. She pulls her skirt up over her hips and wraps her legs around my waist, leaving me centered perfectly to take her, to rekindle the desire that I know we both share.

Her fingers are in my hair while I grind against her. She pushes down on me, and I moan. When she whimpers, I thrust my hips, dry humping the fuck out of her so she doesn't forget about me when she's sleeping tonight.

"Fuck, Saylor, I want you so bad." She tightens her legs around my hips, using her crossed ankles to push me harder into her. Her head falls back, giving me access to her neck. With each bite and kiss I place, she mewls louder, and her hips buck. She needs this as much as I do.

The slamming of the door has her squirming out of my hold and both of us in a panic. I turn, angling my body to protect her as I face the newest visitor. It's the off-season, and hardly any of the players are in town, which is why I came here today. I wanted to be alone and not have to answer questions from my peers.

"Kidd," Wes Wilson, the manager of the Renegades, says as he comes around the corner. I hide my bloodied hand behind me and use it to continue to touch Saylor.

"Hey, Skipper. Didn't expect to see you here today."

Wilson came on last year, about midseason, after our manager suddenly retired. I've never had any issues with him, but I have a feeling that is about to change. He's angling his body, trying to see past my shoulder to find out who is hiding behind me. Thing is, if he wants to know that bad, he's going to have to come and force me to move. Embarrassing Saylor isn't high on my priority list. She may be willing to fight the pull that we have toward each other, but I'm not.

"Vacation was cut short."

I nod, understanding exactly what he means. He's here because of me. I open my mouth to tell him I'm sorry, but I don't want it to be an invitation to stay and talk. He takes my silence as his cue to leave.

"We have a meeting in thirty. Make sure your plaything is gone."

My blood boils at his comment calling Saylor a plaything. She's anything but, except she won't see it like that. Not now. If I made any progress with her, it's disappeared. I wait until the door closes again before walking around the corner to make sure he's gone.

"The coast is clear," I tell her, coming back around the corner. She's fixing her hair, even though she didn't need to. That's a part of her that I hadn't gotten to yet because I was too consumed with kissing her and feeling her rub against my dick to even put my hands in her hair. Next time, though.

Saylor brushes past me without making eye contact; I reach for her, grabbing her wrist as she walks by. She stops, keeping her back to me.

"Saylor."

"That was a mistake."

"No, it wasn't," I counter, trying to keep my voice from carrying. "Look at me, please."

She shakes her head and pulls her arm from my grasp. "I came here to tell you that we were meeting with Wilson and Stone. What we did—"

"What we did was perfect. I don't know why you keep fighting it."

Saylor turns and looks at me, her eyes cold and her stance rigid. "There's nothing to fight. I won't lie and tell you that I'm not attracted to you. I am, but I shouldn't act on it. It's unprofessional, and you're…" She takes a deep breath. "You're Travis Kidd, and that is enough to make me run the other way."

Before I can rebut anything she's said, she's gone, and the door is slamming, leaving me alone with my thoughts, with a bloodied hand and a hole in the wall.

Defeated, I hang my head and ask myself what the fuck is going on with my life. Up until the other day, my biggest worry was finding a place to eat dinner while my housekeeper is on vacation. And now? Maybe I should run off to Florida and bask in the sun. Live like a bum on the beach and hide from everyone. I'm not under arrest, so technically I can leave, but what does that do? It makes me look guilty as fuck, and I'm not.

After a quick shower, a shitty hand job to ease the tension left over from my make-out session with Saylor, and a half-assed wrapped bandage on my hand, I find myself sitting at a long table with the Renegades general manager Ryan Stone, Wilson, Saylor, and Irvin. I have a team of legal beavers, all meant to protect me from people who want to take advantage, and yet here I am.

"Now that Travis is here, we can get started," Saylor says. I'm hoping that she'll look at me, but she doesn't. Her eyes are focused on Stone and Wilson. "We think it's best that Travis make some special appearances. I've gone through a few of the events coming up in the area and am confident that I'll be able to secure him an invite."

"Even with the news that more women are coming forward?" Wilson asks. I liked him up until now, and now I want to smash his smug face into the table.

"Mr. Wilson—"

"Hold up," I say, interrupting Irvin. I adjust in my seat to face Wilson, making sure he knows I'm speaking to him. "This accusation is only that. A made-up fucking story because I didn't want to take her home the other night. I never touched her in any inappropriate manner whatsoever. I rebuffed her, and she got pissed. And suddenly there are all these other women supposedly coming forward? Why now? I've never had to beg for sex." Everything I've said is true, minus the begging part. I'd get down on my knees and crawl if that's what it took to get Saylor back into bed with me.

The room grows quiet, and I like that I've stunned everyone. I fiddle with the pen in front of me, pushing the top up and down. The clicking is annoying, but I don't care. Right now it's soothing.

"Saylor, you were saying?" Stone says, breaking the silence.

She clears her throat. "Obviously, my plan will change if the DNA test comes back positive, but I don't believe it will."

I glance up immediately and find her looking at me. I try to smile but fear it's more like a grimace than anything. She believes me, and I wonder if she'll ever know how much that means to me.

"Anyway, I'd like to get Travis out in public. Continue his charity work and make sure that he's mingling with people who will support him."

Irvin sighs and leans forward. "It's an election year. With these other women coming forward, the district attorney is going to have a field day."

"I didn't do anything to them either," I say, defending myself.

"You don't even know their names," Irvin adds, but that doesn't make a difference.

"Well, the way I see it, it's her word against mine. Witnesses in the bar will see that I left without her. Besides, I didn't give the police a DNA sample, so they'll have to arrest me before I give that up."

I push away from the table and walk out the door. I can't take any more of this shit. This bitch is fucking up my life, and there isn't anything I can do about it.

BOSTON RENEGADES

The bad news keeps piling up for Travis Kidd. It's being reported that more women have come forward with similar allegations. Our attempts to reach Kidd or Irvin Abbott, his lawyer, have been unsuccessful.

Under the condition of anonymity, an employee of the police department has said an arrest is imminent as the evidence against Kidd continues to pile up.

After a call to the BoRe Organization, we were told that *everyone* was on vacation and to call back later.

We'll update you when we have more information.

The BoRe Blogger

EIGHT

Saylor

The articles about Travis are getting worse, and now the blog that covers the Renegades exclusively is reporting that an arrest is coming, which will make it almost impossible for me to do my job. Deep down, I know he didn't do this, but I'm not certain that he didn't do something to the others. I'm so torn on what to do, but coming forward with what I know isn't worth the risks that I face.

My apartment isn't big by any means, but it's warm and homey, and as I look at the Christmas tree with its lights twinkling against the rain-pelted window and the fire as it emits a soft glow over my living room, it shows me everything that I've worked hard to build. And I'm not willing to lose it because I was in the wrong place at the wrong time. The urge to even go into the bar was stupid. I should've walked past and kept going until I was home, but the letter from Lucy's father really threw me for a loop.

That letter sits on my coffee table next to my glass of hot apple cider, taunting me. I've read it over and over again, and each time it breaks my heart a little bit more. I know that I have to let him see her, to allow him to be a part of her life, but why now? How come the prior years weren't enough for him to want to see her?

I pick it up again and read *Dear Saylor* only to put it back down and grab my cider. It's warm and somewhat satisfying but not strong enough to numb the pain and anxiety I feel. This week, I want a redo.

The knock on my door is soft and sends my heart racing. I look over my shoulder and swallow hard before getting up and tiptoeing toward it. I'm not expecting anyone, and it's far too late for company. My breath catches when I look through the peephole and see Travis standing on the other side. He's wet from the rain and looks like he's shivering. I rest my hand on the doorknob and pray that he goes away. Part of me wants to open the door and let him in, to let him finish what he started today, but I can't. It's unprofessional and against my contract. Fraternizing with the athletes will get me fired. I knew this when I slept with him the first time, and yet I risked it. But never again.

He knocks again. It's quiet and soft but enough for me to gasp and jump.

"Saylor," he says, his voice muffled by the door. "I know you're there. I can see the shadow of your feet. Please, I have nowhere else to go."

I rest my forehead against the door while my hand moves slowly over the locks. First the chain, followed by the dead bolt, and finally the knob as I have an internal battle between right and wrong. I crack the door open, and the muted hallway light provides a path into my apartment. He's been here before, a few nights after we got together. I refused to let him in, didn't want him to see the damage that I had done to myself when I crashed my car. I didn't want him to know that I regretted ever going home with him.

He steps in and closes the door behind him softly. Is he being conscientious of Lucy, knowing that she's sleeping, or is this how he is all the time?

"Thank you," he says, even though I haven't done anything. Since he walked out of our meeting earlier today, I haven't heard from him. My call to him went unanswered, and the message I sent, never replied to. I figured he needed time to decompress and I didn't want to bombard him. The business we have to tend to can wait.

"For what?"

"For letting me in. I know you don't want me here." His voice breaks, and his head hangs. This man's world is falling apart, and I could fix it, but I'd lose mine in the process. I reach behind him and lock the door, not because I plan on letting him stay, but because if any fans or members of the press followed him up here, I don't want them trying to get into my place.

"It's not that, Travis. Let me get you a towel." I leave him standing by the door while droplets of water start to pool at his feet. When I return, he's taking off his hat, jacket, and shoes. "Here ya go," I say, handing him the towel. "I'd offer you a change of clothes, but I don't think you'd appreciate wearing yoga pants and a sweatshirt that would barely cover you."

He laughs. It's the first time in a couple of days that I've heard it. Usually, Travis is cracking jokes and making my eyes roll with his one-liners and classic schoolboy antics. There have been many rumors that he's the jokester in the clubhouse, which I have no doubt are true.

"Let me take your stuff." He hands everything to me, and I hang the clothes in my bathroom to let them dry and turn my heat lamp on. He's still standing by the door when I come back into the room.

"Do you mind if I take off my pants?"

"Travis."

"It's not like that, Saylor. I'm cold and..." He shakes his head, and that's when I see him shiver.

I nod quickly. "Let me grab you a blanket." I run to my room and pull the quilt off my bed. When I return, he's on my couch with his arms extended, one to hand me his jeans and the other to take the blanket from me.

"Thank you."

"What are you doing here?" I ask as I curl up at the end of my sofa, leaving a full cushion between us.

"I had nowhere else to go."

"What about your house?"

He snuggles under the blanket, trying to get warm. I reach for the remote to turn the fire up, knowing that it won't take much time to raise the temperature of the room.

"It's crazy there. The press is camped out front. They're always talking and have their lights flashing into my windows. People walk by and scream at me, calling me names. I can't do anything or go anywhere without them following me. I can't even order food without it being on television."

Anxiety starts to overtake my thoughts. "So they followed you here?"

"No; I snuck out my back door and took the alley. I needed to get out of there."

"But why here?"

Travis looks at me with his disheveled hair and five o'clock shadow. "Because you believe me."

His words are heart crushing and cause me to choke on the air I was exhaling. I try to make my cough sound like an ailment and not a reaction that I've been caught off guard. He pats my back as I cover my mouth, waiting for the tickle to subside. I reach for my glass of cider only to realize there is hardly a drop left.

"Can I get you something to drink?" I'm off the couch in a flash, not waiting for him to answer.

"A beer or something very hard so I can forget everything."

I ignore his request and brew us both a cup of coffee instead. I have a feeling it's going to be a long night of sitting around, with minimal talking and a lot of thinking. With two mugs in my hand, I offer him one. "Sorry, I don't drink."

"Really? Since when?" I know he's remembering our night together. We drank a lot that night, and neither of us was in any shape to drive, but I did.

"It doesn't matter. Alcohol is the last thing you need right now." He takes the mug and brings it to his lips, sipping quietly.

"Is Lucy sleeping?"

"Yeah, she is." Most of my clients have met Lucy. We've attended a lot of the family events that teams hold or she'll go to games with me. I try not to let family and work mix, but there are times when it can't be avoided.

"Look, about earlier today—"

"I know," I say, cutting him off. He doesn't have to tell me that the heady kiss was a mistake. I already know it was and can't happen again. The fact that I'm attracted to my client is a no-win for me, and I really need to find a way to overcome the desire I feel for him.

"You know what?" he asks, meeting my gaze.

"That what we did was a mistake."

He chuckles, reaffirming my feelings. At least that's what I think he's doing until his laughter almost sounds sarcastic. Travis sets his coffee cup down on my table and sits back against the couch, running his hand through his damp hair. "Nothing about what happened today, with us, is a mistake, Saylor. I like you a lot, in case you haven't figured that out yet, and short of skywriting it, I don't know how else to show you." He's looking at me as if he can see right through me.

I swallow hard, and my hands tremble as I try to pretend that he doesn't have any effect on me, but he does, and I hate it. He makes me feel both weak and desired. Both are emotions that I shouldn't feel when I'm around him.

"We can't."

"I know, you keep saying that, but I don't understand why. I know you feel something for me."

Why can this man read me like an open book? I've tried to stay shut off from him, avoid being the PR member that has to deal with him, unless directed by Jeffrey. And yet, here I am smack-dab in the middle of his biggest crisis, eager to help him, desperate for his attention, and determined to keep him a mile away from me. "It's not about what I feel or don't feel, Travis. It's unprofessional for us to be involved."

"So I'll use another firm."

I shake my head and place my mug on the coffee table. "Switching now would not be beneficial to your career or the case pending against you. Drastic measures such as that usually lead people to think you're guilty, and that's the last thing we want. Besides, who's to say we'd even work out as a couple? You like women far too much."

He looks away, unable to deny my statement. The last thing I would ever do is enter into a relationship with him, knowing that he has a wandering eye and hands that can't seem to stay at his sides.

I take our mugs back into the kitchen and busy myself with washing them, even though they can go into the dishwasher. Being away from him allows my mind to clear and my body to stop trying to pull him near. I jump when a strong arm wraps around me and the other shuts off the water. I'm cocooned in a blanket of warmth as he presses into my back. My traitorous body sags against his as he nestles into my neck.

"Travis."

"I only want to hold you," he says, his words ghosting over my shoulder. I can give him this moment while we're protected in my home, but nothing else. My heart would never survive being broken by him, but right now he needs some comfort. And I rather enjoy the way his arms feel around me. I wrap my arms around his, and he squeezes me tighter. His body sighs, while mine goes a mile a minute, reminding me that he isn't wearing any pants, and my lady bits scream out for attention.

Earlier in the gym, I let him get the best of me. From the moment I saw his sweat-laden body, mine craved his, and I think he knew it. When he kissed me, I gave in to temptation, submitted to the desire that I feel for him each time he's near, and more so since I've seen him more in the past few days than I have in months.

He turns me in his arms, and his erection brushes against me. Travis's hand cups my cheek as his lips descend onto mine. The kiss is tender but full of emotion, and when his tongue enters my mouth, I whimper.

I want more when he pulls away. His thumb caresses my lip as he smiles, even though there's sadness in his eyes. I want to take it all away for him, but I can't.

"I would never hurt you, Saylor."

Believing him, trusting him with my heart, would be stupid. I did that once with Lucy's father, and while I may have won in the end with the birth of Lucy, the heartbreak was almost too much to handle.

"I want to believe that is true."

"I'll prove it. If you give me a chance."

I shake my head, causing him to drop his hand from my face. Instead of stepping away and asking him to leave, I guide him over to the couch and pull him down next to me. I can be here for him and provide him comfort, but opening my heart to someone like him is impossible.

It's late, and I know I have a busy day ahead of me, but the thought of leaving Travis alone doesn't sit well. Reaching for the remote, I turn on the television and flip to a movie channel that I know won't show anything about the scandal.

"I think I've seen this one," he says, causing me to look at him. "The wife had an affair, and the other wife goes after the mistress's husband."

My mouth drops open as I look at him, and he shrugs.

"What?"

"You watch Lifetime?"

"Of course—how else do I know what women want?" He kisses me again, quickly, even though he knows nothing will ever come of it. I shake my head and laugh. Who knew that a guy like Travis Kidd was in tune with his feminine side?

NINE

Travis

Sneaking out of my house is something I've never had to do, even when I was a teenager. My parents didn't care what I did, as long as my grades were kept up and I wasn't breaking any laws. At other people's houses, I've definitely jumped out of windows and shimmied down drainpipes. I even busted my arm sliding off the roof of a house of some girl I met at a basketball game. That act alone almost ruined my chances of playing ball my junior year of high school.

When you're running because you're trying to escape parents who came home too early, there's an exhilaration that courses through your body. Your adrenaline pumps, and you feel invincible. That all changes when you're forced to sneak out of your own house to escape the onslaught of media and the names being hurled in your direction from onlookers. It makes you feel worthless.

Walking the darkened streets of Boston, hidden under a baseball cap with my jacket pulled up against my face to thwart off the wind and rain, I felt hopeless and found myself staring at Saylor's apartment building. I had been here a few times before, but only as far as her door. The night she left me opened my eyes. I didn't want her to be a one-night stand, or even two nights. I wanted to get to know her, and not only in the carnal way.

If I ever thought that Saylor was a sure thing, I would've been fooling myself. She's far more mature than I am. She's career minded and focused on raising her daughter. And determined to keep me on the periphery of her life. Even as I sit next to her, with my arm resting on her shoulder and my fingers playing idly in her hair, this is as close as she'll let me come. With the exception of what transpired earlier today and the kiss we shared in her kitchen.

She yawns, and I use this opportunity to adjust the way I'm sitting and pull her closer. Never mind the fact that she's fully clothed and I'm clad in a somewhat damp T-shirt and my boxers. There's something definitely wrong with this picture. It's like my role in life has been reversed. Usually, it's me who is fully clothed and about to walk out the door, leaving behind a barely dressed woman. But something tells me that this is the way it needs to be, even if she won't tell me why.

I know my reputation scares her. Fuck, it scares the shit out of me. Branch Singleton, the Renegades' designated hitter and one of my good friends, has often said I was going to end up in trouble. Well, the fucker was right, because look at me now—dealing with what I never thought would happen: a rape accusation that I can't even defend against yet, and other women claiming the same thing. Irvin says we have to wait and see if the district attorney is going to proceed with bringing charges against me. Until then, I'm supposed to keep a low profile and stay out of trouble. What better way to do that than in the arms of my publicist?

But here I sit, holding the woman that I have a massive crush on, and who keeps telling me we can't be together. I can't tell if this is some twisted irony or a wicked, shitty hand being dealt my way. Either way, I don't want to give up the fight. Deep down, I know it can be a number of things; my job and schedule aren't exactly conducive to dating, but her job affords her the ability to be at my games. My reputation and my antics off the field aren't doing me any favors. I know that Saylor needs someone who is going to put her first—hell, even put her daughter first—and I want to be that person. I'm not sure how, though.

At some point during the night, Saylor leaves me on the couch. The house is quiet, and the fireplace is still glowing, letting off enough heat to keep me warm. With the quilt wrapped around my shoulders, I walk over to one of her two floor-to-ceiling windows and look out over the city. While Boston isn't Vegas or New York City, we still have the ambience of a city that never sleeps. Lights dance off each other, guiding early morning travelers to their destinations while off on the horizon, the sun is starting to rise, and horns blow in the harbor as boats prepare for their day's journey.

My arm brushes their Christmas tree, and my fingers pull on the needles. It's fake, but who cares? The fact that she has one up speaks volumes. It's been years since I've even seen a tree, because I spend most of my Christmases on my parents' yacht in the middle of the Gulf of Mexico. I reach down and plug the tree in. It sparkles as the white lights glow throughout Saylor's quaint living room. Compared to my house, her apartment is small, but I feel more at ease here than I do in my own. I can feel the love that has been poured into this place to make it a home.

Above the fireplace, Lucy's school picture is front and center. Her toothless grin is contagious, and I find myself smiling back at her. I pick up another framed photo and run my thumb over Saylor's face.

She and Lucy are posing with a reenactment solider, and they look happy. And I want that. I want to be a part of something where love is given unconditionally.

I look back at what became my makeshift bed and notice my jeans are folded and resting on the arm of the couch, and my shoes are sitting on the floor next to it. I should dress and leave before Saylor wakes, but I want to see her. I want to be part of their morning routine and see if I can fit in with them. It's selfish of me to stay, but I need the normalcy. It's also presumptuous to think that someday I'll be here permanently, but I have hope. And right now I need a lot of hope to get me through the day.

I dress quickly, shocked to find that my jeans aren't stiff like cardboard, and slip my shoes back on. Folding the blanket, I slip it under the sofa to ward off any ideas that Lucy might have about me being here and pull my phone out to order breakfast. It's the least I can do for Saylor after she opened her home to me.

Once I have breakfast laid out, it's only a matter of time before they both wake up. After I ordered, I stood in her doorway with the door cracked, waiting for the deliveryman. The last thing I wanted was for him to knock and wake either of them. Not only was Saylor up late with me, but it also probably would've scared the shit out of her.

The aroma of the pancakes, bacon, sausages, and eggs makes my stomach growl. I rush to the couch and turn on the television when I hear a door open. I don't know who it is, but I'm hoping that whoever comes around the corner is happy to see me. I try to keep my eyes focused on the news, but I can't. I'm watching the doorway like a hawk.

"I expected you to be gone when I woke up," Saylor says as she ties the belt of her bathrobe into a knot. The sight of her in a fluffy robe to ward off the chill really turns me on. Who would've thought that thick winter wear would be a turn-on?

"I didn't want to leave your door unlocked." It's a lie, but a good one.

"Oh," she says, looking at the door. Is that my cue to leave? Probably, but I was acting dense, like I wasn't following.

"I took the liberty of ordering breakfast for you and Lucy." I point over to her island where mounds of takeout containers sit. "It's a peace offering for letting me stay the night."

Now would be a good time to leave, but instead I stand and go over to the island and open one of the containers. "Do you want me to fix you a plate?"

"No; you need to leave before Lucy wakes up."

I nod, knowing this. I close the container and make my way toward her. She steps back, shutting me out in an instant. "Thank you for last night, Saylor," I say. I want to kiss her goodbye or at least feel the softness of her cheek against my fingertips. As slowly as I can, I head to the door, knowing that she's following me. She unlocks it as I slip on my jacket.

"Will I see you later?"

She nods but doesn't make eye contact with me. I sigh and step out of her apartment. She shuts the door, and then I'm met with a series of noises indicating she's locked it. I rest my hand on the thick piece of wood and imagine she's doing the same, even though I have a feeling she's not. After a long minute, I make my way down the hall only to realize that I've forgotten my hat. In an instant, I'm back at her door and knocking.

"What?" she asks, opening her door in a huff.

"I forgot my hat."

She steps away, leaving her door open and giving me a chance to watch her walk around. Lucy appears in the hallway, claiming that she's starving and asking her mom what smells so good. I can't help but smile because I know that I did that.

Saylor freezes when she sees Lucy. She looks back at me, to my hat in her hand, and to her daughter. Saylor quickly stuffs my hat into her pocket before facing her daughter.

"Hi," Lucy says, giving me a small wave. She's dressed in a light-blue nightgown with a princess on the front, and her hair is a crazy mess of brown locks.

"Hey, Lucy. Do you remember me?" I've had the privilege of meeting Lucy a few times during the Renegade family functions or when Jeffrey has a party and invites me. I've also seen her in the stands, stuffing her face with pink cotton candy and pretending to give a shit about baseball.

She shrugs and walks toward the door, but her mother stops her before she gets too close. "Maybe. What's your name?"

"Travis," I tell her. "I'm on the baseball team."

Lucy pretends to think about it, which makes me laugh. Little kids are the cutest, and honestly I wish we had more of them around. I'm looking forward to Cooper Bailey's twins being older so I can play with them. Right now they sleep, eat, and shit, and when they aren't doing any one of those three things, they cry.

"Oh yeah—I remember. Do you want to have breakfast with us? We're having…" She pauses and looks up at her mom. "What are we having, Mom?"

"Um…"

"Breakfast sounds great. I'm starved." It's evil, and I know Saylor will kill me for it, but I invite myself back into their home. I take off my jacket and hang it on the hook next to Lucy's. Seeing it there reaffirms my desire to be in Saylor's life. I know it's random to think of myself as part of their little family, but I want to. I want to feel secure, loved, and needed. I also know in order to do that, especially where Saylor is concerned, I need to get my shit together and stop acting like a college kid with a walking fucking hard-on all the time. She deserves better.

Lucy meets me halfway and walks me toward the kitchen. I know better than to look at Saylor, because if I do, I'll see how angry she is. I know I should've told Lucy no, but who in their right mind can say that word to a little girl who looks like a miniature version of the woman you want to get to know? Hell, maybe I can find a way into Lucy's heart, and Saylor will open up to me.

"Come on, Mom," Lucy says as I help her climb onto the stool.

"Yeah, come on, Mom," I add with a wink, and am rewarded with the most epic eye roll. Saylor marches into the kitchen and makes a cup of coffee with so much force that Lucy whispers to me, "She's grouchy without coffee."

Duly noted, kid. Next time, I come with coffee. Something tells me that if I can get Lucy to like me, she'll spill all the secrets about her mother. All's fair when it comes to love, right?

TEN

Saylor

"I like Travis," Lucy says as she skips along the sidewalk while holding my hand. The arm-jerking motion is wearing, but I allow her to do this. I like Travis, too, but I don't tell her that. She has never seen me with a man, and honestly I don't know how I would explain dating to her if I were to start. She's always been my priority, aside from my job.

"He's nice," I tell her.

"Is he coming over for dinner?"

"No. I'm sure he's having dinner at his own house." Which, according to his press release, is probably takeout from the local Chinese restaurant like the other day.

"We should invite him over. I think he would like chicken fingers," Lucy says, as if everyone in the world loves chicken fingers. Thankfully, we arrive at her school, and her suggestion is thwarted.

"Have a good day, sweetie. Grandma will pick you up later." I kiss her on the nose and wait for her to move toward her cubby.

"Maybe my new friend Travis can pick me up."

I groan internally and make a mental note to thank Travis...for what, I don't know. Lucy is five and infatuated with everything new that comes into her life. By the time I get home from work tonight, she'll have forgotten about Travis, and we can move on.

Except after last night, I'm torn. He makes me want to try with him, but it's impossible. I'd have to give up my job, and while others may be able to do this and have another job waiting in the wings for them, my reputation would be tarnished. I don't think he understands that. And he can't give up his, not that I would ever ask him to. I have to accept the fact that everything between us needs to remain professional.

I wave at Lucy, and she reminds me to ask Travis to dinner by yelling across her classroom. I try not to roll my eyes at the thought, but there's no way in hell I'm inviting him over. Last night was a fluke. He came to me in a time of need, and hopefully he won't do it again, even if I want him to.

As I walk among the crowds of people trying to make it to work, my phone rings with an unknown number. It's not uncommon, and usually I send them to voice mail, but with the case against Travis and my determination to paint him in a bright, shining light, I answer. "Saylor Blackwell."

"Hello, Saylor."

I abruptly stop, and the person behind me crashes into me. He mumbles something unintelligible, and all I can do is offer him a smile in return while I hold my phone to my ear.

I haven't heard the voice of Elijah Henry in years. Not since I told him I was pregnant, to which he replied, "I'm married." For eight months we dated, attending social events throughout the city, hand in hand, posing for pictures that made the front page of the newspaper. The prominent lawyer from Virginia who came to Boston to teach for a semester caught my eye. I was in my second year of law school when we met, and I fell in love hard.

Our romance was a whirlwind, fairy-tale story. I moved out of my drafty loft and into his high-rise penthouse. He helped me study and ace my exams and took me on a cruise for Christmas. Even though we had just begun dating, I expected a ring. He had hinted at it a few times, and I tried not to let my sadness show when he placed a diamond necklace around my neck instead.

Absentmindedly, my hand goes to my neck to feel for the necklace that no longer hangs there. When he left, I had no choice but to sell it. I was homeless, without a job, scared, and pregnant. If my mother hadn't moved to Boston, I don't know what I would've done.

"Saylor?" He says my name again, but this time with a sigh. I don't care if I'm making him wait. I need to get over the shock of hearing his voice. I need the memories of him to stop flooding back so I can focus on why he's calling. Lucy. He wants to see her, according to the letter he wrote.

"What do you want, Elijah?"

"Is that any way to treat me?"

I scoff and blurt out, "Yes, it is." I don't need to remind him that he left me, that he cheated on me with another woman and married her while we were still together. He bed hopped, going from her to me, and never thought once about how that would make me feel. There's a part of me that thinks if I hadn't gotten pregnant with Lucy, we'd still be together, living a lie.

"Look, what happened in the past...it's water under the bridge."

"What do you want, Elijah? I'm busy, and now isn't a good time."

"Make the time, Saylor. I'll be in town at the end of the week, and I want to see you."

So he wants to see me, not Lucy? Not that I want him seeing her, but why doesn't he ask about her? I start walking again and head toward my train station.

"I'm about to enter the station. I'll call you later," I tell him, hoping that he gets the hint.

"I'll call you when I land," he says as he hangs up. I squeeze my phone in my hand and grunt. People stare, but it doesn't bother me. I have no doubt they can see how angry I am. Someday I want to grow up and be like Elijah. Be someone who doesn't care about anyone, bosses people around, and has my demands met. Best of all, what would it be like to go through life and not have a care in the world? It must take a lot of brass balls to be someone like that.

Instead of heading to work, I take the train to Irvin Abbott's office. He wants to meet and go over Travis's case. Technically, I don't have to be there, and under the circumstances, I wish I weren't. My job is to make Travis look good, to remind the community of the man he is when they need him the most. As much as I loved studying law, Elijah ruined that for me.

Abbott and Abbott is a family-run business with an impressive client list. They represent mostly actors, politicians, and athletes. The receptionist greets me by name when I walk in and tells me that Irvin is going to meet me in conference room 3. I've been here enough times to know where the conference rooms are and easily make my way to our meeting point.

I'm the first one to arrive, and that affords me the opportunity to decompress. I'm still reeling from my phone call earlier, and knowing that Elijah is coming to Boston has me on edge. Never mind the fact that it's close to Christmas break for Lucy, and I have a feeling he's going to ask to take her back to Virginia for a visit. The answer, of course, would be no, but he knows I don't have the money to fight him in court.

Irvin walks in with nothing more than a folder and laptop in his hand. Usually, his arms are stacked with books and he's trying to balance a cup of coffee.

"I see you're missing a few files," I say in greeting.

"Yeah," he says, looking flustered. "This is something new the office is trying. You know, to go green." By the look on his face, he doesn't seem too impressed. I happen to agree with the initiative but would find it hard to go paperless if I were practicing law.

"So what can I do for you today, Mr. Abbott?" Over the years, he's asked me to call him Irvin.

He waves his hand, as if dismissing my comment. "Please, call me Irvin. Mr. Abbott is my father. Word from the DA's office is that the rape kit is coming back today, and they'll subpoena Travis for a DNA sample," he says, sighing. "We'll comply, but I want to make sure that the media sees him going in, and have him answer a few questions as he walks by the reporters."

I look at him questioningly, wondering why he'd subject Travis to something like this. "I'll bite. Tell me why, because I'm not so sure this is in his best interests."

Irvin opens the folder and slides a single sheet of paper over to me. It's a list, numbered one through twenty, starting with Jane Doe 1. My hand covers my mouth as my eyes scan over each entry.

"Surely this can't be serious."

"I'm afraid so, and each story is worse than the previous. The DA hasn't given me the names yet, but he'll have to if he arrests Travis. I have a feeling he's building a case, and if he can't nail Travis on the first charge, he has nineteen others waiting in the wings."

The list makes my stomach revolt, and I excuse myself to the bathroom. Inside, I wait for the contents of my breakfast, the one Travis had delivered for us, to come back up, but it never happens. The bathroom is quiet, and I use the peacefulness to look at myself in the mirror. My fingers trace over my lips, remembering the way he kissed me yesterday, and last night. My eyes close as I recall the way he held me and fell asleep with his arm wrapped around me. I've told him no, repeatedly, and he hasn't forced himself on me. I had him in my home, sleeping on my couch, and he didn't do anything to make me feel uncomfortable.

I could clear his name of the first allegation, but not the others. And one may not be enough to make this all go away.

When I get back to the conference room, Travis is there. His head is downcast, and when he looks up at me, his eyes are bloodshot. *This* is not the man who left my house hours ago.

"Sorry about that," I say, taking my seat, and thankful that Travis is across from me. "When do you expect him to be subpoenaed?"

"Tomorrow. Knowing the DA, he'll hold a press conference first thing in the morning while the police go to pick up Travis." The thought of Travis being escorted out of his house by police sickens me.

"What if we beat them to the punch?"

"What do you mean?" Irvin asks.

"Travis voluntarily gives his DNA. We'll hold a press conference at the clinic, where he publicly tells everyone that he's not guilty and is going to prove it."

I look to both Irvin and Travis for their approval. It's risky, but the preemptive strike by Travis will show everyone that he has nothing to hide.

"I'll do it," Travis says. "I've been waiting to tell my side of the story."

"You won't say anything that isn't scripted," I tell him. "This has to be straight and to the point, no questions. And you know what, we'll do it at the station where you went in for questioning. The media will have a field day with this. No one ever voluntarily gives DNA."

"It's risky," Irvin says.

"The only risk is if Travis raped the accuser. He says he didn't, and I believe him. These other women, unless they had rape kits done, won't have his DNA, and the evidence will be unsubstantiated."

Irvin stands and paces the room. Each pass by, he huffs, as if this is his way of contemplating. I try not to stare at Travis, but his eyes are boring into mine. Gone is the sweet man who entertained my five-year-old this morning, and in his place is a man who is watching his life slip away. I may not be able to come clean about what I know, but I can do this. I can bring him in front of the camera and show the world that he's not the monster the state's attorney is making him out to be.

"You'll stay on script?" Irvin asks Travis, who nods eagerly. "I don't like it, but it's better than the police showing up at his door."

"Great, I'll get to work."

ELEVEN

Travis

"Are you ready?" Saylor asks after she's closed her laptop. For the past few minutes, I have watched her multitask like crazy. She went from her phone to her computer without losing focus. "I sent your speech to your phone. Read it. Know it. You want to sound confident and self-assured. Let the people see the same Travis Kidd that they see on the field. The one facing his nemesis when the game is on the line."

I nod, but I'm not so sure that I am any of those things she listed. Irvin leads us out of the office, and I follow behind, watching the sway of Saylor's ass in her skirt. Days ago, I would've reached out and tapped her rear to get her attention, but now I can't do that. I can no longer be the person I was because of what this rape accusation is doing to me. Even after I'm proven not guilty, people will be waiting for me to fuck up. All eyes will be on me, watching my every move. The Travis Kidd who could joke with women, pick them up in bars, and have a good time with them is dead. A new one has to take his place, because this shit isn't worth it.

Saylor and I wait outside while Irvin takes care of something in his office. We stand side by side, pretending that there isn't any tension between us. I put my hands in my pockets and let out a sigh, hoping to get her attention. When she doesn't look at me, I decide I've had enough. "You're fucking sexy when you work."

"Excuse me?" She finally looks at me for the first time since we've stepped outside. I move closer to her and lean in, inhaling her perfume. The fresh scent of gardenia mixed with honey sends a jolt to my crotch. I want to spend hours nuzzling her neck until I smell like her.

"Back there in the office, when I said I had something to tell you and would tell you later. That was it. Watching you in action is mesmerizing. Have dinner with me tonight?"

She shakes her head.

"Why not?"

"Because I have a standing dinner date with Lucy."

"So bring her, too," I tell her. I know what comes with dating a single mom, and I'm game for it. Lucy is a kick-ass kid and had me in stitches this morning.

"We can't, Travis. It's crossing the line."

I look away, pissed that she keeps bringing up this imaginary line. Doesn't she understand that I want to get to know her? That the person being accused of this horrible crime isn't me?

Before I can say anything else, Irvin comes out, talking on his phone. Saylor falls in step behind him, and once again I'm following behind her. Only now I can't watch her ass, because her black wool coat covers it.

We pile into Irvin's car, with Saylor and me in the backseat while Irvin stays up front. He tells his driver to take us to the police station, and my stomach drops. I start reading through the words that Saylor penned for me, as the dread continues to grow. What if I'm making a mistake by giving them my DNA? What if this backfires? "What if this isn't a good idea? What if I'm setting myself up?"

"Did you rape her, Travis?" Saylor asks, looking square into my eyes.

"No, I didn't. You know I didn't."

She looks away and nods. "You'll be fine."

"And what if I'm not, Saylor? We could walk into that police station and give a statement, and this whole thing goes away."

Saylor turns and glares at me. Her eyes then fall on Irvin, who is still on the phone. She shakes her head and pulls her coat tighter around her. "You won't understand."

"Try me, because right now I'm scared fucking shitless to walk into that station."

"You have nothing to worry about," she whispers.

"Right. That's really easy for you to say. You can clear my name, and yet you keep telling me that you can't. If there is something wrong, then let me help."

Her head turns toward the window, effectively shutting me out. I want to punch the seat in front of me but hold back. The driver didn't do anything to warrant my anger. Saylor has, though, and I want to know what is going on in her world that she's willing to let me go down in a blaze when she knows she could help me.

As soon as we pull up to the police station, many media agencies are outside and ready. Saylor laughs, and for the life of me, I can't figure out why.

"What's so funny?"

She nods toward the station. "I'm willing to bet that officer has been tasked with keeping the media in order. Not an easy task sometimes."

I frown as I get out of the car and run around the back to Saylor's door to help her out. As I reach for her, she sets her hand in mine, and I close my hand around hers. She stands, chest to chest with me, and even in her heels, she's still shorter.

"Let me in," I plead. It's not because I need her to clear my name but because I want to get to know her. Waking up in her house, even though it was on a couch, was the best thing that has happened to me in a long time.

"I can't."

Saylor steps away, and my only condolence is that I get to watch her walk up the steps. I follow quickly and take my place next to her as she stands in front of the camera marked ESPN.

"Thank you for coming here on short notice. My client Travis Kidd has a statement to make. Once he has concluded, I will take only a few questions related to his statement."

Saylor steps away and motions for me to start. I have what I'm supposed to say memorized, but the words seem fuzzy in my brain. The cameras start flashing, and I imagine the video feeds are rolling.

"For days, I have kept my silence while the police investigated me on the accusation of rape. I'm here today, of my own accord, just like I was when they questioned me, to submit my DNA sample. I want to clear my name, and this is the way to do it. Thank you."

Immediately my name is called out, and questions are thrown my way. Saylor stands front and center, poised and perfect.

"Paul," she says, pointing at the man whom others are surrounding.

"Travis, have you met with the Renegades? What's your status on the team?"

Saylor nods, so I answer. "We've met, and I'm an active member of the team."

Once I finish, the questions are once again being yelled at me.

"June," Saylor says, signaling to a woman off to the side.

"Travis, your name has been added to the Cancer Center's annual ball. Can you confirm that you'll be in attendance?"

I give Saylor a sideways glance to see if I'm going. She nods. "Yes, I'll be there."

"Kenny." Saylor points to a man in the back. There's something about his face that makes me feel uneasy.

"Travis, you have twenty women coming forward, stating you've raped them. Why would you voluntarily give your DNA? Why implicate yourself?"

My hands grip the sides of the podium, and my teeth clench. Saylor rests a reassuring hand on my back but I still can't find the words to answer. I want to yell out that I'm innocent, that the only thing I've done wrong is become a womanizer, but the words escape me.

"That'll be all. Thanks for coming," Saylor says as she grabs my arm and pulls me toward the door.

As soon as we're inside, I realize what she's done. While her intentions may have been in my best interest, I look guilty as fuck to the people out there and the ones watching at home. "What the fuck, Saylor? Let me defend myself." I point toward the door and step toward it but she stops me. She may be short but she's strong, and I'm weak when it comes to her.

"You froze, Travis. I was protecting you. As of now, Irvin doesn't have any idea who these other women are, and for all we know, they could be after money. Let Irvin and me do our jobs. It's what you pay us for. Can you please just trust me?" she asks softly. She pleads with me to do this because then she doesn't have to. I will get to the bottom of why she can't come forward, and it will be tonight.

Irvin motions for me to walk down the hall and points toward a room that I enter, with Saylor following behind. A female police officer is there, waiting for me.

"Sir, before I begin, can you confirm that you are here under your own free will?"

"Yes," I say.

"Please open your mouth." I do as she says, and she takes a long cotton swab and sticks it in my mouth, rubbing it against my cheek. And within seconds, it is done. She slips the stick into a bag and exits the room.

"That's it?"

"Yeah, that's it," Saylor says with a sigh.

Irvin walks to the window and lifts a slat in the blinds to peek outside. "Everyone is still outside. I was hoping they would leave."

"I figured. They'll have questions, but we are going to ignore them. We'll walk out there with our heads held high and with smiles on our faces," she states as if nothing is wrong.

We do as she says. Saylor even waves at a few of them. I think about flipping them off but figure that would be all over social media, and right now I don't need any more negative press.

Irvin offers to have his car drive us to our respective homes. When his driver pulls up in front of Saylor's apartment complex, I get out to help her out of the car. As soon as she's on the curb, I tap the car and watch it speed away.

"What are you doing?"

"Taking you to an early dinner. I need to thank you for today, for believing in me."

"It's my job, Travis."

I pretend that her comment doesn't sting, but it does. I want her to believe in me as a person, not the athlete. "Well, as your client, I would like to take you to dinner."

"Travis!" The little squeal catches my attention. By the time I can react, tiny arms are wrapped around my legs, and I stumble slightly.

"Hey, Lucy. What are you doing out here by yourself?" I look at Saylor, who looks pissed.

"I'm with my grammy," she says, pointing behind her. Saylor follows her daughter's finger and shakes her head. I wave at Saylor's mom, Norma, remembering her from previous encounters.

"Lucy, you shouldn't run off like that," Saylor scolds. She says something quickly to her mother, who waves goodbye.

"But, Mommy, I was so excited that you invited Travis for dinner that I forgot."

I look up and can't keep the smile off my face. Saylor is fuming. Her toe is tapping, and if I'm not mistaken, she's clenching her jaw rather tightly by the look on her face.

"What's for dinner?"

"Chicken nuggets," Lucy says with a shrug.

I squat down so I'm her height, and while looking between Lucy and Saylor, I say, "How about we go out for pizza? I know a great place that I think you and your mom will like."

TWELVE

Saylor

She's five. That is what I keep reminding myself. And to her, Travis is like a shiny toy. An annoying doesn't-ever-shut-off toy that is trying to weasel his way into my life despite the fact that I've told him nothing is going to change between us.

This is one of the hazards of my job. The too-cute, too-sweet athletes who try to sweep me off my feet and show me that they're interested in me. I'd be interested, too, especially with Travis, if I knew the outcome. If I were guaranteed a happy-ever-after, I'd jump at the opportunity. Unfortunately, not even Travis can give me that.

Travis holds Lucy's hand all the way to the restaurant. Watching them together really makes me long for a partner, someone for Lucy to have in her life. And maybe even have another child. When I found out I was pregnant with her, I imagined a life with Elijah, with a house full of love and children. Sadly, I don't see any of those dreams coming true, and I'm okay with that. I'm happy with my life, happy with it being Lucy and me.

He holds the door for us and places his hand on the small of my back when he steps in behind me. The thick fabric of my coat acts as a barrier, preventing me from feeling his hand against my skin. Last night, when he held me, my skin ignited. The warmth that he made me feel by that simple act was enough to make me run from him. It would've been so easy for me to sleep there, nestled in his arms, but I can't do that to myself.

Travis asks that we be seated in the kid section, causing me to give him a confused look. Even parents don't like sitting there, but we do because it makes our children happy.

Lucy's eyes light up, and she starts clapping. "Mommy, can I go play?"

"Yes, but give me your stuff first," I tell her as I reach for her hat while she takes off her coat and mittens. Her hair is standing every which way due to static, and I try to tame it before she runs off.

"My hair used to do that when I was a kid," Travis says as he takes his cap off and runs his hand through his hair.

"It still does." I sit down across from him and remove my scarf and unbutton my coat.

"Nah, now it's cool for a guy to have hair like this. They call it sex hair." He smiles, and against my better judgment, I smile back. We stare at each other. His blue eyes dance around, taking in the way I'm looking at him. His eyes seem to change color, maybe with his mood, but tonight they're vibrant and full of life. Nothing like the dull version they were earlier. Or maybe it's the fluorescent lights playing tricks and I'm making excuses to stare at him, because there's no way his crooked smile is reeling me in, except it is, and I know that I could easily get lost in him, in his world.

His hand reaches across the table for mine. Before I let him take it so I can torture myself with what I can't have, I look around the section we're in and see that the only other family here is tucked into the corner. They seem lost in their own world and not paying attention to the man sitting across from me. Our fingers thread together, and his thumb brushes idly against my skin.

That night with him is so vivid in my mind—the way he made me feel like I was the only one that mattered to him. I knew what I was doing when I left with him. I wanted it. I needed the escape from my reality. And I was lonely. Travis filled that void. As his knee brushes mine under the table, my leg slides forward and rests against his. The subtle flirting is agonizing and needs to stop, but he makes me feel desired, and that's something I haven't felt since the last time we were together. He doesn't need to know that I haven't been with anyone since him.

"Can I take your order?" The young waitress interrupts us, causing us to break apart. I feel the loss of him more than I care to admit.

"Uh, yeah," Travis says as he reaches for the menu. "What kind of pizza does Lucy like?" he asks.

"Cheese is fine."

"And you?" he asks, looking me in the eye.

"I'll have a salad."

He shakes his head and orders our dinner and drinks while I focus on Lucy. She's playing with a few other children. Their laughter carries throughout the room, and it's heartwarming to see her enjoying herself. We don't get to do things like this often.

"Thank you for bringing us here," I say to Travis. With my hours, by the time I'm home it's a quick dinner if she hasn't eaten at my mother's. Even my weekends can be consumed by work.

"It's my pleasure, Saylor. Lucy looks like she's having a good time."

He motions toward her, and I turn around to watch her again. Now she's with a few kids, riding the mini-carousel. "She is. I try to do things like this for her, but being a single mom is hard some-times."

"Where's her father?"

His question gives me pause. I slowly turn back around to face him as the waitress delivers our drinks. He's ordered us water and a pitcher of root beer, because everyone needs the frothy soda with pizza. "He's in Virginia with his wife."

"Oh." His tone makes me feel that he's thinking the worst about me.

I shake my head, hoping to stop where his mind is going. "It wasn't like that. The relationship was still taboo, but he wasn't mar-ried when we started dating. Honestly, I don't know what he was doing. He was my professor. We started dating and moved in with each other. I thought he was going to propose, and I was going to live this fairy-tale life. When I found out I was pregnant, it was like life was lining up, only a bit out of order. Anyway, I told him, and he replied that he was married."

"And that's it?"

"Yeah, pretty much." I don't tell him that I was depressed for months after the fact or that I was homeless for a time. Or that I gave up a career in law because keeping my baby was more impor-tant to me. And I definitely don't tell him that Elijah is coming to town this week and that I'm scared he's going to take Lucy away from me.

"Well, since you gave me something about you, here's something about me."

"This isn't a tit for tat, Travis."

He shrugs. "I want you to know me. The real me," he says as he leans forward. Instead of having his hand on the table and reaching for mine, his fingers graze my knee and continue to do so as shivers run up and down my spine.

"My home life was shit. My dad owns multiple Ford dealerships. I own a Chevy because I know it pisses him off. He worked all the time and was never home. There was always gossip when I was growing up about him cheating on my mom. My mom believed that he was faithful, but rumors…Well, you know what those do to people. Anyway, I did whatever I could to stay out of the house, so I played baseball, basketball, and football. I was the all-American kid with a supportive mom in the stands and a father who couldn't come see his kid play because he either screwed someone on a deal or they were part of the rumor mill and he wouldn't do that to my mom." Travis shrugs.

"Is that why you are the way you are?"

Travis pulls his hand away from my leg, sits back, and finishes off his glass of water. He fiddles with the straw wrapper that sits on the table. "It's not like that."

"It's not?"

He shakes his head. "These women…"

"Look, you don't have to explain yourself to me. The question was rude, and I'm sorry for asking it."

Travis reaches for my hand, and I give it to him willingly. "I want to, Saylor. I never set out to be a womanizer or anything like that. When I first entered the league…the women—they chased me. At first, I was focused on my career, but I gave in to temptation. I dated a few of them but never longer than a few weeks, because they would whine about my schedule and I didn't have time for that. So I started having one-night stands because they're free of drama, at least up until now."

"But she wasn't a one-night stand?" I refuse to say Rachel's name in public. By the look Travis gives me, he knows who I'm referring to.

"No, she wasn't. I became interested in someone else," he says, dropping his voice low. It's easy to see why women gravitate toward him. Not only is he very good looking, but he's also charming and has a smile that makes you weak at the knees. It would be so easy to fall into his arms. It would be so nice to be the one who comforts him during this crisis, to be the one he comes home to at night. It's not only my job keeping me from him; it's also the fact that I'm not sure I could trust him enough.

I look around the room for Lucy, spotting her instantly. I need to be in mom mode and not under the spell of Travis Kidd. I keep my focus on her so I don't have to face him, because every time I do, I start to remember how I ended up here. If Elijah hadn't sent the letter, I wouldn't have gone to the bar and run into Travis. If that hadn't happened, he wouldn't be in this mess and we wouldn't be sitting across from each other, sharing subtle glances and shy touches. I shouldn't be here, but honestly, I like where I am.

"What do I have to do, Saylor?"

Turning back to face him, I get lost in his eyes. My head is screaming that he's doing everything right, that he's making his intentions known, and he's where he should be when I least expect him. But I can't. The little girl running around and telling everyone that her name is Cinderella depends on me. And I refuse to ask her father for any more child support than what he already pays. I can't let my heart get in the way of my job. Besides, who's to say he'll feel this way next week or next month?

"Are you in a relationship with someone else?" he asks.

I shake my head quickly. "It's not that."

"Look," he says. "I don't blame you for telling me no. I can't make any excuses for my reputation, but I can promise you that if you give me a chance, I won't let you down."

"It's not that, Travis."

"Then what is it?" he pleads.

Before I can answer, our food is delivered, and my stomach embarrasses me by gurgling loud enough for him to hear. He laughs and motions toward Lucy. "I'll get her," he says as he slides out of the booth. I can't help but follow him as he goes to my daughter. She comes running to him and jumps into his arms. I need to caution her on some boundaries, except the look on not only her face but his as well makes me feel differently. She doesn't even know him, and she's smitten with him.

I work quickly to put Lucy's plate together, making sure the pizza is cut into bite-size pieces, and pour her a small glass of root beer. She rarely gets soda, but tonight is special, even if I don't want to admit it.

"I'm so hungry," Lucy says as she climbs into the booth, choosing to sit next to Travis. I shouldn't let it bother me, but it does. I've never had to share her except with my mom.

"Do you mind watching her so I can go to the salad bar?" I ask, waving my plate in the air because I'm suddenly nervous.

"Of course," he says, and as I step past him, he grabs my wrist, stopping me in my tracks. "I want to make myself very clear here, Saylor. I would do anything for you and Lucy. I want to be here with the both of you."

I nod and stumble away in a daze, wondering who the hell Travis Kidd is. I only know him as my client, someone I'm required to keep in a positive light with the media. As I look back at Lucy and Travis, his head is turned toward hers, and she's talking animatedly. Not once does he take his eyes off of her. He doesn't frown or try to eat his own food. He's totally lost in the world of my five-year-old daughter, and she in his.

He's exactly what she needs in life.

After dinner, Lucy is able to convince Travis that he needs to play with her. I start to open my mouth to remind her that she should ask first, when Travis winks at me and slides out of the booth.

For most parents the reprieve is nice when you visit an eatery that has a room for children to burn off energy, but because it's my daughter and the man who is trying to win my affection, which under normal circumstances I'd be willing to give, I feel anything but abated, because I can't take my eyes off of them.

Lucy squeals in delight as Travis chases her around the jungle gym in what looks to be a game of tag. Each time it's her turn to go after him, he dodges her a few times before letting her win the game.

"Excuse me, but is that Travis Kidd you're with?"

I startle at the man who is standing at my table, who seemingly appeared out of nowhere, or has he been here the entire time and I've been too focused on watching Travis and Lucy that I didn't see him approach me?

His question puts me on alert, and I shift into work mode. "Who's asking?"

He laughs, not in a ha-ha-funny sort of way, but in a menacing way, causing the fine hairs on my neck to stand tall. I try to seek out Travis, but the man is blocking my path.

"Why are you with a rapist?" he asks in the same moment that Travis steps up to him with my daughter in his arms.

"That's enough," Travis says to the man. I motion for Lucy to come to me and she does as Travis hands her easily to me. "I suggest you leave," he tells the man, going chest to chest with him.

"Or what?" he asks.

"Or I'll make you," Travis warns.

I work quickly to get Lucy's coat on and when Travis turns to look at me, I see anger. While my body is coursing with fear, Travis's has to be filled with murderous rage.

THIRTEEN

Travis

It's been two days since I've seen Saylor, and not by choice. She has other clients that need her attention today as well. I try not to let the fact that she's with other men today bother me, but it does. I know she's not exclusive to me, but it would be nice if she were.

We are still waiting for the rape kit analysis to come back, along with the DNA test that I took. Irvin doesn't understand the holdup and has been on the DA's ass to make everything public. I want this nightmare behind me. I didn't do what I'm being accused of, not to Rachel and definitely not to anyone else, so the fact that it's taking so long is really starting to make me worry. I have a feeling that the state's attorney is sitting on something huge. Otherwise, why's he stalling? There are so many questions that I can't get answers to, because no one knows.

I'm back at the clubhouse today. This is the only place aside from Irvin's office that I can have any privacy. I was stupid to take Saylor and Lucy out to dinner the other night. Halfway through, a patron was brazen enough to go up to Saylor. I had spotted him earlier, lurking in the corner of the kid room but without a kid. I was careful to keep an eye on Lucy, more so than Saylor and I had done earlier before dinner came.

When I had gone to play with Lucy, the man approached Saylor. It was only a matter of seconds before I had Lucy in my arms and back at the table. One second later and I would've been able to prevent Lucy from hearing the man ask Saylor why she was with a rapist. But I couldn't prevent Saylor from hearing those words. The look on her face—it killed a piece of me. I know she believes me, but having a question like that asked really gives someone pause, and when she looked at me, I could see in her eyes that she was wondering the same thing. Our night was cut short after I threatened the man, who in turn promised to go to the police.

And now I picture his face as I shadowbox in the mirror. The urge to hit something repeatedly is growing day by day. My level of frustration is about to reach its breaking point. I want to wake up from this nightmare and go about living my life. I'm tired of the media camping out on the sidewalk in front of my house, and I'm sick of walking by the creepy, black, nondescript van that is parked only two doors down, the occupants of which are always hiding something when they see me head their way. I've seen enough movies to know they're taking pictures, but of what? It's not like I'm going to bring someone home, or even try to hook up with a random female.

There's only one person I'm interested in, and if she'd give me a chance, there's no question about me changing my ways. For her, I'd do it in a heartbeat, and I wouldn't miss any of the lifestyle I've been leading. Saylor would be worth it.

The door opens to the gym, and two voices try to talk over my music. I stop fighting myself in the mirror and go over to the sound system and turn it down.

"You stupid fucker," Ethan Davenport says as he turns the corner, followed by Cooper Bailey and Branch Singleton. I must look shocked, because he shakes his head and says, "Shut your mouth. You're not my type."

"That's not what your wife said," I add, confident that he knows I'm joking.

The guys make their way over to me, and we hug it out man style. I get a bit choked up that they're here and have to clear my throat before speaking. "What's going on?"

Cooper squeezes Ethan's shoulder. "This asshole thought you could use some company."

"Yeah, but you didn't have to take time away from your family and your kids." I look at Branch and Cooper especially. Branch has been trying to spend as much time with his son as possible, but the boy's mother doesn't make it easy. And Cooper's twins aren't more than two months old.

"I'll fly back to Seattle before Christmas," Ethan says.

"And Ainsley and the twins are here. They came with me," Cooper adds.

"My boy is with me until spring training starts," Branch states.

"No shit?" I say to Branch, who nods. Having his son here is a huge milestone for him, and I know he has to be overjoyed.

"Well, fuck, I don't know what to say."

"How about you tell us you're fucking starving and in need of a beer?" Cooper rubs his stomach while the guys laugh.

"Yeah, I could go for some grub."

The guys help me close up the gym and wait for me to change back into my winter wear before we head out for some lunch. We head to the Bleacher Bar, a place we'd like to enjoy during the season but never can. The back wall of the bar opens up over the stadium and center field, giving the diners a unique ambience. Of course, when there's a game, we're always playing.

"Hey, you guys…oh, wow." It's clear the waitress knows who we are when we walk in. The four of us smile and follow her to a table. Of course, she gives us one that overlooks the field. "What can I get for you?"

"I'll have a water," I say, while the others order beer. This is part of keeping my nose clean. If my brain isn't fogged up with booze, every decision I make can be done with a clear head.

As soon as she walks away, Branch leans in. "What the fuck is going on?"

I fill him in on what I know, and on the day I went in for questioning. Everyone seems in agreement that it's strange that it's been almost a week and the results haven't been made public.

"Do you think they don't have enough to charge you?" Ethan asks.

"They can't charge me with anything related to my DNA, because I didn't touch her. But I'm assuming she took my jacket home. I'm not really sure because I haven't heard whether the police were able to retrieve it from the bar."

"How'd she get your jacket?" Cooper asks.

This is where I have to be careful with my story. I still don't know why Saylor won't come forward, and I had planned to find out the other night at dinner, but the nice gentleman who stalked us ruined that for me.

I lean in farther so we're huddled together, and speak quietly. "I left the bar to speak to someone else, and the chick came after me, which pissed me off. So I bailed, leaving my jacket in the bar. And now she has it."

"And now she's crying rape?" Branch tsks as I nod. "That's fucked up."

"That's the tip of the iceberg," I say, righting myself. "I'm sure you've heard that others are coming forward, saying the same thing."

"Man, I told you this shit would catch up with you." Branch slaps me on the back, reminding me of the many times he told me to curb my partying and I didn't listen. He was an example of what not to do—a cleat-chaser he hooked up with ended up pregnant.

"And I'm paying the price for not listening."

The server returns with our drinks, and we place our order. We watch *SportsCenter* for a few minutes before the conversation picks up again.

"How are the twins?" I ask Cooper, who beams at the mere mention of his children.

"Hands down the best and hardest accomplishment of my life. Ainsley's a fucking machine when it comes to the babies. She has everything down to a T."

"And you come in and fuck it up, right?" Ethan says, laughing.

"You know it. I have learned not to announce that I'm home by yelling loudly and slamming the door."

The four of us laugh, and as I look around the table, I realize I'm the odd man out. Even though Ethan doesn't have any children, he has a niece that he dotes on. Hell, most of us love her because she's such an amazing kid. This could all change for me if Saylor gives me a chance. I know the stakes in dating a single mom and how reserved they are about falling in love, because it's not only their hearts that get hurt if things end badly. I need to step up my game where she's concerned, though, because I want so much more after spending more and more time with her.

A group of fans walk in and spot us immediately. Within seconds, we're signing autographs and posing for pictures. Honestly, I'm surprised I was asked, considering all the negative media about me right now. One fan even said that she didn't think I did it, because her friends are always trying to land an athlete. Really? This is the kind of world we live in?

I know the day will come when I can tell the truth, and I plan on it. I'll stand on the highest rooftop and shout my innocence when I'm given the green light. Irvin says it'll be soon, but I've come to the realization that his definition of "soon" and mine are vastly different.

Our food is delivered, causing us to turn into barbarians. The first bite is always the best, and there's nothing like a greasy burger to make your day better. I have to admit that having the guys here has really lifted my spirits, and while I don't want them to miss time with their families, I'm happy to have them with me.

"This burger," Ethan mumbles as he puts it back onto the plate and wipes his hands. "I love my mom, but she's on this health kick and Daisy has joined her. I don't even have my winter fat yet because I'm eating egg whites and lean meats when all I want is a juicy steak. My dad, Mike, and I have been trying to sneak out for pizza, but my mother has junk-food radar right now. I'm freaking starving," he says, stuffing fries in his mouth.

"At least you're eating. Ainsley wants to try and do everything herself and sometimes she's too tired to cook, and I can't even make toast, so it's been a lot of takeout," Cooper adds.

We look to Branch and wait for his story. He shrugs. "Chicken nuggets and pizza have become staples in my house."

I open my mouth to tell them about my dinner dates last night but keep that to myself, although I'd love to introduce Branch's son to Lucy. They're close in age and would probably get along.

"And we all know how you've been eating, Kidd. I can't believe you held a press conference to get some food," Ethan says.

I shake my head and set my burger down. "They didn't give me a choice. They were either going to follow me there or harass the person delivering it, so I tried to beat them at their own game."

"How'd that go for you?" Branch asks.

"Perfect," I tell them, laughing. "Food was delivered, and I think the restaurant saw an increase in sales that day from the news crew." Giving them the publicity is the least I can do if I'm not able to eat there like usual. In fact, the restaurants I have been frequenting are mostly in Saylor's neighborhood, increasing my chances of running into her. Can't say that's working out for me either. If it weren't for Irvin, dinner the other night wouldn't have happened. I should send the man a thank-you card.

"So what's next?" Cooper asks.

I set my napkin down and clasp my hands in front of me. "After we finish, I think we order dessert. What kind of friends would we be if we didn't allow Davenport to get his winter fat?" Everyone laughs while Ethan tries to push me out of my chair.

FOURTEEN

Saylor

I have purposely avoided my phone today. Elijah threatened that he'd be in town, and I'm hoping that I can avoid seeing him by not answering any calls or text messages. It's foolish, but it's the only thing getting me through the day. I've also been able to ignore Travis for the last couple of days. That hasn't been easy, but I have a job to do and everything can't revolve around him, even though that's what he'd like. My other clients need my services, have crises, have events that need to be RSVP'd to, or have contracts that need to be looked over. My co-workers could help me out, but passing off my clients in favor of one isn't the smartest thing to do.

A quick glance at the clock lets me know that the office will be closing shortly. It's Friday, the one day that Jeffrey insists that staff leave at five. Every other day, we stay until the job is done, whether it's in the office or out in the field. But on Fridays, he wants to make sure we can relax before the hectic weekend of sporting events starts. Not that the weekdays are any less crazy, but Sundays are the worst during the winter. We have football, basketball, and hockey, and luckily for me, aside from the issues with Travis, none of my clients should need me this weekend. Although, in this business, you never know until you get that call.

The downside of not having to work is that I can't use it as an excuse if Elijah does show up. I contemplate calling ahead to get Lucy and me tickets for an event, anything to get us away from Elijah, and as I pick up my phone to do so, a shadow appears in my doorway.

"Hello, Saylor." His voice is something I'll never forget but wish every day that I could. Many times it's the voice I hear in the middle of my nightmares when he tells me he's coming to take my daughter away from me. I liken it to the way Anthony Hopkins voiced Hannibal Lecter, creepy and bone-chilling.

I sit up as straight as I can and try to calm my nerves. I have often thought that if I ever saw him again, I'd crumble, that my heart would betray me and I'd fall back into his arms. But seeing him now, standing in my doorway with his designer trench coat folded over his arm, and those plastic covers that men put on their shoes instead of changing into boots, makes me laugh. These past few days, not once did I see Travis worry about his shoes. And the more I look at Elijah, the more I question what I saw in him all those years ago.

"Elijah," I say curtly as I try to peer through my blinds to see where Wanda is. Normally she would call ahead to announce a guest, but I can't see any sign of her, which means he walked right past her desk in search of me.

I don't invite him in or ask him to take the empty seat in front of my desk. For all I care, he can stand there while my co-workers brush past him, wondering who he is. Unfortunately for me, he doesn't care that I haven't extended an invitation or that I don't want him in my office.

As he moves toward my desk, I angle the picture of Lucy so only I can see her. Never has he asked for a picture of her, and I never post any of my child on my social media pages, unlike the way his wife is always posting photos. I've seen pictures of their kids, one born only a few months after Lucy, and the other within the last year. Sometimes, at night, when I'm feeling particularly bad about things, I compare their pictures with Lucy to see what traits they share. I know that someday I'll have to tell her about them, and about her father, but that day is not now. She's five, and her biggest worries are whether or not her Cinderella dress is clean and if her new best friend is going to eat breakfast or dinner with us again.

"I've been trying to call," Elijah says, sitting down and crossing his leg. Again, I find myself laughing because none of the men I'm around sit like this. They're casual, even in the most formal of settings. Right now, Elijah looks like a yuppie.

"I'm working, Elijah."

He sighs, as if I'm the one bothering him. And because I want to irritate him, I pick up my phone and bring it to life. Sure enough there are a slew of missed calls from him, but it's the text messages from Travis that make me smile. I open those because he could need something from me or have news that I should know about.

Dinner tonight?
I hope you're having a nice day!
I'm craving chicken fingers in the shape of funny characters!

Rereading these makes me smile, even though I shouldn't. I have yet to tell Travis everything, other than our relationship can't work. I don't want him feeling sorry for me or showing me any pity. The mistakes I made are on me, not him. He doesn't know that one night with him would lead to a life-altering situation that could cost me my job, my freedom, and my daughter. He doesn't need this type of drama in his life right now.

"Do you think you could flirt with your boyfriend on your own time and not on mine?" Elijah asks, clearly exasperated already by my attempts to ignore him. I open my mouth to correct him but don't. If he wants to think I have a boyfriend, I'm going to let him.

"Actually, you're on my time," I tell him as I set my phone down. "What do you want?"

"I want to see Lucy."

"You mean you want to meet her," I point out, hoping he feels the verbal jab.

He brushes off my comment and pulls at the pleat in his slacks. "She's four, Saylor. Moving forward, I'm building memories with her."

I stare at him, trying to come up with a reasonable response, but words fail me. I open my mouth to say something, only to close it right away. Elijah rolls his eyes, growing exasperated with me as quickly as I am with him.

"Is it money, Saylor? You know I pay my child support. I don't know what else you want from me."

"Nothing," I tell him as I clench my hands. "Absolutely nothing, which should be your clue that you need to leave my office and forget she even exists."

He shakes his head, and if I weren't watching him like a hawk, I would've missed the sly smile that formed before it disappeared. "You have no problems accepting my money."

I hate that he's right. I need it to pay for her education. The tuition at her private school is a bit out of my reach, and I figured his money would go to something good.

"Elijah, I don't have time for your games. I have work to do."

This time he nods, drops his leg back to the floor, and leans forward. "I saw that one of your clients is in trouble."

"And?" I ask, leaning forward to match his stance.

"And I know that you've been seeing him."

"Excuse me?" I scoff, hoping to convey that he's grasping at nothing.

"A colleague saw the three of you together."

I stand and decide to pace around my office. It's smaller than Jeffrey's but still allows me to walk off any nervous energy.

"So let me get this straight. A friend of yours saw me with my client, and my daughter happened to be with me?"

"Yes."

"When?" There has only been one time, and that was dinner earlier in the week. It's not unheard of, having dinner with clients or even having them at our homes for the holidays. There is no way Elijah knows that Travis is interested in me.

"A few nights ago, and you can imagine how upset I am that you're allowing our daughter to be near an accused rapist."

Now I'm seeing red. The fact that he thinks I'd put my daughter in harm's way really pisses me off, but I can't tell him that. I need to keep my cool, remain calm. The last thing I want is for him to accuse me of being overly emotional.

"How dare you assume that I would put *my* daughter's well-being at risk. You have no leg to stand on when it comes to parenting Lucy. You don't even know how old she is. And you don't have any clue about what type of parent I am. I have raised her, by myself, since she was born."

Elijah leans back in the chair and crosses his leg again. My phone chimes, and I go to it, finding a text from my mother telling me that she's sick and asking me to come get Lucy. I'd love to, and would normally drop everything, but I'm not ready for Elijah to see her. I close my eyes and think, and as my fingers hover over my phone, I know that what I'm about to do might change everything. I reply to Travis's messages, asking him to go to my mom's and get Lucy, explaining that my mother has fallen ill.

Of course.

Relief washes over me, and while this isn't ideal, it's the only thing I can think of. And I know Travis will treat Lucy as if she's the most precious person in his life. I tell him that my mother lives in my building and give him her apartment number. I also let him know that he can get the key from my mom to gain access to my apartment. It's risky, but the alternative is telling Elijah I need to go and having him follow me.

"Sorry, that was business," I tell him, offering him a smile that I can only hope placates him. I know that I have to play nice in order to keep him at bay.

"Back to my visitation. I figure that I'll come up one weekend a month until school is out, and then she can come to Virginia for the summer. Renee would really like to be a mother to her. I'm sure you can understand."

My mouth waters, and not in the way that it does when I see Travis, but the way it does before I'm about to throw up. That is what I want to do right now, hurl into my garbage can or all over his lap. He can't be serious with this pile of shit he laid out for me.

"I think I need a minute, Elijah."

I leave my office, taking my picture of Lucy and my cell phone with me for good measure. I wouldn't put it past Elijah to snoop through my desk while I try to regain my composure. In the bathroom, I lean against the door and try to catch my breath. I knew this day would come, but honestly I never expected it. I figured—had hoped—that he was content with his new family and wouldn't want to interrupt mine.

Heading to the sink, I splash water on my face and pat it dry, trying not to ruin too much of my makeup. Elijah doesn't need to see that he's getting the best of me. I return with my head held high as I strut back into my office. Sitting back down, I face him.

"First off, Lucy has a mother; it's me, and I don't give a rat's ass if your wife wants to be a mother to my daughter—it's not going to happen. Second, if you want visitation, you will have to follow the court order that has been in place since she was six months old. Had you been following it right all along, I might have been amenable and let her spend a week or so in Virginia, but you haven't, and one weekend a month isn't going to change that. Third, I am never going to understand anything when it comes to Renee or you, for that matter. As far as I'm concerned, she has no say in what goes on in Lucy's life."

"Don't test me on this, Saylor. She's my daughter, too."

I should take his threat seriously, but I don't. "Then act like it, Elijah. Until then, we have nothing to talk about."

"Except, I'm here to see her."

I pick up my phone from off my lap and look at my calendar. "Tomorrow we'll be at the indoor play palace. You can see her there."

Elijah stands and slips on his coat. "Don't make this harder than it needs to be. One call and her bags are packed and she's on the next flight with me."

He doesn't give me a chance to respond before he's walking out of my office. I'm frozen in my chair as his words replay in my mind.

There's no mistaking that threat. If I don't give in to his demands, he's going to call in a favor. He did that many times when he was living here, often with his corrupt friends. Elijah said that's how you made it to the top, how you became powerful, trading favors for favors.

I grab my coat and lock up my office. The trains will be crazy at this time of the day, so I hail a cab, only to get stuck in traffic about halfway from home. I get out and walk as fast as I can through the holiday shoppers, and in high heels. In hindsight, I should've taken the time to change my shoes, but I want to get home to Lucy. I need to hold her, feel her in my arms, and know that she's safe.

When I open my door, Travis and Lucy both stare at me. Christmas music is playing, and our tree is lit. Travis smiles, and I cover my mouth to hide my laughter. This man, who has been telling me that he wants something, anything, with me is sitting on my couch wearing a tiara. His lips are painted ruby red, and the blue eye shadow he has on really makes his eyes brighter.

Somehow he knew that this would make my day better.

FIFTEEN

Travis

By the mixed expression on Saylor's face, I can tell something is bothering her even as she tries to mask the turmoil at my current state. I slowly slide the tiara off and set it on the table before scooping Lucy up in my arms and carrying her over to her mother. Don't ask me why I felt the need to do this, as opposed to letting Lucy walk over, but something inside told me that I needed to deliver Lucy into her arms.

They both collapse into each other while I stand by awkwardly. This seems to be a private moment that I shouldn't witness, and yet here I am, wanting to envelop both of them in my arms. In the matter of a week, these women have wrapped me around their fingers, and there isn't shit I can do about it.

Saylor lets out a sob. It was quiet, but I heard it. As she sets Lucy down, she shyly tries to cover her eyes so that I don't see her tears.

"Do you want to talk about it?" I ask as I reach for her hand.

She lets me hold it, only briefly, until she's pulling away and wiping her eyes. "Stressful day."

"Thankfully, it wasn't anything I did," I tell her jokingly. She smiles, only it doesn't reach her eyes. I'm not sure what happened today at work, but whoever fucked up did a number on her.

"Mommy, Travis let me do his makeup."

Saylor looks at me and laughs. I curtsy and wish I still had on the tiara so I could twirl around like a ballerina.

"His makeup looks great, sweetie."

Lucy beams with pride and runs off to her room after Saylor asks for an "adult" minute.

"I need more than a minute, Saylor. I think you know that." I waggle my eyebrows at her, causing her to half laugh, half cry. I pull her into my arms, and she nestles her head into my neck. "Do you want to talk about it?"

She shakes her head and pulls away from me. "I can't take you seriously with that crap on your face. Follow me—I'll help you clean it off."

I don't think Saylor realizes that I'd follow her anywhere, especially if she's leading me down the path of righteousness. For her, I'd be a better man. All she has to do is say the words, and I'll enter every self-help program available to be the type of man she deserves. But something tells me that she likes the bad boy in me and that she craves the dirty-talking, cocky man that I am.

Her bathroom is decorated in a Disney theme, and earlier when Lucy was giving me the grand tour of their two-bedroom, one-bath apartment, I noticed that Saylor's life has been overcome by Lucy. I don't mean that in a bad way, but I do know that women like to have space to go and relax, and Saylor doesn't seem to have that. Every inch of their apartment is "Lucy," whether it's toys, books, or decorations.

Saylor motions for me to sit on the pink-covered lid of the toilet as she digs under the counter for something. I watch her prepare a handful of cotton balls with some type of liquid, as if it's pure science.

"Close your eyes," she says. The liquid is cool against my eyelids, and the pressure she's applying is soft. "I'm sorry she did this."

"I'm not. It was fun. I've never done anything like this before."

She moves to my other eye and follows the same technique. "You could've told her no."

I smile and rest my hands on her hips. I feel her lean closer as she continues to rub the cotton ball over my face, removing the remnants of Lucy's makeup job.

"This shouldn't feel good, but it does," I whisper into thin air. I'm afraid to open my eyes, fearful of her expression. Sometimes my little comments make her happy, and other times they make her step away.

"This might taste funky, so try not to lick your lips." She starts working on my lips and scrubs a bit harder.

"Ouch," I mumble as my bottom lip is tugged across my face.

"Sorry, she really caked this crap on."

"Where'd she get it from anyway?" I ask in between swipes.

"My mom. Lucy isn't supposed to use it without permission and supervision." Saylor continues to work at removing the lipstick. She steps out of my hands, and I open my eyes to find her staring at me. I'm tempted to pull her onto my lap so she can straddle me and have another heavy make-out session, but with Lucy in the other room, I can't imagine Saylor would even kiss me right now.

"I was supervising," I say with a laugh.

"Right, and what if I couldn't get this off?" she laughs.

I shrug and stand to look at myself in the mirror. Aside from my lips being stained red, the makeup is gone. "Then the media would've had a field day with me." I wink at her in the mirror, and she blushes. "Do you want to talk about what has you all upset?" I ask as we leave the bathroom. She shakes her head and motions toward the door.

"I need to give Lucy a bath, and I'm tired. Do you mind?" As soon as the words are out of her mouth, she's covering her face and shaking her head. "I'm sorry—that came out wrong."

"It's fine, Saylor." I bring her to my chest and hold her tightly. After a few seconds, her arms snake around my waist. Kissing the top of her head, my lips linger there for a moment until they move down to her temple, cheek, and finally to her lips. Her quick intake of air isn't lost on me as I try to fight back a smile while I kiss her. "Good night," I tell her as my lips hover over hers. "Lucy has already eaten dinner. I am the master at fish sticks and fries."

"Good night, Travis, and thank you for saving me today."

"You save me every day." I leave her with those parting words, hoping that she understands what I'm saying to her. Hell, sometimes I don't even understand what I'm saying except when it comes to Saylor. I know that she likes me, but something is stopping her from pursuing a relationship. It could be a number of things—my reputation is probably the biggest hurdle—and I hope I'm doing everything right when it comes to showing her that I've put that life behind me, more so for her than anything.

Instead of taking a cab or calling for an Uber, I walk home. The night air is brisk, and the wind is holding steady. I can't get my mind off Saylor and how I'd much rather be in her tiny apartment than home alone. Their home is filled with love, warmth, and it makes you feel welcomed, while mine is a designer slab of bachelorhood.

I groan when I see the same trucks parked outside my house, not to mention the surveillance van sitting a few doors down. They think they're subtle and that I don't notice them. I've been tempted to play practical jokes on them but have refrained. It's part of my trying to turn over a new leaf. The Travis Kidd from a week ago would've stuck a banana up their tailpipe, had copious amounts of food delivered, and probably even ordered them an escort.

My name is called as I near my house. Someday I'll be able to answer all their questions, but until then, I stuff my hands in my pockets and keep my head down.

"Travis, are you still a Renegade?"

"Do you know what's taking the DA so long?"

"Are you nervous that your arrest is imminent?"

The last question has me stumbling over my feet. A reporter reaches out and grabs my arm to help me straighten up. "Thanks," I say as I adjust my coat and start walking up the stairs to my door. Unless this woman somehow stole my jizz, there is no way they can pin her rape on me. It's unfair that I'm being hounded when there hasn't been a peep about her or her credibility.

As soon as I'm behind my closed door, I lean against it and sigh. I want to scream, throw things, and stand in front of my large picture window with my middle fingers up, telling them all to fuck off. Somehow I doubt Saylor would approve of a stunt like that, though, and the damage I would do with the media would probably be beyond repair.

Instead, I move through my darkened house, turning on only the television for light, and slip into my bathroom to take a shower. There isn't a thing sitting on my countertop, and my walls are decal-free. In fact, looking around I feel as if the gray-and-white décor is boring and lacks life. Saylor's may be cluttered, but it feels homey.

After a long, hot shower and a self-induced facial to make sure the makeup is in fact gone, I park myself in front of the television. Thankfully, I'm not the headline on every channel tonight, but the alternative is Christmas movies. I search in hopes of finding something like *Die Hard* to watch, but I can only find the sappy love stories that are meant to make women weep and send men running.

Except I don't want to run anymore, but I'm not sure I want to settle down either. I do know that Saylor is someone that I want to explore a relationship with, but I also know that exploring isn't an option for her. She comes with Lucy, and loving one means loving both. There's no doubt in my mind that I can love them both, but I'm not sure love is enough.

My phone rings, and Branch's name and ugly mug appear on my screen.

"'Sup," I say as I continue to flip through the channels.

"I have a suite at the Bruins game tomorrow night. You interested?"

"Is this a date?"

"Fuck no. I'm taking my son and thought you'd like to meet him. Plus, it's probably wise for you to be seen with your teammates. I've read some shit that says we've all turned our backs on you, and—"

"I know you haven't," I tell him before he can finish his sentence. "Can I bring someone? Well, two someones?"

"Kidd, are you saying you have a girlfriend?"

The thought of Saylor being my girlfriend brings a smile to my face. "Nah, she's my publicist, but she has a daughter that's your son's age. Maybe they can have playdates and shit while you're here."

"The more the merrier. Coop is bringing Ainsley, but not the twins. The fucker got Wilson to agree to babysit."

I laugh as images of Wilson changing shitty diapers play out in my mind. "What a kiss-ass."

"Who? Bailey?"

"No, Wilson," I say. "Who the hell volunteers to babysit twins?"

"Dunno. So you in?"

"Yeah, I'll be there for sure. Put me down for three just in case."

"Righto. Peace," Branch says as he hangs up. I don't even hesitate to call Saylor, and when she says hello, a jolt of excitement hits my dick, causing it to wake up.

"Fuck, you sound sexy when you answer the phone."

"Travis..." She draws my name out, making me pray that she's been thinking about me.

"Fuck, Saylor." My hand palms my growing erection. "Don't you just want to fuck and get rid of all this sexual tension between us?"

The line goes silent until I hear her sigh and mutter, "Yes."

"Me too, but not a one-night stand. I want more."

"I can't," she says, killing the small buzz I had going over the thought of us knocking boots.

"Right, I forgot," I say, clearing my throat. "Branch's son is in town, and he's the same age as Lucy, or close to it. He's invited me, or us, to the hockey game tomorrow night. He has a suite. Do you want to go?"

"Travis—"

"Look, I'll leave your name at the will-call window if you want. I thought I'd offer, but I realize that you can get tickets to any event you want. So, good night, Saylor." I hang up, wondering how she can go from night to day so damn fast. One minute she's asking me to watch her daughter and doesn't balk when I kiss her, but then she won't go to a hockey game with a bunch of baseball players.

Am I missing something? Or am I so wrapped up in her that I'm not seeing what's right in front of me—a woman who has told me nothing can happen?

SIXTEEN

Saylor

My phone vibrates beside me, and a quick glance shows a text from Elijah instead of Travis, like I had hoped. All morning I have contemplated calling him to apologize for my behavior last night, but I'm a coward. I can't bring myself to tell him that, while I'm interested, he's not worth the risks, and I can't find the right words to convey that to him without hurting his feelings. The last thing I want to do is hurt him, but I have to tell him. I can't continue leading him on, even though each kiss brings me closer to succumbing to him.

Elijah's face lights up my screen, this time by calling. I dread speaking to him, so I send him to voice mail and open his text message instead. He's asking when and what the address is for the play palace, and honestly I was hoping he would've forgotten or decided Lucy wasn't worth the headache and returned to Virginia, back to his picture-perfect house and Stepford wife.

I decide to wait until about five minutes before we leave to let Elijah know where we'll be. It's mean on my part, but the man deserves to be kept on his toes where Lucy is concerned. All the way to the play palace, she yammers on about Travis and how he's her best friend and how she wants him to come over again. Secretly, I do, too. I haven't slept well all week, not since the night he came over, and I have never felt more alive than the day we made out at the gym. When I'm alone, thoughts of the night Travis and I spent together keep me yearning for him, and no matter what I do to quell those visions, there are more waiting in the wings to take their place. Not to mention the anticipation of what could happen if I let go of my inhibitions and gave in to him.

Last night when he called, I almost gave in and invited him to come back over. He's right—the sexual tension between us is thickening day by day, and I'm on the verge of combustion. Travis has a knack for taking a word like *fuck* and turning it into the most sensual expression ever. When he asked me if I wanted to fuck, to be with him longer than one night, I nodded yes while my mouth muttered the words *I can't*.

I can't replayed over and over in my head as I achieved my own orgasm while imagining it was him between my legs. I have never been one to resort to self-pleasure, until this week, and now it is an automatic response after he's left or after he's invaded a dream. While I may know my body, Travis mastered it in one night, and I'll never be able to duplicate what he did.

My level of anxiety grows as we enter the palace. I pay our fee, our hands get stamped, and I quickly usher Lucy over to a locker where we can store our stuff.

"Travis would love it here," she says as she takes off her winter wear. I look around and agree. Deep down he's a big kid, at least where Lucy is concerned.

"I'm sure he would."

"Maybe next time he can come." She looks up at me with her

blue eyes, eyes that are the same color as Travis's. That thought alone gives me pause. I don't see him as a family man, but I see pride in his eyes when he looks at Lucy. I push her brunette locks out of the way and give her a kiss on the nose.

"Come here. Let me fix your hair." Her hair is full of static from her stocking cap.

Lucy does as I ask, turning around and tipping her head back so I can redo her ponytail. When I was young, I used to dream of having a daughter so I could do her hair, and now that I do, I realize how much of a pain it is. *Everything* gets in your hair when you're little.

"All set," I tell her, and move us along until we're in the play area. "I'll be right here." I point to the table where I'm going to sit and read while she plays. I like the security of the play palace, knowing that Lucy can't leave unless the stamp on her hand matches mine. This allows her to get out the energy she has from being cooped up during the winter, and I can catch up on some reading.

I try not to watch the door, wondering if Elijah is going to show. I don't want to believe that he's changed, that he's willing to make Lucy a priority. I want him to forget about her, pretend she doesn't exist, but I know he won't do that.

I'm lost in the pages of my book when I hear his voice. A quick glance tells me he's not thrilled to be in a place like this. It's noisy, dirty, and there's a mob of children running around freely. I'm laughing on the inside because this is perfect. *This* is Lucy. If you're not playing dress-up and willing to be a kid, then you won't end up being her best friend.

"Do you plan to stay here all day?" he asks, standing next to me.

"You can sit down, ya know," I say, pointing to the seat in front of me. He hesitates and brushes the chair off with his hand. I can't help but laugh at how out of place he looks in his suit. It's the weekend. He needs to lighten up. When we were together, he used to wear jeans and loafers. Never sneakers. Now that I think about it, it drove me crazy back then.

"This place is filthy."

"She loves it."

"I had rather hoped you meant a sophisticated learning facility, not a jungle full of—"

"Children, Elijah. You have two of them at home."

"Renee and I don't allow for this type of debauchery."

I close my book and slip it into my bag. "You don't allow your children to play?" I ask, taking mental notes of his demeanor. How in good conscience would I ever agree to let him take my daughter for a week, let alone months, if she's not allowed to play?

"In a controlled, sterile environment."

Shaking my head, I scan the crowd for her. She's at the top of the jungle gym, about to jump into a pit of foam balls. On the inside I'm encouraging her and tempted to make Elijah watch. Maybe it'll give him a heart attack, and he'll bail on her. "So boring and stuffy, like you."

He glares at me, and I shrug. I don't care if Lucy rolls in dirt, kisses frogs, or jumps in rain puddles. It's a part of growing up and being a kid. It's hard for me to fathom that this is the man that I wanted to spend the rest of my life with, the man that I wanted to have a house full of children with. We're nothing alike, and our views on parenting vastly differ.

"Where is the child? I would like to meet her."

It's in this moment that I decide I'm going to give him a run for his money. Had he referred to her by name, I probably would've called her over and introduced them to each other. Not as her father, of course, but as Elijah.

"She's playing over there," I say, nodding toward the massive jungle gym. He turns and sighs.

"Stop the bullshit, Saylor. I don't have time for this."

"Well, if you want to see her, make the time. Go on; go find your daughter."

I owe him nothing, yet everything. He's missed every court-appointed holiday and visitation. Birthdays have come and gone without a card, but the monthly support payment is made without hesitation. His money is the only thing I can count on from him. I have no doubt he could destroy me in court, with the people he knows, but I would do everything I could to make it a long, drawn-out battle so that when it was over, Lucy would be of age to tell the judge what she wants to do.

Elijah walks to the center of the room before going over to a random girl. She looks to be about eight or so and wants nothing to do with him. He does this to two or three more girls before I decide to intervene. As fun as it would be to see him get tossed out of here, the last thing I need is for him to take me to court. Truth is, I wouldn't be able to afford to fight him, and he knows that.

"Lucy," I yell as I stand next to him. He glares at me once again, and I shrug. "All you have to do is ask for a picture every now and again, and you wouldn't look like a creepy pedophile."

Lucy comes running and grabs my hand, leading us toward the back of the room where the food stand is. She probably thinks it's lunchtime, and a quick look at the clock tells me it is. That is something Elijah can take care of while he's here.

He follows us, standing behind me while we wait to order our food. "What are you hungry for today?" I ask.

"Um…" she says, tapping her index finger against her cheek. "I think a corn dog and fries."

"Hi, can we have a corn dog and cheeseburger, both with fries and two bottles of water?" I step aside and motion for Elijah to go. He looks at me like I have two heads, while shaking his. "Suit yourself, but you're paying." I smirk, daring him to tell me no.

Elijah steps up and places a mumbled order that I'm unable to hear and brings a table number back to where we've been sitting.

"Who are you?" Lucy asks as she scoots closer to me. Her legs swing back and forth, and I know exactly when she pops him in the knee. I can't help but laugh, because she's doing everything that I want her to.

"I'm Elijah Henry."

"I go to school with a boy named Henry, but sometimes he goes by Hank."

"Is he your friend?" Elijah asks.

Lucy shrugs. "Sure, everyone is. It's a rule. But he picks his nose, and that's gross."

"It's disgusting. You shouldn't hang out with boys like that," he says, causing me to frown.

She stops talking as our food arrives. While Lucy and I went for what I call "fair food," Elijah has opted for a salad. A few other moms walk by and give him a look that has me chuckling under my breath. He has to be *that* guy all the time.

"Why are you here?" Lucy asks.

"I came to see you," he says, setting his fork down.

"Oh. But why are you dressed for work? Today is Saturday. It's a play day."

He looks down at his clothes and back at me. I cock my eyebrow, letting him know that I agree with her.

"This is how I always dress."

Lucy seems to accept this answer and goes about eating her lunch, never asking him another question.

His phone rings halfway through, and he answers. By the responses he's giving, I'm assuming he's talking to his wife, and I don't like what I hear, such as "dirty environment," "out of control," and "processed foods."

"Sorry about that," he says, hanging up.

"Sure you are." I gather my and Lucy's empty baskets and leave Elijah at the table while I take Lucy to the bathroom to clean up.

"Who is that man?"

"A friend, I guess." I don't know how to answer her, because I'm not going to be the one who tells her that he's her father. Those words need to come from him, and when she asks where he's been all her life, he can tell her. I'm going to end up taking the brunt of the emotions that will come after the fact. I shouldn't have to be the one to deliver the news, too.

"I don't like him," she says as she washes her hands.

I don't either, but I can't tell her that. As much as I don't want to, I have to be an adult in this situation, when I really want to stick my tongue out at him and tell him to fuck off.

"Sometimes people hang around even when you don't like them," I tell her, hoping my five-year-old can understand the gist of what I'm saying.

"I like Travis. Can we go see him?"

She holds her hands out for me to dry, all while her eyes plead with me. He invited us to hockey, but I didn't exactly give him an answer. It would be nice to see Branch and maybe talk some business with him. We've been trying to land him as a client for a few years, especially after he signed his recent deal with the Renegades, far under his market value.

"I don't know, Lucy. We'll see, okay?"

She sighs but places her hand in mine. When we get back to our table, every sign of Elijah is gone. I tell Lucy to run and play as I reach in my pocket for my phone. I have one missed call and a text from him.

I will be reevaluating my stance.

"Fucker." I slip my phone back into my pocket and return to my book. Only, the words are a blur, and I can't concentrate. It's a damn good thing he pulled this shit before he told her who he was. I can't imagine what she'd think if she knew and then he bailed on her.

SEVENTEEN

Travis

Shaun Singleton is the spitting image of his father, and for two people who haven't spent a lot of time together, they sure act like each other. Seeing Branch interact with his son shows me another side of him. I'm used to the baseball player, the most feared designated hitter in the American League. He's usually stone-faced and lacking emotion, unless he's brought in the winning run in the bottom of the ninth.

Tonight, the Branch Singleton sitting in the suite is different. He's relaxed, joyful. Dude looks happier than a pig in shit.

I feel bad for Ainsley Bailey, though. I had thought Saylor would want to come and had hoped she'd be around to hang out with Ainsley. Saylor is used to sports and understands them. Ainsley is somewhat new, even though she went to a lot of our games after the All-Star break. Instead, she's watching the Bruins warm up while her husband prattles on with his teammates.

"Hey, Kidd, why don't you go pick up some chick and bring her here so Ainsley has someone to talk to?" Cooper asks, patting me on the back.

I shake my head and sip on my water. "As much as I'd like to help you out, cleat-chasers are way too risky for me right now."

He hangs his head in shame. "Sorry, man. I forgot."

"It's cool." But seriously, how can you forget that shit? It's the reason he's even here right now and not living the life in Florida where it's warm and the sun shines every day.

"I thought you were bringing someone," Branch says, digging the knife that Cooper already stabbed me with even deeper.

"She couldn't make it."

I decide that talking about who I was going to bring isn't the conversation for me right now and walk to the front of the suite, taking a seat next to Ainsley.

"Hey, Travis," she says, giving me a hug.

"How are my niece and nephew?" After Cooper made me go to Lamaze class with him, I took an interest in the twins. They're cute as hell, but Uncle Travis isn't taking on any duties until they're fully potty trained and the projectile vomiting has stopped. I swear that Cal was born from the exorcist or something equally evil. Janie, on the other hand, loves me and makes eyes at me whenever I see her.

"They're good. They're with Wes tonight."

"Yeah, why is that?" I ask. "They're super-tiny humans, and he doesn't strike me as the type to babysit."

She shrugs and looks behind her, I'm assuming for Cooper. "Um…he and Coop have spent a lot of time together, and he asked. I mean, it's only for a few hours, and they'll probably sleep through most of it, and…well, maybe I should leave and go get them, right?" Ainsley starts to stand, but my hand comes down on her arm, keeping her in her seat.

"It was only a question. I'm sure Wilson is capable of being a great babysitter. Besides, I'm sure you need a few hours without them."

"I do. I really do," she says, nodding. I think I probably scared the shit out of her, but that wasn't my intention. I just find it odd that Wilson, of all guys, would want to babysit.

General manager Ryan Stone and his wife, country music superstar Hadley Carter, walk into the suite. A few people who can see inside notice her right off and start chanting her name. As much as I don't want to, I stand and go over to greet him. The last time I saw him, I was storming out of the conference room in a heated fit.

"Mr. Stone," I say to a man who is younger than me. We shake hands, and he reintroduces his wife. She and Ainsley had babies on the same day. "How's your boy?" I ask, giving her a kiss on the cheek. Stone is a lucky bastard being married to one of the hottest chicks around.

"He's really good. Thanks for asking." Hadley sees Ainsley and waves before kissing Ryan and leaving the suite with a few security guards. The second Ryan focuses his attention elsewhere, I turn to Cooper.

"I didn't know Stone was going to be here," I say to Cooper, who nods.

"Hadley is singing the national anthem tonight, so Branch invited them to hang out with us."

"Gotcha."

"You nervous?" Coop asks me.

I shrug. "Everything about my life makes me nervous. I hear someone say my name and I'm afraid to turn around, or they ask if I read something online and I'm afraid to look, because I don't want to see what people are saying about me. The stuff I have read is bull-shit. Everyone is concerned with the victim and assumes that I've done something wrong." I down my water, wishing it were something stronger.

"It'll work out," Cooper tells me.

"And if it doesn't?" I say as Cooper and I both turn and look at Stone, who is immersed in conversation with Branch.

"I'm trying to remain optimistic for you. Hell, you helped me with Ainsley. I'm only trying to return the favor."

I can't help but laugh. "I didn't do shit when it came to Ainsley except give you a hard time."

"You didn't chase after her, and that says a lot to me about a person."

Putting my arm around Cooper, I pull him into a headlock and rub my knuckles on his head. "That's the one thing I'll never do—touch a teammate's girl."

"But others are fair game?" he asks.

"I suppose," I say, shrugging. "Maybe that's my problem."

"Yeah, maybe."

I follow Cooper down the few steps and take a seat one away from him and Ainsley. I don't want to intrude on their date night and don't mind being a loner for the evening. We stand for the national anthem when Hadley's name is announced. We all scream loudly for her, and Ainsley lets out a whistle that makes us all cower and cover our ears.

As soon as the puck drops, the sound of Saylor's voice catches my attention. I turn around to find her being greeted by Stone. Lucy is with her, and when she sees me, she comes running.

"Travis," she says as her tiny arms wrap around me in the fiercest hug I have ever had, and one that I needed desperately.

"What are you guys doing here?"

"Dunno. Mom said we were coming to hockey, and you are here."

"Well, I'm happy you're here," I tell her as I pull her into my lap. I start talking to her about the game, explaining how hockey works.

"But you don't play this one?"

"Nope, only baseball."

"But why?" she asks, putting her hands up.

"Well, because when I was your age, hockey wasn't an option for me. And I don't know how to skate."

"I do," she says, turning in my lap. "I will teach you."

"I would like that, Lucy. Hey, do you want to meet my friends?"

"Okay, sure."

I turn her on my lap to face Cooper and Ainsley and introduce them to her. I also add that Ainsley has two babies at home, and Lucy asks if she can go see them. Of course I tell her yes, because I'm going to do whatever I can to spend time with her and her mother.

Halfway through the first period, Saylor joins us down in front. I know that I have to remain professional, but man if I don't want to reach for her hand or place a kiss on her sweet lips.

"Glad you could make it."

She smiles and leans toward me. The attempt is subtle, but I notice it. "I wasn't sure if this was a good idea or not."

"It's only a hockey game, Saylor. And my teammates are here. It's not like I'm going to take advantage of you."

She blushes at my comment, and I want to reach out and stroke her cheek but keep my hands firmly planted on the armrests. The Garden erupts, and Lucy jumps off my lap and starts cheering right alongside Cooper.

"I think she likes hockey," I tell Saylor, who shakes her head.

"She likes everything. Ballet, dance, gymnastics. If someone is taking a lesson, she wants to sign up."

"What does she do now?"

Saylor looks down at her jeans and brushes her hand along her leg. "Nothing."

"Why not?"

Her eyes close briefly, and I already know the answer before she says it. "Those activities cost money, and right now, I'm not in a position to pay for them."

The only thing I can do is nod. I know I could offer to pay for Lucy, but Saylor would tell me no. And it's not the same type of no as when she tells me that we can't be together or when she tells me that I shouldn't kiss her. This would be crossing the line and could very well ruin the relationship I'm trying to build with her.

"What about her dad?"

She shakes her head, and her eyes go from me to Lucy. Lucy is busy talking to Cooper and Ainsley and not paying attention.

"Sore subject?"

"You can say that," she says.

The buzzer sounds, and I scoop Lucy up into my arms and put her over my shoulder, much to her squealing delight. She's laughing so hard that I start to as well. I set her down, and she pushes her hair out of her face.

"That was fun, Travis. Let's do it again."

I kneel down to her level. "After I introduce you to my friend. His name is Shaun, and he's here visiting his dad for a bit, so he doesn't know anyone, and I thought you guys could be friends."

"Okay," she says, shrugging. Life as a five-year-old is simple. I

take her over to where Branch is still talking with Stone and introduce Lucy to everyone.

"Shaun, this is my friend Lucy."

"Hi," he says quietly.

"Hi," she replies, grabbing my hand.

"Shaun's dad plays baseball with me. Do you remember Branch?"

"Hey, Lucy."

She waves, suddenly shy. Well, this isn't going like I thought it
would.

"Shaun brought his iPad if you want to play a game with him,"
Branch says, pointing to the table. She nods and follows them, climb-
ing up into the chair next to Shaun.

"Lucy, I'll be sitting by your mom, okay?"

"Yeah." Lucy never looks up as Shaun starts scrolling through
his games. Within seconds, they're deep in conversation about who
knows what.

Branch pulls me close and nods toward Saylor. "You banging
her?"

Oh, how I want to lie right now but don't. "Nope; she's my publicist. Saylor actually works for my manager, and she's been assigned
to babysit me until this shit clears up."

"She's actually really good at her job, Branch," Stone says, joining
in on our conversation. "You may want to consider setting up a
meeting with her and Jeffrey. He's expressed an interest in you, and
Saylor has done a lot for Travis's public persona. Jeffrey's firm does
more than public relations. He runs a full-scope business management firm."

I look at Stone oddly, wondering why he would encourage one
of his players to seek another agent. Everyone knows that Branch

got screwed on his current contract, saving the Renegades a shit ton of money. Of course, that benefited the organization but not Branch.

"Let me introduce you," I tell him. He follows me over, and Saylor stands when she sees him.

"Saylor Blackwell, this is Branch Singleton, and for some reason, our GM thinks he needs Jeffrey as an agent, manager, or whatever you guys are calling yourselves these days."

They shake hands. "Stone is right," she says. "Let's talk."

Before I can even blink my eyes, Saylor and Branch are off in a corner discussing business, and Lucy is preoccupied with Shaun. I'm back to being a loner, and while the thought is slightly depressing, at least I'm doing it in the same vicinity as the two girls I wanted to spend the night with. That makes me feel a little bit better.

I sit down next to Cooper and sigh.

"Dude, you're banging your agent's assistant?"

"No," I say, shaking my head.

He laughs, and it makes me want to punch him in the junk. "What the fuck ever, dude. It's written all over your face. If you're not dipping yet, you will be soon."

"I don't know what you're talking about." I'm trying with all my might to keep a straight face, but shit, it's hard. I want to gossip like a high school girl after her first kiss under the bleachers, but I can't. The last thing I need is the media running with a story about Saylor and me. She doesn't need that kind of publicity, and I certainly don't. Right now, I'm branded a rapist, and for all intents and purposes, she should steer clear of me.

"Whatever you say, man." Cooper goes back to talking to Ainsley while I sulk. It's what I'm good at—feeling sorry for myself.

Before I know it, the game is over, and the Bruins have won. There will be a celebration down the street at the local bar where my nightmare began a week ago.

Tonight, I think I'll walk Saylor and Lucy home and hopefully to their door, where I may be able to steal a good-night kiss from the woman that I desperately want to be with.

BOSTON RENEGADES

A press conference was held today in the pending case against left fielder, Travis Kidd. The state's attorney said that the results of the rape kit were inconclusive and further testing will be done using the DNA sample that Kidd voluntarily provided.

The members of the media were not allowed to ask questions and were left dumbfounded by the statement. Many of us asked questions anyway, but we were not acknowledged. We would like to know why Kidd hasn't been cleared if the test is inconclusive. Our legal expert says that the state is likely trying to make an example out of Kidd.

Irvin Abbott, who represents Kidd, stated that he had no comment but promised that justice would prevail. Our calls to Kidd went to voice mail.

On a side note:

We want to let Travis know that everyone at the BoRe Blog believes in him, and when he's ready, we're here to tell his side of the story.

The BoRe Blogger

EIGHTEEN

Saylor

The streets of Boston are bustling with holiday shoppers, reminding me that Christmas isn't that far off, and that means my vacation is coming up. This year, I'm taking time off while Lucy is home on winter vacation for some mother/daughter time. She's growing so fast that I don't want to miss these small moments with her, and thankfully my employer is flexible enough to let that happen.

Cinching my coat closer, I try to ward off the wind that is blowing in from the harbor. It's my dream to one day live in the south, a place where the sunshine brings you warmth almost daily. Deep down, I know I would miss the snow during the holidays, but I wouldn't miss the cold.

A cab finally pulls up, and I slip inside, giving the driver my destination. Irvin and I are meeting today. It's been about two weeks since the accusation, and the DA's office has yet to file any charges. We're all tired of the cat-and-mouse game that is being played. A man's life and his career hang in the balance. And while he is far from perfect, he deserves justice.

When I arrive, Travis is outside. I assume he's waiting for me, but we haven't really spoken since the hockey game. Honestly, I miss seeing him, and so does Lucy. She asks about him all the time, and I don't know what to say. I can't be honest with her and tell her that I chased him off, because she won't understand.

"Morning," I say as I walk up the steps. I'm greeted with his panty-dropping smile as he hands me a cup of coffee. My body rejoices at both the needed dose of caffeine and him. It pains me to admit that he's consumed my every thought for the past couple weeks. "Thank you."

Travis nods but says nothing as he opens the door to Abbott and Abbott. Inside, the office is warm, and I quickly unbutton my coat and remove my scarf. The receptionist tells us where we're meeting. Travis follows me to the conference room, shutting the door behind him, blocking us from the people walking up and down the halls.

"I know you're frustrated," I start, but close my mouth as he stalks toward me. He takes the paper cup from my hand and sets it on the table, along with my messenger bag. "Travis…"

"I've missed you," he says as his eyes wander from mine to my lips and back again. Or is it my eyes doing the wandering, needing to know where he's looking?

I pull my lower lip in, biting it with my teeth in order to keep my thoughts bottled up inside. The slight nod is an automatic response and one that can, and likely will, get me into trouble. "I can't," I tell him in a whisper.

Those words cause him to step back and move to the other side of the room. He's not given a chance to say anything, because the door opens, and Irvin, along with his team, comes barging in. They seem to be eager as they take their seats, talking loudly among themselves. This reminds me of the war room, where sports teams strategize for that key player. I've been in a few, negotiating last-minute contracts on Jeffrey's behalf. It's stressful and not my cup of tea. I'd rather dress the athletes up and have them attend galas and high-society functions where they're required to open their checkbooks and donate to amazing causes. That is where my talents are—making the athletes shine.

"All right, the move by the DA this morning is nothing more than a ploy to get more time. Travis, you're releasing a statement, letting the fine people of Boston know that you're innocent." Irvin sits down in a huff, holding his head in his hands. When he looks up, everyone is staring at him. "Right," he says, starting again. "I'm pissed, and this has gone on long enough. My source down at the lab says the report is inconclusive because the rape kit is missing."

My mouth drops open, and there's a collective gasp throughout the room. I glance quickly at Travis, who seems to be gritting his teeth. If we were in a cartoon, steam would be billowing from his ears.

"Mr. Abbott, what do you mean?" one of the young lawyers asks.

"The DA and I spoke this morning, minutes before he went live, and he indicated that the rape kit had been tampered with. He said that they've pulled all the surveillance footage from the lab and will be following up on leads."

"Is that what you think?" Travis asks.

Irvin shakes his head. "I think that the results came back, and you don't match. As I've said before, the district attorney is up for reelection next year, and this is shaping up to be a high-profile case. Your past isn't exactly your friend, and if he can make a case stick, he wins the women's vote, and he forces teams to take a hard look at punishments. As of right now, the Renegades have yet to make a statement, and in the court of public opinion, that doesn't look so good."

"I didn't rape her. Hell, I didn't even leave with her. I left with someone else."

I try to remain composed even though my heart is racing and my palms are sweating. I'm afraid to move from my spot along the wall, afraid that I'll draw some unwanted attention.

Irvin tosses a legal pad toward Travis, along with a pen. "I want her name and number. If she can give you an alibi for that night, I want to talk to her today."

Travis nods but doesn't make a reach for the yellow paper or the pen that he could use to end my career—and permanently alter my life. I need to speak to him before he decides to hand me over to the wolves. Maybe speak to Jeffrey and let him know what's going on and, most importantly, meet with my probation officer. I fight back the tears and swallow the frog that is currently residing in my throat.

"Maybe we should delay the press conference until after I've spoken to this other woman. What do you think, Saylor?"

I clear my throat and nod. "One more day or so isn't going to hurt. We can utilize some sports blogs to leak some information. This will keep his fans and the general public happy. My suggestion would be to use the BoRe Blogger. They seem to have the largest Renegade following and expressed their support for Travis this morning after the press conference."

"Work that angle, will ya?" Irvin asks. "So, change of plans. Travis is going to give me the name of his alibi, I'll meet with her, and we'll release a statement after the fact."

Everyone stands, and the level of talking increases again. The legal pad is eyeing me, mocking my presence in the room, and all I can do is hold my phone in my shaky hand as I stare at my e-mail contacts.

When the door closes, I jump, dropping my phone. Travis is there to pick it up for me. He hands it to me but does so in such a way that his hand lingers against mine. My already rapidly beating heart picks up speed, if that is even possible.

"You have to help me, Saylor."

"I can't, Travis. You don't know what you're asking of me." I grab my things and leave the room, hoping that he stays behind. If he gives me up, so be it, but I'm praying that he doesn't. He's innocent, and that will come out sooner or later, with or without me.

I hustle away from Abbott and Abbott and hail a cab a few blocks down the street, asking to be taken to my office. My phone pings with messages from Travis, asking where I am, but they go unanswered. I need to prepare for the inevitable. In the grand scheme of things, it's not going to matter what Jeffrey says—he can't have a felon on his payroll, and that is what I'll be if word gets out that I was in the bar.

Everything about that night comes rushing back. I chose to walk home, in a daze after reading Elijah's letter, and stopped there. I didn't even take a sip of alcohol, knowing that I was making a mistake. And when I saw Travis, I couldn't leave. I was cemented to the bar stool, watching his interaction with that woman, wishing it were me in his arms. But it wasn't me. He chose her. And now both of us are going to pay the price.

Jeffrey is out meeting with clients when I return, leaving me no choice but to wait. I don't even know what I'm going to say to him. How do I tell him that the night I crashed my car was a night that I spent wrapped in the arms of our client? I can't. It physically pains me to know that I have to look him in the eyes and tell him what's going on.

On my desk is the picture of Lucy that I hid from Elijah. She's my reason for living, and with the fear that Elijah could take her from me weighing so heavily on my mind, I can't let Travis tell Irvin that I was there. We have to find another way to clear his name. I slip the picture of Lucy into my bag and text Travis to let him know that we need to talk. I tell him that I'm coming to his place. I don't ask him if he's told Irvin yet, because I don't want to know. If he has, he can ask his lawyer to forget he's ever said anything. He responds instantly.

I'll come to your house. Too much media at mine.

I sort of liked the idea of the media being there as a buffer, ensuring that I would leave in a timely manner. Having him at my house, being near him, makes me weak in the knees. I'm vulnerable when he's around, tempted to give in to the desire that I feel for him.

Hurrying out of the office, I rush to the train station and weave in and out of the tourists who are lingering on the streets. The midafternoon commute by train is easier than a taxi, and by the time I'm at my stop, my heart is all but beating out of my chest.

As I round the corner to my apartment, Travis is standing out front. In his hand is a bouquet of flowers. And unless he has a date after our meeting, I'm assuming those are for me.

"Hey," he says, meeting me halfway.

"Hi, sorry for running out like that. I needed to think."

"I'm going to pretend that I understand, but I don't. And I need you to tell me."

"I know, and I will, once we're inside."

"These are for you," he says, giving me the roses. They're red and smell heavenly. I head toward the main entrance to my building, and he falls in step behind me, resting his hand on my back. The doorman opens the door and ushers us inside, where we wait for the elevator.

"What time will Lucy be home?"

"Not until later. My mom takes her to the library after school. This is usually my late night."

I smile at the people getting off and step in. The confined space of the elevator is making it hard to focus. Travis's cologne overpowers the scent of the roses, and I find myself leaning toward him to get a better whiff. I'm tempting fate, I know, but I can't help it.

We're silent as we walk down the hall to my apartment, and once inside, he goes over to my tree and turns on the lights before bending down onto the floor.

"What are you doing?"

"Checking the water level."

"It's fake," I tell him with a laugh.

"Right—I think I knew that."

I hang up my coat and motion for his. He hands it over. "I'm going to cut to the chase, Travis," I say as I hang his coat next to mine.

"That would be nice."

"Right," I say, wringing my hands together. I go to the couch and sit down, and he follows, except he takes the middle cushion, leaving no space between us. When his hand rests on my leg, my mind goes fuzzy. "I can't think when you're this close."

"Why not?"

"Because…" I shake my head and turn my gaze away from him.

"Why?" he asks again.

"Because I like you, Travis, and you make it hard to focus on the objective."

"Which is?"

When I look at him, he's smiling. But he won't be after I tell him what happened and why I need to stay away from him.

"That night, the one we spent together, it's been one mistake after another. Not only can I lose my job for being with you, but I can also lose everything. After I left, I wrapped my car around a telephone pole and was arrested for a DUI. I lost my license and am on probation. The night you saw me...I'm not allowed to be in bars, Travis. If you tell Irvin, I could go to jail." A single tear falls down my cheek, and before I can wipe it way, he's doing it for me.

NINETEEN

Travis

"Why did you leave that night?" I ask, needing to know if it was something I did. I tried my damnedest to make her feel special. To show her that she meant more than any of the others I had been with, that she was different.

When she walked into the fund-raiser, all eyes were on her. The royal-blue dress accented her olive skin, and I found myself drawn to her. We had worked together in the past, and she'd always been on hand for my screwups but seeing her in that room, and watching all those men flock to her, I grew jealous. I've always been attracted to her. It's hard not to be when someone looks like she does with that long, dark hair and eyes so light blue that I sometimes mistake them for hazel or even gray.

Saylor sighs and brings one leg up underneath her other one. "I had gotten up and made the mistake of checking my messages. Jeffrey had texted that an associate let him know that we had left together. He didn't need to remind me that I'd lose my job if I slept with one of our clients. But I knew that's why he had sent me a message."

"I asked you not to leave. Hell, I think I begged you," I say to her.

I had never begged anyone until that moment. I didn't want her to go. I wanted to wake up with her in my arms and feed her breakfast in bed.

"I was so upset and angry at myself for going home with you. I was crying and still drunk when my car struck the telephone pole. I had minor scrapes and a few bruises, but I blew over the legal limit and was hauled off to jail.

"I lost my license and was given probation for five years. One of the conditions is that I'm not allowed in bars or where alcohol is served. I have to get permission to attend work functions, and Jeffrey almost fired me because of this. He put me on probation for a year."

"That's why you called and asked me for help the next morning, isn't it?" I ask as the realization sets in. I knew I let her down but wasn't aware of the magnitude.

She nods. "I thought I could get the charges dropped and figured…"

"That since we had been together, I would help?"

"Yes, but not in the way you're making it sound. I was hoping, since we were drinking at your place so heavily, you wouldn't mind making a phone call."

"But I told you I was busy?"

"Yeah, and that was the end of it."

"Shit." I'm such a fucking dick. All I had to do was call Irvin and save her all of this pain. "Wait—what about dinner the other night? And the hockey game?"

She shakes her head. "I wasn't allowed to go to dinner but did anyway because I didn't want to tell you. The hockey game was business."

Saylor covers her face with her hands and groans. My fingers wrap around her wrist to pull them away so I can see her. "Does Jeffrey know about us? About that night?"

"No," she says, shaking her head. "Or if he does, he has never said anything."

"I'm really torn up on the inside about this, Saylor. I had no fucking idea. And here I am pressuring you to come clean because it saves me, but it can destroy you. There has to be a happy medium here."

I look away and focus on her fireplace. I'm so torn and don't know what to do. I want this investigation to stop, and Saylor could help. But she's right—I'm a risk, and one she's not willing to take.

"Fuck, Saylor, I'm sorry. I'm going to make it better," I say as I get up and start pacing around her living room. The lights from her Christmas tree twinkle, and I absentmindedly rub one of the branches between my fingers. Her ornaments have a homey feel to them, not like the celebrity trees you see where everything matches. A few of them look handmade by Lucy, and there's a series of them that mark each of Lucy's Christmases.

"You have a beautiful tree." I have to change the subject because I'm starting to overthink how I could save her. Right now, the only thing I can come up with is to put money in her bank account, but that only helps so much if she's unemployed or in prison.

"Thank you. Have you put one up yet?" She comes over and stands next to me, straightening out an ornament that only twists back around.

"Nah. I never do. I usually spend Christmas out in the middle of the ocean with my parents. They live on a yacht and are constantly sailing."

"But not this year?"

I shake my head. "I thought I wanted to stay here and experience winter, but well…anyway, I can't leave until everything is squared away, which I'm hoping is soon."

"It will be," she says, placing her arm on my bicep.

I pull her into my arms and hold her. I feel her body sag against mine and know that she's comfortable. Hell, I'm comfortable. Every time I'm near her, I'm at ease and not afraid to be myself. Saylor sees a whole other side of me that even the guys on the team don't see.

"Can I ask you a question?" I say. We both pull back so we can look into each other's eyes.

"Of course."

I break eye contact to push her hair behind her ear, exposing her neck to me. She swallows hard and shifts her weight from one foot to the other.

"If you didn't work for my manager and have to put up with me, knowing what you know about me, would you want to be with me?"

I look into her eyes and wait for her answer. Her grip around my waist becomes tighter, and her chest slightly heaves. "Yes," she says breathlessly.

My hand cups her cheek while my thumb brushes across her lips. They part, and I take that as my invitation to kiss them. I move slowly, testing her reaction, until I feel her fingers push into my hair and pull me closer.

She wants me, probably not as much as I want her, but the feelings are there, and I'm going to take every little bit until she tells me otherwise.

The second our lips touch, the surge I feel is indescribable. This kiss is different from before. The longing is greater, as is the feeling that we could be together if our situations were to change.

We move in sync, and my hand now cradles her head, angling her perfectly to me while her hands roam freely over my chest, into my hair, and onto my waist. Her fingers inch under my shirt and graze my stomach.

I want to lift her up and take her to her bedroom. I want to worship her and make promises that I know I'll have to work hard in order to keep. She deserves someone better than me, but I want the pureness that she brings into my chaotic world.

Breaking away from her lips, I taste her neck as she whimpers, tilting her head to the side to give me better access. Her hands trail down my arms until her fingers are lifting the hem of my shirt and I have no choice but to stop kissing her and help her pull my shirt over my head.

Saylor looks up at me as her fingers dance over my skin, tracing the outline of my abs and my tattoo. She places an openmouthed kiss on my chest, sending me into overdrive. I scoop her up and head toward her room.

"Remind me…which way?"

"To the left," she says as she tugs at my earlobe with her teeth.

I kick her door open and stumble my way into her room. Her legs hitch over my hips, grinding her core against me. I had hoped to be smooth and set her down gently, but nothing ever goes as planned and I end up falling on her.

Saylor starts to laugh, and while that action could devastate a man, I find myself laughing right along with her. I stay centered between her legs and gaze into her eyes. If she has any doubts, I don't see them.

My eyes close as she tickles the scruff that I've been letting grow the past few days. Normally I grow a winter beard but have been shaving in anticipation of kissing her more. Looking at her swollen lips, I can see where I've roughed her up a little bit. Truth be told, I like it—a lot.

Lowering my head, I kiss her again, but her response isn't as enthusiastic as I would like. "We can't do this, can we?" I ask, without leaving the comfortable spot that I've created.

She shakes her head, and I roll off of her. "Please," she says, reaching for me.

I turn and look at her. "Please what?"

Saylor sits up and attempts to straighten her hair. It's wild, and perfect. "I like you, Travis, but if Jeffrey found out, I'd lose my job."

"What if we kept us a secret?" Even as I make the suggestion, I know I wouldn't be able to. I would want to parade her around, be there for her and Lucy. I would want them at my house and in the stands wearing my number. "Yeah, I guess you're right." I scrub my hands over my face and groan. Saylor snuggles into me, and it feels damn good. I roll slightly and pull her into my arms.

"I'm sorry," she says.

"Don't, Saylor. I'm going to find a way to make this work."

She pulls back and looks at me. "You can't fire Jeffrey. If we started dating, he'd know. He'd fire me anyway."

She's right, and I hate it. I want to think that there's a way around our situation. Never mind the fact that in order for her to get me out of my mess, she'd have to face jail time. I could never do that to her or Lucy.

We stay like this, with her head on my chest and my fingers playing with her hair. I could fall asleep, and no doubt it would be the best sleep I've had since the night before I walked into that bar and everything changed. It's funny to think that my life has been vastly different since that moment. A false claim that could end my career has been eye-opening and made me take a serious look at the lifestyle I've been living. I've made changes, not only for me but also to try and prove that I can be the man Saylor needs me to be. Right now, I can't imagine being anywhere else, other than where I am now, except maybe between Saylor's legs and making her scream my name.

She sits up and smiles before leaving me in her bedroom. When she returns, my shirt is in her hand, and all I can do is picture her wearing it to bed.

"Thanks, babe," I say, letting the term of affection slip out. I can tell by the blush in her cheeks that she likes it, and I make a note to say it more when we're in private, because yes, I will be doing everything I can to show her that I'm interested. I just have to find a way to make a relationship with her work where she doesn't have to risk anything but her heart. Something tells me that she's worth it, and I will prove to her that I'm worth every risk she's willing to take.

We've just barely stepped back into the living room when the door opens and Lucy comes barreling in with her grandmother on her heels.

"Travis!" Lucy squeals as she launches into my arms.

"Hey, pretty girl."

"Are you staying for dinner?"

I glance over at Saylor, who nods.

"Yeah, I am. Should we order something?" The last thing I want is for Saylor to have to cook, although having a home-cooked meal would be very nice.

"No, Mommy will make 'ghetti." Yes! Now I want to squeal like a five-year-old.

"Lucy Lou, come give Grammy a kiss."

I let Lucy down, and she runs over to her grandmother.

"Mom, do you remember Travis Kidd? We've been working on his publicity events." Saylor trails off…as if she's trying to find an excuse as to why I'm here, instead of telling her mother the truth, although I'm not sure what that is. For me, I'm here because I want to be with her. For her, I want it to be the same, and maybe it is or could be, if the circumstances were different.

I go over and shake her hand. "It's very nice to see you again under better circumstances," I tell her.

"You too. Lucy hasn't stopped talking about you since you played dress-up with her."

Lucy beams as she looks up at me. I tap her nose with my index finger and pull her into my side.

"Will you be joining us for dinner?" I ask Norma, who shakes her head.

"No, tonight I play bridge with the ladies. Have a good night." She turns to leave but peeks her head back in before shutting the door. "Don't do anything I wouldn't do, Saylor."

My mouth drops open as Saylor's face turns red. I waggle my eyebrows at her, only for Lucy to interrupt every dirty thought I was starting to have.

"What does that mean?" she asks, causing Saylor and me to burst out laughing.

TWENTY

Saylor

The bell chimes, letting us know that we can go out onto the ice. Ever since the hockey game, Lucy has been asking if we can go skating. I readily agreed, and she invited Travis. Deep down I knew she would, and I didn't balk or try to tell her otherwise. Truth is, I want him here. I may not be able to be with him romantically, but I can be his friend, and sometimes that is more important.

Lucy tilts her head back and sticks out her tongue, catching the falling snowflakes and laughing when they land on her cheeks, forehead, and eyelashes. Travis copies her, chuckling right along, while I stand back and watch the one person I love most in the world bond with a man whom I could so easily fall in love with.

Even though he knows we can't be together, that hasn't stopped him from coming around. It's not every day, but it's enough to keep the interest I have in him growing to the point that I've found myself looking for another job. Not that I want to quit working for Jeffrey, but the thought of being in love intrigues me. I've only been in love once, and that didn't turn out so well for me, with the exception of having Lucy. Love scares me, but I'd put my heart out there for

Travis because I think he deserves it, and I know he'd love Lucy with everything that he is.

"Are you two yo-yos ready?" I ask, reaching for Lucy's gloved hand. She smiles and wipes her face with her other one before grabbing Travis's hand as well. The three of us make our way onto the ice, holding hands like a family. It'd be a picture-perfect moment, something for a Christmas card, if our situations were different.

Travis wobbles, causing Lucy to laugh. I've brought her to the Frog Pond every winter since she could walk so I could teach her how to skate. This is another activity she's asked to participate in, but all I can afford is the public rink. Maybe if Elijah were a better father, he'd be willing to pay for lessons. The thought has occurred to me to ask, but I'm afraid of what he'll ask for in return.

"Watch me, Travis," Lucy says as she lets go of our hands and skates forward. She spins in a small circle, twirling like a ballerina.

"You're amazing," Travis says as he claps. He tries to bow but begins to lose his balance. His arms start to flail about, and I do my best to help him right himself, only to go down in a heap, landing on top of him.

"Are you okay?" I ask in between giggles. He groans and wraps his arms around me, preventing me from moving.

"Perfect," he says, meeting my gaze. That's when I see the longing he feels in the depth of his blue eyes. It'd be so easy to give in to the temptation, the desire burning within, but I could lose my job. I need to be stronger around Travis, yet I find that I don't want to be. When he's around and we share moments like this, I forget about the responsibilities I have.

He licks his lips, and I consciously follow suit, eager to taste him once again. Before I can protest or roll out of his arms, his lips are pressed to mine, and people around us are cheering. I pull away and try to hide my embarrassment by keeping my eyes focused on the ice, praying that no one with a camera caught this moment.

Travis is able to right himself before I stand, and he helps me up, refusing to let go of my hand once he does. He pulls me to him, cupping my cheek and guiding my face up so I have no choice but to look at him. "I'm sorry. I couldn't help myself."

I nod and offer him a small smile. I wouldn't have been able to help myself either, and maybe that's why I'm upset—because he did it first when I wanted to?

"You guys kissed," Lucy snickers, adding to my embarrassment. *She* should've been my first thought, but she wasn't. My job was. And tonight when I tuck her in, I'll explain to her what happened, even though I don't know how to tell her. She's five, and I don't want her to think it's okay for her mother to go around kissing men.

Travis leans down and kisses Lucy on the cheek. "Now I've kissed you," he says as she squeals in delight. We link hands again and continue to skate. Each time we go around the rink, someone recognizes Travis. A few have tried to stop him to take pictures, but he nicely asked them to wait until the break because he's with his family.

His family. That is how he referred to us. He could've easily left that part out or called us his friends, but he didn't, and now my mind is filling with doubt and my heart is asking what the hell I am doing by pushing him away. We can't help who we fall in love with. That is evident by my colossal mistake with Elijah.

Lucy skates ahead of us again, and this time Travis links hands with mine as we follow her around the rink.

"People are going to talk, Travis. We shouldn't be holding hands."

"Are you worried about Jeffrey?" he asks.

"I have to. I can't afford to lose my job."

He sighs but doesn't let go. And I don't want him to. I'm comfortable like this. Even if thick winter gloves are masking our connection, I can still feel the heat radiating between us.

This is my idea of a perfect date, with the white lights adding to the ambience of the holiday decorations. Christmas music plays from the speakers, and couples who are in love, or starting to fall in love, skate together.

The logical part of me is telling me to let go of his hand, to keep a safe distance between us, but I don't want to. In fact, being this close to him isn't enough right now.

"Will you stay, after we get back to my place?" The words slip easily from my mouth, and as his eyes light up, I can tell that he's surprised. Probably more so than I am.

He stops skating and clumsily maneuvers himself to stand in front of me. "I'd love to."

I feel like I should add that we'll be sitting on the couch, drinking hot cocoa and keeping our clothes on, but I have a feeling he knows that. And if he doesn't…well, he'll learn quickly that I want him there to keep us company. And by us, I mean Lucy and me, until she goes to bed, and then he'll go home. Even as I have these thoughts, I know I'm lying to myself. I want him at my place so he can hold me, kiss me, and make me long for a time when I'd be free to submit to him.

We continue to lag behind Lucy until the bell chimes, letting us know that our time is up. As soon as we sit down to remove our skates, a couple of kids come rushing over without a parent or adult in sight, asking Travis for his autograph. Behind us, I hear a few snide comments, but the kids don't seem to be aware of Travis's current controversy. I have no doubt he's going to oblige each and every child, which will prolong our night here. I shouldn't be jealous, but I am.

I help Lucy remove her skates and take her with me while I turn them in. When we return, he's still signing autographs and posing for pictures, and this hits home for me. For a brief moment, I imagine what it would be like to be with him, and right now it'd be great, until baseball season starts and he's running ragged. Baseball is his passion, and the schedule is hectic. I know many wives don't mind it, but I'm not sure how I'd feel being second.

I sigh heavily as I sit down, pulling Lucy next to me.

"Mommy, why can't he say no?" she whines as she pushes into me. I know she's tired, and probably cold. Travis glances over his shoulder at me, and I can't decipher the look on his face.

"Okay, guys. I have to run," he says, much to the displeasure of the crowd, which grew exponentially while I was gone. He turns to us and scoops Lucy up in his arms and reaches for my hand. "Sorry," I hear him say to Lucy. I can't hear if she says anything back, but when I look over, she's nestled into his shoulder and her tiny arms are wrapped around his neck. I'm going to have to explain that she has to share her best friend with all of Boston because of his job, and I have a feeling that she may not like that too much.

I half expect Travis to grab a cab, but he continues to walk. His pace is brisk, but I'm able to keep up with him step for step. When we arrive at my apartment, I hold the door for him, because he refuses to put Lucy down.

"She's sleeping," he says while we wait for the elevator. All I can do is nod since my tongue is tied, and I really want to cry. She's never had the opportunity to fall asleep in any man's arms, only mine and my mother's. I'm not jealous but heartbroken. I haven't been able to offer her a father figure, and it seems that Travis is trying to fill that void, whether I let him into my life or not.

I find myself leaning up against him in the elevator, closing my eyes for the brief ride. He kisses the top of my head as the doors open for my floor. The window at the end of the hall shows our reflection, and if I didn't know any better, I'd say we were a family. My heart skips a bit faster at that notion, and I find that the idea of being with him like that excites me, but is it enough to say goodbye to my job?

Travis carries Lucy to her room with me hot on his heels. He gently sets her down on her bed and pulls her stocking cap off. Her hair is matted to her face and he's the one to brush it away.

"I'm going to leave so you can change her," he says, quietly shutting her door after he steps out. I start to change her clothes, which is harder than one would think. A five-year-old's body isn't nearly as flexible as a newborn's.

"Where's Travis?" she asks. Her voice is groggy, and her eyes are still closed.

"In the other room."

"Can he tuck me in?" she mumbles, causing my heart to skip again. Yet another first, and it's being done by a man that I can't let into our lives, at least not in the way he wants to be.

I continue to change her clothes, making sure that her nightgown is pulled down before I pull the covers over her. Most likely she'll kick them off in the middle of the night and her pajamas will be hiked up to her neck.

Opening the door, I'm startled to find Travis standing in the hallway. His coat is off, but the expression on his face is like nothing I've ever seen. He looks hurt, and for the life of me, I can't figure out why.

"She's asking for you," I say, opening the door wider. He brushes past me but not without touching me. It's subtle, but noticeable.

"Hey, Lucy," he says as he kneels down next to her. "I'm really sorry about those other kids. I promise that next time I'll tell them no, or ask for your permission first." As tears fall from my eyes, he leans forward and gives her a kiss on her forehead. I don't know if she's heard him or not, but she rolls toward him, snuggling under her blanket.

I can't seem to tear my eyes away from Lucy until Travis tugs on my arm, pulling me out of her room. He shuts off her light and closes her door.

"Was I out of line?" he asks when we enter the living room.

"No," I say, shaking my head as I look at him. "She likes you. She may even love you."

"And what about you? Do you like me?"

I nod but decide the subject needs to be focused on her. "I think you're giving her something that I haven't been able to."

"And what's that?" he asks, stepping closer.

"A father." My voice cracks, but the title isn't lost on him. He knows what I mean.

"Honestly, Saylor, I like the thought of being someone that she depends on. I know the deck is stacked against us, and I've only been coming around for a few weeks, but she has me wrapped around her finger. And the way I see it, either I leave and never come back, so I can break these bonds, or we do something about it."

"I think we should do something about it."

"Like what?" he asks, inching closer to me.

"Take me to bed." With my heart pounding in my throat, I know this is what I want. My body craves his touch, and if tonight didn't prove that he's committed to Lucy and me, I don't know what else he can do to show me.

Travis doesn't say anything. He cups my cheek and gently presses his lips to mine before picking me up and carrying me to my room.

TWENTY-ONE

Travis

It takes me a moment for her words to register, but once they do, I'm pursuing her. I don't know what changed, and honestly I don't care. Being with her, in any way she'll have me, is all that I've been asking for. When she called me earlier, inviting me to go ice-skating, I jumped at the opportunity, even though I can't skate for shit, because it was a way to spend time with two of my favorite women.

And now I'm kissing her, and she's kissing me back with pure, unadulterated passion. Her fingers are tugging, pulling, and grasping as I carry her to her room. She moans into my mouth, encouraging me to move faster, but I don't want to. I want to savor this and burn each moment into my memory so that when I'm alone, I can recall how I felt when she finally gave herself to me.

The moonlight shines through her window, guiding me through her semidarkened room. Our kiss is sensual and exciting. There isn't anything urgent about this moment right now. And for the first time in my life, I'm going to make love, and it's going to be with this incredible woman. Our first time was lust filled and muddled by my sense of humor, because until her, I haven't been able to take anyone seriously. Normally, I hide behind corny one-liners and half-assed jokes and treat the women I've been with like one of the guys. Not this time, and not with her.

I gently set her down and step away from her. She reaches for the hem of her sweater and pulls it over her head, leaving a turtleneck in place. I cock my eyebrow and smirk, only for her to remove the next piece of clothing. Saylor sits in front of me clad in her bra and jeans, looking unsure.

My sweater and shirt are now in a similar pile on the floor, next to hers. When she stands, I start taking off my belt and slowly undoing the buttons on my jeans. Her hands mimic mine while my dick is screaming that we start humping already.

That's not what I want to do, though. That's not the type of woman she is. I want her to know that she means everything to me. I want her to feel the desire I have for her and how it's been building for weeks. Saylor needs to know that the night in the bar, regardless of the outcome, is what has brought us together. That one look at her and I knew she was the one I wanted to be with.

Our jeans fall to the floor—well, mine fall while she shimmies out of hers. It's cute, watching her hips move back and forth, and while I try not to laugh, I can't help it. I kick mine off and palm my hard-on, watching her expression as she catches what I'm doing.

"Are you sure about this?" I ask, needing to know before we go any further.

"I am, but—"

"But no one can know."

She nods and a bit of life fades from her eyes. I step forward and lift her chin so she can look at me. "If it means that I get to be with you, I'll keep the secret."

"Travis." Her voice is quiet and causes my erection to jump. She breaks my gaze and reaches out to touch me. Even with the cloth barrier preventing skin-to-skin contact, I can feel the heat from her. Saylor rubs the outline of my dick through my boxer briefs, while I stare at her hand.

"Every night since I saw you in the bar, I've dreamed of this."

"Me too," she says as her fingers push into the waistband of my boxer briefs, pushing them down so I can kick them off. "Do you want me, Travis?"

"You have no idea," I tell her, reaching around and grabbing the clasp that keeps her bra together and flicking it loose. I pull the lace away from her body, and her nipples harden from the cool air as my fingers trace the outline of her breast. "You're so fucking beautiful."

My mouth is on a nipple before she has a chance to respond, and her fingers are in my hair while I massage her other breast and covertly pump my erection for some relief. Moving to her other breast, I swirl my tongue and gently bite her, causing her to gasp.

"Get on the bed, Saylor."

She does what I demand, scrambling away from me, but not before my hands grip her panties and slide them down her legs. Saylor gets under the covers, pulling the side back for me.

Before I join her, I dig through my pants in search of a condom. I won't bother telling her that I've put one in there every time I've come over in hopes that we'd find ourselves here. "I want to taste you, make you come on my tongue, but I think I want to feel you wrapped around me first. What do you want, Saylor?"

She pulls me to her, and her lips hover over mine. "You. I want whatever you want to give me." My heart. That is what I want to give her, but I fear she may not give me hers in return, and even the macho bastard that I am doesn't want to get hurt.

My fingers caress her hip, her ass, and move over her thigh. She parts her legs, welcoming me as my featherlight touch makes her skin pebble with goose bumps. I groan when I reach her core and my digits slide between her folds. Her eyes close as she widens for me. "Fuck, Saylor," I say, latching on to her breast.

Her hand has a steady grip on my hair, and her back arches with each swipe my finger makes over her sensitive flesh. I can only take so much before I'm pulling away and sitting back on my knees to slide the condom over my erection. Saylor watches my every movement, licking her lips in the process.

"Come here," I say, grabbing her leg and pulling it over my hip. My thumb brushes over her clit, and she bucks her hips in anticipation. I center myself, pushing in gently. "Fuck, fuck, fuck," I mutter as I become fully sheathed in the woman who has been driving me crazy for the longest time.

I'm slow and methodical, making sure she feels every inch of what I'm giving her. Saylor hitches her other leg over my hip, changing the angle of penetration, and that movement causes me to move faster.

Lowering my head, I capture her lips, sliding my tongue deep into her mouth and swallowing every gasp, moan, and mewl. My hand grabs on to the headboard while her nails dig into my ass, pushing me deeper. I grip her leg for leverage, and she pulls my hair, making me want to scream.

Saylor breaks away from our kiss and arches her back, giving me ample space to kiss her neck. "Shh," I remind her when she cries out.

"I'm close," she tells me.

Sitting back on my knees, I pull her hips to meet my thrust. My thumb once again brushes over her clit as she covers her mouth with a pillow. She bucks wildly, and her legs quiver as her walls squeeze me for everything that I can give. Each pump brings me closer to the edge until I'm falling on top of her and groaning into the same pillow she used to capture her cries.

I'm breathing heavily as I roll off of her. She removes the pillow and sits up. "Where are you going?" I ask as panic starts to set in.

She looks at me over her shoulder and smiles, removing any doubt that she might regret what happened between us.

"To find something to sleep in."

"My shirt works," I say, winking at her, but she shakes her head.

"I don't want Lucy to see me in that. She'll ask questions, and I don't know what to tell her."

"Fair enough." I roll to the side and pull the condom off. I look around her room for something to put it in, only for her to hand me a tissue. "Thanks." I put my boxer briefs and my T-shirt back on before sneaking off to the bathroom, surprised to find Saylor following me.

I barely have enough time to dispose of the wadded-up tissue when she shuts the door, enclosing us in the tiny space. "What are you doing?" I ask her in a voice barely above a whisper.

"I wanted to see you in the light," she says as her hands move up my chest. She's killing me, because all I want to do is jump into the shower with her and take her again, but this time I want to fuck her Travis Kidd–style. When she reaches into my boxer briefs, I have to step away.

"I only had one condom, Saylor."

"Oh," she says, backing up. I reach for her before she gets too far.

"Listen to me." I cup her cheek, holding her in place. "I'd do this over and over again in a heartbeat, and I promise to make it up to you tomorrow. I'll make love to you first and then finish the night by fucking you senseless. I remember how you like it from behind, how you loved it when I pulled your hair while I drilled into your pussy." Her cheeks flush as she swallows. I kiss her hard, plunging my tongue into her mouth while she collapses into me. I swat her bottom, making her yelp. "Do what you need to and meet me in your bed. I'll be waiting to tease you while you sleep in my arms."

It's only a matter of minutes before she returns and crawls right into the open space, snuggling in next to me. "Roll over," I tell her so I can spoon her. "Do you feel that?" I ask, thrusting my erection into her ass.

"Travis."

"Yeah, baby, that's how much I want you right now. Be prepared for tomorrow night." I kiss her behind her ear and pull her closer to me.

I close my eyes but never find sleep. My mind is plagued by thoughts of Lucy complaining to Saylor about what happened with the kids at the ice rink. The last thing I want to do is hurt either of them, and that is exactly what I did tonight. I put the fans first because that's what I'm used to doing, but I can't continue to do that if I'm going to be in Lucy and Saylor's lives. They deserve my undivided attention, no matter where we are.

Saylor's door swings open, and the shadow from the hallway shows a tiny person. And like I did in high school, I'm off the bed and hiding on the floor while Saylor sits up.

"What's wrong, Lucy?"

I close my eyes and hold my breath, praying that she doesn't walk over to this side of the bed to climb in. This must be what others have said about dating a single mother—the trials and tribulations of late-night visits from children. I don't give a fuck, though, because I love the fact that I get to be the man Saylor needs and be a father figure to Lucy. Being with them is going to make me love harder and put more effort into building a relationship.

"I heard some noises."

I stifle my laugh and make a mental note to add music next time we're getting busy.

"Well, I don't hear anything. I'll tuck you back in."

"Where's Travis?" she asks. I want to yell, "Looking under your mom's bed for monsters," but realize that Saylor may not appreciate my humor.

"I'm sure he's home."

"Well, he forgot his coat. I bet he gets a cold."

Once the door shuts, I sit up and laugh into the comforter that's hanging over the side of the bed. When Saylor returns, she's muttering something unintelligible.

"What are you still doing on the floor?"

I reach for her, pulling her into my lap. "I was thinking that maybe I didn't satisfy you enough and thought I could at least get you off with my fingers." It's not the first time I've used sex to defuse a situation.

"What if I want more?" she asks, grinding into me.

"Fucking, dirty vixen."

She nods and raises her arms so I can take her shirt off. Her breasts bob up and down as she rocks against me.

"Keep your panties on, please. I don't have much willpower when it comes to you."

"No promises, Travis."

I fear that I have unleashed a horny beast by the name of Saylor, and if I'm not careful, she's going to slay me.

TWENTY-TWO

Saylor

My body is sore, but not in the way you feel after a hard workout at the gym or after running a marathon. Not that I would know what the latter feels like, because I've never done one, but the discomfort in every muscle in my body is a stark reminder of what I did last night. What *we* did last night.

And I don't regret it.

Those words are easy for me to say while I lie snuggled in his embrace. The feelings of warmth, satisfaction, and, dare I say, love keep me safe and calm in this bubble. I know that once I step outside of it, life will be different. Reality will set in, and Travis and I will have to answer the blaring question "What comes next?"

How easy would it be to fall into a blissful routine with him? Easy, that's how. And let's not forget dangerous. I don't care that he's facing this ridiculous charge of rape, which in my opinion is dragging on for far too long. The DA is hell-bent on making an example out of any sports figure he can. Anything he can do to pad his election results. At least that's my view.

The streetlights still shine through the slats of my blinds, and the red numbers on my clock tell me that I need to get up soon. I'm already fretting about what to say to Lucy when she wakes up. She's far too observant and has already pointed out that Travis left his coat here. I roll my eyes at the thought of having to hide him from her, knowing how she feels about him, but she's far too young to understand adult needs and why her mommy had a sleepover.

Travis pulls me closer and snuggles into my neck. I've never been one to cuddle while sleeping, but being held in his arms last night was something I could see myself getting used to. I felt like he was protecting me from everything that we're going to face, now that we've done this. And as much as I'd like to say this wouldn't happen again, I'd be lying to myself. I like this man—a lot.

My fingers trail up and down his forearm as I prepare to say the words I dread. "You have to leave," I whisper.

He groans in response before sighing. "I know, and for the record, I don't want to. I want to get up, make my girls some breakfast—and by make, I mean order in—and sit on the couch with Lucy and watch cartoons."

My eyes grow misty as I fight to keep the tears away. What he wants to do is my picture-perfect Saturday morning, and it's mocking me, waving its hands to show me that it's there, but I can't have it. I want it and the moments that come with having a man around.

Travis must sense my anguish, because he moves me underneath him and is kissing away my fears. "We'll be fine," he vows, breaking me even more on the inside. How he can be so confident when his own life hangs in the balance is beyond me.

He slides out of bed and quickly starts dressing. Part of me feels dirty for ogling his butt, and instead of calling him back to bed, I get up and change into some sweats. Travis meets me at the end of my bed and gives me a searing kiss, morning breath and all, before nodding toward my door. This is the ultimate walk of shame, hiding from your five-year-old daughter.

As soon as we enter the hallway, I hear her bed squeak, and the pounding of my heart seems to echo throughout my apartment. Travis tiptoes as fast as he can out of sight, and I pray that he's able to get out before she sees him.

"Good morning, sunshine."

"Morning," she says through a yawn. I spread my arms out for a hug, but she bypasses me and heads straight to the living room. I follow and collide with her when she stops suddenly. "Did you bring me pancakes again?"

I look up and see Travis frozen in the doorway, the hallway light illuminating him.

"What are you doing here so early?" I ask, trying to play it off.

"I…uh…"

"He forgot his coat, Mommy."

"Yes—see, I forgot my coat last night and was coming to pick it up," he says, stepping back into my apartment.

"But you didn't bring pancakes?" she asks with a shrug.

"I wanted to make sure you were awake first. I didn't want them getting cold," he tells her.

"Oh." She climbs up onto the couch and snuggles into one of the pillows. I turn the television on for her and retreat into the kitchen to make coffee.

"Sorry," Travis says as he comes up behind me.

"For what?" I ask, waiting for the pot to start filling.

"For not getting out sooner."

"It's fine, Travis. But you better order her some pancakes," I say with a wink as I quickly move the glass pot out of the way to fill my mug. I need the caffeine to start my morning off right. He makes the all-important phone call, telling the restaurant that he'll pay double if they're here within the next fifteen minutes before he heads into the living room.

Once I'm a few sips into my coffee, I head back to the living room, where I find Travis sprawled out on the couch, fast asleep, and Lucy resting comfortably on his chest, zonked out, too.

This is how he wanted to start the morning, and I'm happy that he's gotten his wish, even if I'm slightly jealous of my daughter. Instead of curling in around them, I opt for a shower, using this free time wisely. Usually, I shower with the door open in case Lucy needs me, but today I quietly shut it and plan to let the hot water massage my achy muscles.

By the time I get out, they're awake and eating breakfast. I guess the restaurant really wanted double, because I thought I'd have more time.

"Smells yum…" My words trail off as I get an eyeful of Travis Kidd standing at my sink, washing dishes. Someone pinch me, because I think I've died and gone to la-la land. Could he be any sexier than he is right in his moment?

"It is," Lucy says with a mouthful.

"Don't talk with food in your mouth," Travis tells her, but he does it in a nonscolding manner. His voice is soft, yet stern, and makes me long to have someone else to help raise her. Being a single mom isn't a cakewalk, and I do my best, but sometimes I feel like I'm letting her down.

"What's your plan for the day?" Travis asks, interrupting my thoughts. When I look at him, he's smiling, and I have a feeling he's up to no good.

"Taking Lucy to meet Santa. She has a list that she would like to give him, and I have a few last-minute things to pick up."

"Do you mind if I tag along?"

"I'm sure you're busy, Travis. You don't have to hang out with us."

He turns from the sink and leans across the island, smiling. "If I didn't want to be with you and Lucy, I wouldn't have asked if I could go with you."

I shrug, acting noncommittal even though I want him with us. Yesterday, everything changed, and I'm not referring to the sex. It was a culmination of being with him—everything from the laughing and skating to the stolen kiss. It was the way he was with Lucy when he realized that she was upset, how he pushed his fans away for her. To me, that means everything, and I know deep down that if I want to give him a chance, I should. Maybe if I talked to Jeffrey, he'd understand. But the likelihood is that he won't, and if I ask him, I'd be putting my job in jeopardy. "If you want to come shopping with us, you can."

His smile turns into a megawatt grin. "Perfect. I'm going to go home so I can take a shower and change." He goes to tell Lucy goodbye, letting her know that he'll be back shortly so we can go shopping. When he gets to me, he leans in and whispers, "I'll make sure I have more than one condom this time," and then he's gone, leaving me speechless and gasping for air. Only the slamming of the door helps me catch my breath.

"Bath time, Lucy." She jumps up and races me to the bathroom. She may be slightly excited to visit the man in the red suit today.

"Do you think Travis will want to sit on Santa's lap?"

I shake my head quickly. "No, I don't think so," I say, trying to stifle a laugh. It's hard to imagine a man Travis's size sitting on the lap of Santa.

"Do you love him?"

Her question catches me off guard. I'm not ready to admit that I'm falling in love with him. It's almost as if saying those words out loud would shift everything that is being built between us. Instead, I lie to my daughter. "As his friend, yes."

Lucy stands in the tub while it's filling. Why she does this, I'll never know. But it's her thing, so I let her do it.

"I love him."

"I'm sure he loves you, too, Lucy."

A few moments later, the bathwater is deep enough that I can start helping her wash. I fill up her cup with water and pour it over her head as she sits down. She spits, sputters, and starts laughing as the water cascades over her head, all while asking me to do it again. And I do, repeatedly, until it's time for me to wash her hair. She can do the rest and prefers to be treated like a big girl.

With her out of the bath and dried off, I have the dubious task of putting on her tights. These contraptions are ten times worse for kids than they are for adults. The crazy amount of wiggling, twisting, and pulling has Lucy turning into a contortionist.

"Mommmiieeee." She drags my name out as I shake her little body into the white nylons.

"There, all done. Now we can do your hair." I tug her along behind me, back into the bathroom so I can blow-dry and curl her hair. Last year I did this and burned her forehead. It was an accident. She sneezed and I flinched, bumping the barrel into her skin. I felt horrible, but she reminds me of it every time I go to do her hair. "I'll do the ends only, okay?"

She eyes me suspiciously through the mirror. I wink and blow her a kiss as I get started on her locks.

Once I have her hair done, I do mine quickly and then help her get into her dress.

"Do you think Travis will think I'm pretty?" she asks as I button the back of her red velvet dress.

"Of course he will. Now step," I say, placing her snow boot on her foot. This is the downfall of having to take the train everywhere—dressing for the outside elements. When we get to the mall, she'll change into black patent shoes.

I send her back to the living room so I can get dressed and finish putting on my makeup. I opt for jeans and a sweater and start laughing to myself as I remember how long it took me to undress for Travis last night. Trying to be sexy during the winter is hard, although you can definitely make up for it when you're sitting by the fire.

A knock at the door has me scrambling to put my boots on, and Lucy yells that she'll get it, even though she knows she's not allowed to. I follow closely behind her and am there when she opens the door. Travis stands there, looking dapper in his peacoat, jeans, and from what I can tell, another sweater. However, what catches my attention are the flowers that he's holding.

"These are for my two favorite girls." He extends both hands, each of which holds red roses—one set for me, the other for Lucy.

"See, I told you he loves me," Lucy says as she takes her flowers. Travis winks, and that simple gesture turns my insides into a quivering mess.

I take the other bouquet and hold them to my nose and inhale. "They smell so good."

"Like you," he says, leaning in and taking his own deep breath. "Fuck, Saylor, I can't wait for tonight."

"And what makes you think anything will happen?"

He steps back and appraises me before smirking. "Nothing has to. I only want to be in the same room with you, and I'll be happy."

BOSTON RENEGADES

While Travis Kidd's future continues to hang in the balance, he's not slowing down. Many have e-mailed to let us know that Kidd has been spending time with a mysterious woman and her daughter. Sources close to the Kidd tell us that the woman in question is his publicist and that she's helping him with his image. However, there is speculation that he is the father of the young child and the woman in question is a former ex. We are unable to confirm the true identity at this time.

Over the course of covering Kidd's career and off-the-field antics, never once have we come across a paternity claim.

In team-related news, the waiver wire is active, and general manager Ryan Stone has been offering deals to some of the best pitchers in the league. Let's hope that Stone can sign some star talent that will put us into the playoffs.

It is also being speculated that Steve Bainbridge will hang up his cleats for a tie, taking a job in the front office. If this is the case, we wish Bainbridge a happy retirement and thank him for staying with the organization.

Happy holidays from the BoRe Blogger

TWENTY-THREE

Travis

I'm the type of guy who brushes everything under the rug. If you don't like me, okay. If you think my game sucked or I didn't do a good enough job for you, fine. If you want to think that I had to rape a woman in order to get her attention, well, that is where I draw the line. And as much as I want to ignore the recent articles about my life, I can't, because they involve Saylor and Lucy. Saylor's biggest fear is coming to life, and I can't bury this or make it go away.

The flowers I brought are a peace offering. It was my intention to tell her everything that I read this morning, until they both opened the door. To see Lucy dressed up and Saylor smile when we made eye contact had me second-guessing opening my mouth. If I did, I'd ruin their day. And mine, but I don't matter right now. My issues are things that I have to deal with, and I knew better than to bring Saylor into the mix. She already has her reservations about us, and now everyone knows about her because I'm selfish and couldn't stay away.

Handing them their roses and seeing their reactions pained me. This could very well be the last time we're together like this. It's not going to matter that I'll promise to protect her and Lucy or make sure that Jeffrey doesn't fire her. I opened her up and left her vulnerable. I encouraged the hand holding, and I kissed her out in public. Because of me, she's on every sports blog and newspaper, being called every name you can think of. And it's being speculated that I'm Lucy's dad, which honestly doesn't bother me.

"Okay, our flowers are in water. I think we're ready to go."

I push off the doorframe and reach for Lucy's hand, and Saylor takes her other one once she has the door locked. Looking down at our conjoined hands, I can't help but smile and think that someday this could be permanent for the three of us. That's if she'll be able to forgive me.

There was a time in my life when I never thought about marriage or a long-term commitment. In fact, I teased the shit out of my teammates for even seeing a piece of ass more than once. My feelings changed when I met Saylor, even though I kept them bottled up. I never told the guys about her, and I continued to lie to myself each and every time I was with another woman. Sure, I've had girlfriends in the past, but nothing that lasted more than a week at best. One night with Saylor made me feel different.

As we walk to the train station, I realize I probably could've driven, but I have opted not to since my life was flipped upside down. Walking allows me to evade the press when they start to follow. It's nothing for me to slip through an alley, disappear into a store, or go in through the back door, much like I did this morning when I returned to Saylor's. By all accounts, I should've canceled, but I needed one last day with them before she shuts me out for good.

The train is packed, causing me to pull my stocking cap down lower than I usually like to wear it. I hang on to the upper rail and hover over Saylor and Lucy while they share a seat with an older lady.

Lucy is prattling on about all the things she wants for Christmas. The list is long and probably what every kid is asking for this year. A quick glance at Saylor shows me that the joyfulness in her earlier demeanor is already gone. You don't have to be a genius to figure out why. Everything that Lucy is listing, Saylor can't afford, which leads me back to a question I asked a while ago—where is Lucy's father?

My name is mumbled among the crowd, but I focus on Lucy and Saylor. I promised Lucy that all my attention would be on her when we're together. I'm not the only player like this either. Steve Bainbridge refuses to sign autographs when he's with his kids. After the other night, I get it. Children don't like to share what's important to them. And honestly, neither do I.

The moment our train comes to a stop, we're in the thick of the crowd trying to get off, and join the massive population of shoppers. Carolers are on one street corner, and a vendor selling roasted nuts is on the other, all while holiday music plays from the loudspeakers. This could be overwhelming for some people.

We duck into Macy's and meander through the overly crowded aisles. People bump into us, some polite, others not so much, and finally we end up at the tail end of the mile-long line to see the man in red.

"You know, I could go up there and tell them who I am, and we'd be able to cut."

Saylor shakes her head. "Can you just be our Travis for right now?"

A lump forms in my throat as I process what she said to me. "Our Travis." I like that—a lot, in fact. I nod and remove my coat but leave my hat on. Some disguise is better than none when I'm out in public like this.

Saylor works to change Lucy's shoes while I help Lucy stay up-right. She gives her mom a bit of an attitude, and I find myself wanting to say something, but it's not my place.

"When's it my turn?" Lucy whines. She crosses her arms and huffs, clearly irritating Saylor.

"Why don't you guys go walk around? I'll hold our place in line," I offer, but Saylor shakes her head.

"If Lucy wants to see Santa, she needs to wait in line with the rest of the kids." Saylor says this while looking directly at Lucy.

"I'm thirsty," Lucy says, but this time she's pouting. I feel like I'm about to cave in when she bats her eyelashes, playing me like a fiddle.

"Um…"

"Don't," Saylor says sternly. I shut my mouth and pretend like my feelings aren't hurt. She crouches down in front of Lucy and straightens out her dress. "I don't know what's gotten into you, but I don't like this little 'tude you're giving me. We can leave if you don't want to see Santa."

"I'm tired," she says, whining again. Saylor nods and goes to pick Lucy up, but I stop her.

"I'll hold her." I hand Saylor my coat and scoop Lucy up into my arms. And much like last night, her tiny arms wrap around me as she snuggles into my neck.

"She's probably heavy."

I shake my head. "I could bench-press her and not break a sweat."

It's almost an hour before we finally reach Santa. Lucy is full of pep as she sits on his lap and tells him everything she wants. I'm mentally taking it all in so I can try to make sure at least a few of these things are delivered to her.

With a happy child between us, we decide to grab lunch. Every place at the mall has a wait, and I finally use my name to get us a table.

"You shouldn't have done that. Other people are waiting," Saylor points out as she places her napkin on her lap.

"I know, but I'm hungry, and I don't like waiting."

She rolls her eyes and I reach under the table and place my hand on her knee. My heart races, knowing that I have to tell her about the shit I read this morning, but this isn't the right time or place to do that. I won't be able to wait once we get back to her place either. If I make a move and tell her afterward, I'll look like a fucking prick.

We place our order and make small talk in between helping Lucy color her kiddie sheet that happens to be a BoRe baseball player. They gave her a red and a blue crayon to fill in his uniform.

"How do you spell your name?" she asks me.

"T-r-a-v-i-s." I say each letter slowly, while Saylor helps her write each one out.

"If you ladies would excuse me, I'm going to use the little boy's room."

Lucy must find this funny, because she laughs so hard that she ends up snorting, which in turn makes her laugh even harder.

A few of the men recognize me on my way to the restroom. I stop and pose for pictures and sign a few autographs. I figure I have a few minutes before my food is supposed to arrive. Guys even follow me to the bathroom to talk about spring training and the retirement of Bainbridge. It's creepy as fuck to be taking a leak while other men are chatting about your stats and the other guys on your team. I take longer than necessary to wash my hands, hoping they'll leave. The last thing I want is for them to follow me back to my table.

With the coast clear, I open the door and run smack into a woman, who hits the other side of the wall from the force of the impact.

"Shit, I'm sorry. Are you okay?" I reach for her arm to help her stand up straight.

She nods and moves her hair out of her face. The recognition is instant. My arm drops, and I take a step back.

"You," I seethe, only to have her smile smugly in return. I open my mouth to say so much more but know that I can't. *She's* not worth going to jail for.

"Won't the district attorney love to hear about this?" she says.

"Excuse me?"

"You pushing me into a wall. It's probably frowned upon."

Before I can react, she's pulling out her phone. I don't stay to find out who she's calling. I can't risk it. I rush back to the table, thankful that our food hasn't arrived, and grab my coat.

"We gotta go," I say, grabbing Saylor's arm to help her stand up.

"What? Why? What's going on?"

I lean over the table and grab Lucy, smacking her legs on the underside of the table. She cries out as I cradle her to my chest.

"Travis, what's wrong?" Saylor asks as she runs behind me, trying to keep up as I rush to the exit.

"I'll tell you in the cab."

As soon as I'm outside, I whistle for a cab that pulls up almost immediately. Saylor gets in, and I hand her Lucy, who has started to cry.

"What the hell is going on?"

I glance out of the back window to see if anyone is chasing us. "When I came out of the bathroom, I ran into a woman. She hit the wall, and when she looked at me, it was her."

"Her who?"

I look at Saylor and see her eyes deaden. She knows without me even saying. "She said she was letting the DA know that I assaulted her."

"What was she doing there?" Saylor asks.

"I don't know, but I'm fucked."

Saylor looks forward, pressing her lips to Lucy's hair. She holds her daughter tightly, keeping her hand locked around her wrist. Something tells me that I shouldn't try to touch her, even though I really need to feel her hand in mine, because I'm starting to freak the fuck out.

TWENTY-FOUR

Saylor

I knew the risks of being with Travis, yet I've continued to allow him into my life, into our lives. I let my feelings for him cloud my professional obligations and once again I found myself in the wrong place at the wrong time with him. Why of all people did *she* have to be there to ruin our day? Everything was going so perfectly, and for a brief moment, I could picture us as a couple. And in the blink of an eye, a random trip to the bathroom changed that.

This is a sign. I know it. I can't be with Travis, not anymore. I have too much to lose, and as much as I hate saying it, no man is worth my job or my daughter. And even as I look over at him, I can see the worry lines in his forehead. He's closed off and angled toward the door as if he's going to make a run for it. I realize we're both scared, but for different reasons.

The taxi pulls up outside my apartment, and while Lucy and I get out, he pays before joining us on the sidewalk. We both go to speak but stop ourselves and smile.

"I'm going to go," he says, pointing over his shoulder. Travis steps away before I can even acknowledge his statement. He leaves us standing on the sidewalk, wondering what the hell just happened.

"Where's he going?" Lucy asks, squeezing my hand tighter.

"I don't know, baby." My eyes dampen with tears as I watch him walk down the street. I half expect him to look back and wave, but he doesn't.

Lucy and I ride the elevator in silence, and even the sound of Christmas music doesn't make me smile when we step off onto our floor. The Christmas spirit I had has been diminished by the past hour, and I shouldn't feel that way. Even Lucy seems melancholy, and she doesn't have a clue about the real reason our day went south.

Inside our apartment, I turn on our tree, letting the white lights sparkle throughout the room. "How about some hot cocoa and *Rudolph*?" I ask Lucy as I help her take her coat off.

"Can Travis come back?"

I quickly shake my head. "Not right now, sweetie." She starts to balk, but I don't pay attention to the impending fit. I unbutton the back of her dress and usher her off to her room to change into her sweats before doing the same thing.

One look at my bed pulls me up short. This morning, we left bed in such a hurry that neither of us pulled the covers back into place, and I didn't make it after he left. Usually only one side is a mess, but now it's the whole bed, the corners untucked and pillows strewn everywhere. Visions of last night run through my mind. My flesh warms as I remember his hands kneading my skin as desire built between us.

I change quickly and grab my pillow and quilt, determined not to sleep in there tonight. I have a feeling a night of Lifetime movies are in my future once Lucy is asleep. It won't be the first time I spent a night like this feeling sorry for myself.

Lucy is waiting for me in the living room, dressed in her Rudolph pajamas with matching slippers. The sight of her makes me smile even if my heart is breaking.

With cups of hot coca, complete with marshmallows, in our hands, we snuggle together through a marathon of holiday movies. Lucy has seen some of them so many times that she knows all the words and recites them as the characters do. Only when I can hear just the voices from the television do I realize that she's fallen asleep. It would be so easy to keep her in my arms, but the truth is that I want to be alone. I want to shed tears and not have her wake and ask me what's wrong. I half expected Travis to call or stop by, and the fact that he hasn't has me feeling like he's used me, but I know I shouldn't feel that way.

After tucking Lucy in, I snuggle under my blanket and get lost in the world of cheesy holiday drama. Each story is the same, second chances at love, and here I sit, hoping for a chance. I thought I had found my forever when I met Elijah. He was paving my way to happiness. I was utterly destroyed when he left me, and I vowed to never let it happen again.

It wasn't supposed to happen, but somehow Travis relentlessly whittled away piece after piece of my resolve. And when I finally opened the door and let him in, he slammed his shut. It seems that I should probably forgo any attempt at falling in love. It's better that way.

The faint sound of my cell phone ringing has me scrambling off the couch and to my purse, dumping its contents onto the floor. My heart races as I'm on my hands and knees, searching through God-knows-what until I pick up the cold metal object. I close my eyes, not even looking at the caller identification, knowing it's Travis calling to apologize.

"Hi, Travis," I say breathlessly.

"Ahem." The throat on the other end clears. "Saylor, it's Elijah. Should I assume that Travis is the man you are representing who is accused of rape?"

Everything in me turns cold as I clutch my phone to my ear. I swallow hard and prepare to save face as much as I can, because the man on the other end can easily ruin the rest of my life.

"Merry Christmas Eve," Lucy yells as she comes running out of her room. I take a big sip of my coffee and close my eyes. My finger presses into my temple as I try to push away my headache.

Last night I had every intention of throwing myself a pity party because of Travis, but instead I paced the floor, taking breaks only to write down everything that I remembered about my relationship with Elijah after we broke up. I had a sinking feeling that I was going to need that list.

He called to tell me that he's back in town and that his wife and their two perfect children are with him, and they're here to meet Lucy. I tried to explain that it's Christmas and that we could set something up for afterward, but my pleas fell on deaf ears. He doesn't seem to care that his family is holed up in a hotel during the holiday.

"What time do you think Santa will be here?"

"After you're fast asleep. He won't come if you're still awake." I pull a bowl down from the cabinet, adding some cereal and milk to it. She looks at me and frowns. "What's wrong?" I ask her.

"I want pancakes."

I shake my head. "We don't have the stuff to make them. I'll go to the store later."

"Order them like Travis does." She puts her hands up in the air, as if ordering takeout is the solution for everything.

"I can't, Lucy."

"Why not? Travis does."

"Well, Travis isn't here. Now eat, because there is someone coming over to meet you." I leave her in the kitchen and retreat to my bedroom, where behind my closed door I let the tears fall. I was stupid enough to have a glimmer of hope in thinking that Travis was going to be my knight in shining armor and that he'd come in and save me from everything, including the Big Bad Wolf that is Elijah, but I was wrong. He was only here to save himself, and when he realized that I wouldn't be the one to do it, he bailed. He has to know that, even after the other day, I won't tell Irvin that I saw him at the bar.

The doorbell chimes, and I angrily wipe away my tears before going back to the living room.

"Are you done?" I ask Lucy as I head toward the door. She nods and gets down from her chair. "Head to your room and get dressed, please. And don't come out until I come to get you."

"But I want to see Travis," she says through gritted teeth.

"Lucy…" I pinch the bridge of my nose in hopes of calming my temper. "It's not Travis. Please go to your room."

Lucy crosses her arms and huffs before stomping all the way down the hall. I jump when she slams the door. "I feel your pain," I mutter to my empty living room.

Elijah presses the doorbell again and does so repeatedly. I contemplate leaving him there but know he won't go away anytime soon. I open the door in a huff and glare at him. "I heard you the first time. You don't need to keep pressing the bell like a petulant child."

"Fitting comment coming from you," he says as he steps over the threshold and into my home. He holds his trench coat in his hand, but I don't offer to take it from him. His comment has me reeling, hating him for bringing up the fact that I did the exact same thing to him once after he left me. It wasn't one of my finer moments, but I was pregnant and desperate.

"Where is she?" he asks as he walks around my apartment. He picks up her school photo and holds it in his hands. He smiles briefly before setting it back on my mantel.

"Getting dressed."

"Did you tell her about me yet?"

I shake my head. "Nope. It's really not a conversation I planned to have on Christmas Eve."

"It gets done today, Saylor, and frankly it should've been done a long time ago."

"And what would I have said about why you missed her birthday, Christmas, and everything important to her over the years?"

"I would've been here if you had asked."

"See? That's the problem, Elijah. I shouldn't have to ask or remind you. You should be here because she's your daughter, not because you got a phone call."

I leave him standing there and go into Lucy's room. She's sitting at her small table, coloring. "What are you coloring?" I ask as I crouch down next to her, only to find a picture of Travis, along with other BoRe players.

"Travis gave it to me."

"That's very sweet of him."

She nods and continues to color his jersey red.

"Come on—there is someone here to see you."

"Is it Travis?" she asks again, and I shake my head, watching as her face falls. She sets her crayon down and places her hand in mine. My heart beats a thousand times a minute while my palms begin to sweat. I swear I'm about to have a heart attack the closer we get to the living room. Elijah owns me right now, and he isn't afraid to make everyone around me pay if he doesn't get what he wants.

Elijah is still snooping when we come back in, and when he looks at Lucy, she molds into my leg. He saunters over, trying to show her that he's a man who should be revered. Too bad she doesn't give a shit.

"Hi, Lucy. I'm Elijah. Do you remember me?" He extends his hand to shake hers, but she doesn't budge.

"Hi," she mutters.

He sighs and looks at me. I shrug, hoping he understands that he's on his own. I'd probably be more willing to help him out if I had kept her from him, but I hadn't. He kept himself from her. I have no sympathy for him.

We stand awkwardly in the middle of the room while he stares down at Lucy. You would think that for a man with children, he'd be less rigid, that he'd be more fatherly, but instead he's all business.

Lucy grows impatient under his gaze and starts to fiddle with the hem of my dress. Normally, I'd find something to distract her, but I'm afraid that whatever I do, Elijah will take it as a sign that he's welcome to stay, and he's not.

"Mommy, can I go back to my room?"

"No," Elijah barks out, causing us both to jump. I glare at him, hoping he can see the rage in my eyes. He has no right to speak to her like that. As far as I'm concerned, she's *my* daughter, not his. Lucy clings to my leg, turning her head away from Elijah. Her soft cries break my heart.

"I think you should go, Elijah."

"You know that isn't happening, Saylor." His eyes are cold and dark. The venom behind his words is meant to threaten me, and it does.

I nod, remembering his threat all too well. The call late last night was not only to warn me that he and his family were coming to town but also to voice his displeasure over Lucy spending time with Travis. It seems that our skating adventure had made it into the papers, unbeknownst to me, and Elijah doesn't want Lucy anywhere near Travis. I defended Travis, letting Elijah know that Travis hasn't been charged with any crimes, to which he replied with a terse "yet" and then proceeded to remind me that he's very good friends with the district attorney. That was enough to give me pause and left me with no choice but to open the door for him today.

"Elijah has something to tell you."

This time he squats down and tugs on one of her curls. I have to stare at Lucy because I don't want him seeing that he's getting the best of me. I feel her head turn against my leg as she looks at him.

"I'm your father, Lucy."

She shakes her head, and big fat tears start to fall. "But I want Travis to be my daddy."

Elijah rises to his feet, towering over me, and even though he's not taller than Travis, he makes me feel three feet small under his murderous glare. I swear there is steam coming out of his nostrils as he bellows at me.

"Fix this or I end him."

He doesn't give me a chance to respond before he's out the door, slamming it hard enough that the pictures rattle against my wall.

TWENTY-FIVE

Travis

This isn't how I imagined I'd spend my Christmas Eve, alone and in the clubhouse. I had hoped I'd be with Saylor and Lucy, or at the very least on my parents' yacht. To say my life is epically fucked up right now would be an understatement. I was stupid to think that my name alone would be enough to clear me of any charges, but as time goes by, so does my resolve.

Irvin tells me that the charges will be dropped if I give him the name of my alibi. He had reminded me that the DA is grasping at straws and that he's using the other women to make me admit to something I didn't do. Until yesterday I believed him. Until yesterday I thought everything was going to go away, but the look in Blue's eyes, or Rachel's, really hit home that this isn't going away and that she's out for blood. She's cold and calculated and clearly a very scorned woman because I didn't take her home. I can't even imagine what my life would be like now if I had, although I can't imagine it could get much worse.

I was tempted to call the guys and see if they wanted to come work out, but the potential rejection was too much to take. Branch has his son, Cooper has his twins, and I'm sure Ethan has returned to

Seattle. They all have lives and don't have time to butter up my ego to make me feel better about myself because I've had another run-in with the woman accusing me of rape.

Honestly, I half expected to be woken up by the police, showing me their shiny handcuffs and reading me my rights. I scoured every online news agency, looking for any sign that the state's attorney is coming after me, only to find the wires quiet.

What I haven't done is call Saylor to apologize for ditching them yesterday. That wasn't how the day, and night, was supposed to go. Everything started out so perfectly, and the run-in with *that* woman changed my entire outlook on life, the day, and who I was dragging down with me in this shit storm of trouble. Saylor and Lucy don't deserve to be in the middle of this crisis, and honestly, I should've listened to Saylor from the beginning when she told me that she couldn't be with me. But I pushed, and to her it probably looks like I got what I wanted and bailed. Classic Travis Kidd move.

The stadium is dark and cold, matching my mood—exactly how it should be. People should be home with their families today or out buying last-minute gifts. I had every intention of ordering everything that Lucy had asked Santa for, but only ended up with a few things before my sour mood last night found me nursing a bottle of vodka instead of trying to make a little girl's Christmas morning more magical. Besides, if Saylor were smart, she'd tell Jeffrey to reassign her and let my public image swirl down the drain with the rest of the sidewalk trash.

As I get closer to the gym, I hear the voices of a few people who are lingering around the stadium, no doubt getting the venue prepped for the annual hockey match they hold the day after Christmas. Lowery Field is one of the few "family-owned" stadiums left in the big leagues, and when the Renegades aren't occupying it during the season, it's rented out. I've been here for weddings, corporate functions, college events, and concerts.

My name is mentioned, causing me to stop dead in my tracks. Eavesdropping is a terrible thing to do, but it can be informative. The voices are around the corner from where I'm standing, and they're loud and clear.

"I can't believe they haven't released him yet."

"You know he's brought women in here before."

"I don't feel safe knowing he can come in here any time he wants."

"He's probably going to have to pay her off."

"I can't believe it's taken this long for someone to report him."

"He's a rapist, and I don't feel safe here anymore."

Each jab cuts deeper and deeper. I have the urge to turn the corner and show my face, but seeing fear in the eyes of the people that work here is not something I want to witness. They can have their own feelings, but I wish they'd consider mine. Although by the words they spew, I'm guilty, so it doesn't matter how I feel.

I turn around and take the long way to the gym, trying to keep my emotions in check. I'm on the verge of beating the shit out of someone, or crying. Fuck, maybe I need to do both. This is my life that's hanging in the balance, and since I saw the victim yesterday, I can't get over the fact that she seemed cocky, undeterred by our chance meeting. Shouldn't a woman fear her attacker instead of threatening him? I'm all for women empowerment, but fuck this shit. Two days from now, this all ends, or I'm going to file a countersuit against her. Of course, that won't go over well with the media, but I'm sick of living this fucking nightmare. People need to know I'm innocent.

As soon as I step into the gym and the lights come on, I'm relieved to see that our punching bag is back. Plugging my iPod in, I turn on my heavy metal playlist, tape my knuckles, and get to work on the bag. It's her face I picture each time I hit the target. I was raised to never hit a woman, but fuck if I don't want to do it now. This game she's playing is fucking with my life.

Each hit is harder than the previous one, and the red seeping through the tape isn't enough to stop me. I don't care if I'm bloodied, if the skin of my knuckles is breaking from each punch—the pain is welcomed. It's needed so I can feel human again, so I can feel what it's like to be hurt and not just broken.

My music shuts off, causing me to turn mid-punch. Standing next to my iPod is Easton Bennett, shortstop and a guy who has his own troubles with women.

"What's up?" I say, nodding toward him and my music at the same time. Seriously, who the fuck comes into the gym and shuts off a man's playlist?

He shakes his head slowly. "Not much. I heard you were here, so I thought I'd come see you."

I turn back to the bag and start punching. "Could've called. I've been home."

"This really isn't a social visit, Kidd."

I stop again and rest my arm on the top of the bag to hold it steady. "If you got something to say, say it."

"Actually, a few of us do." That's the voice of Kayden Cross, and Bryce Mackenzie follows him into the open space of the gym.

"What's this, a fucking intervention?" Three of my teammates stand shoulder to shoulder, glaring at me. I step up to them, letting them know that I'm not afraid of them.

"As captain, I'm asking you to stay away from the clubhouse and stadium until Stone has issued a release stating that you're still an active member of the team," Bennett says.

"Excuse me?"

"Being charged with rape—" Cross starts to say before I interrupt him.

"Accused. There's a difference, scum jammer," I say to Cross. "Know the fucking facts before you start spouting off through your whore fondler."

"Kidd, do you take anything seriously?" Mackenzie asks.

"Yeah, I do. Like right now with my motherfucking teammates coming at me with this bullshit. I've met with Stone, and unlike you, he's not willing to throw me to the wolves for something I didn't do."

"Your reputation is enough for everyone to be concerned. As your team, we feel it'd be best if you didn't come around until you were clear of all the charges," Bennett says.

I laugh and take the tape off my hands. Once it's wadded up, I throw it at the guys. "You know, next time you might want to make sure you have the entire team standing behind you, because as infielders, I don't give a fuck what you think. The captain of the outfield has my back, and so does our third baseman. Not to mention the man who we all depend on to bring in the runs. So the next time you want to be a fucking douche farm, better make sure you have every single team member's backing."

I leave the men I once considered my friends standing there as I calmly walk out of the gym. They don't need to see that I'm more upset than I'm showing or see that their words tore at my heart. We are supposed to be a team, and teams stick together through thick and thin.

On my way out, I call Jeffrey and leave him a message. "I want a trade." That's all I say before hanging up. I can't play with a team that doesn't have my back. My next call is to Saylor, but that goes to voice mail as well. I tell her that I'm sorry for yesterday and ask her to call me. More than anything I want to spend Christmas with her, Lucy, and her mother, even if it's only for dinner.

I thought it would be a benefit to have my car back. I thought I'd be able to come and go from my house and no one would notice. Except the reporters who are hell-bent on following my every move have put eyes in the back alley. I don't know what they're waiting for. Do they expect me to have an orgy at my house? For me to parade a harem of women in and out of here every night?

"Don't you have a family?" I ask as I get out of my SUV.

"Sure do, Mr. Kidd."

"Then go the fuck home. It's Christmas," I say as I step through my gate. I make sure it's locked before going into my house and right out the front door. As soon as I step out onto my stoop, everyone is scrambling for position.

They all look confused and shake their heads. "What a bunch of scum fuckers you guys are. Seriously, go home. I can promise you that you won't miss anything."

Stepping back in, I slam my door. It's dark and dreary inside my house, making me long for Saylor's. Even the few presents I did manage to buy for her and Lucy don't brighten my place like I thought they would. Just as I pull out my phone to call her, I hear a knock at my door. Peeking through the blinds, I'm surprised to find Saylor standing there.

"Hey," I say, reaching for her arm to pull her in, but she avoids my reach as she steps inside. "I just called you," I say, closing the door behind her.

She smiles, but it doesn't reach her eyes. "Jeffrey called."

"And that's why you're here?" I ask, only for her to nod. "Do you want to take off your coat and stay for a little while?"

Her smile fades as she shakes her head. "I can't, Travis."

"Can't or won't?"

"A bit of both, I guess." Her lips go into a thin line, telling me that whatever I thought we were building is now gone, but I don't want to believe her.

"I'm sorry about yesterday." I hedge, hoping that my attitude is the reason for her reluctance to be here.

"I'm here because Jeffrey called. He's away on vacation and asked me to stop by. Are you sure you want a trade? You have two years left on your current contract, but there's an out if you want him to execute it."

I reach for her again, only to have her shy way. "Saylor?"

"You're my client, Travis." Her voice breaks when she says this, and I know something has happened since I left her. It can't be because of what happened at the restaurant. She's believed me from day one, so I know that hasn't changed.

"I'm more than your fucking client, Saylor."

"You can't be," she says, looking away.

I go to her and pull her chin up so she can look me in the eyes. "This again? Tell me why not."

She shakes her head and steps away. "So about your contract—"

"Fuck my contract, and fuck this bullshit. I don't want to talk about baseball. I want to talk about us."

"There is no *us*, Travis." Her words are the final nail in my coffin. I stand there, staring at everything else but her as her words reverberate through me. *There is no us.* But there was, and we were going to create fucking magic together.

I glance at the presents, wrapped with pretty bows, mocking me. "These are for you and Lucy," I say. I pick them up and hand them to her, honestly surprised that she's even accepting them.

"You didn't have to buy her anything."

I bite my tongue, keeping the slew of words locked inside my brain. "Right, well, Merry Christmas, Saylor. It's been a pleasure working with you, but you can call Jeffrey and tell him I want to get the fuck out of Boston before spring training starts."

As soon as she steps out, she turns and looks at me. I take one last look at the woman I could've fallen in love with and slam the door.

"Merry fucking Christmas, Kidd." Those are the last words I speak before my lips touch a freshly opened bottle of vodka.

TWENTY-SIX

Saylor

I sit on my sofa with my afghan over my legs, wishing I had a glass of wine in my hands. Beside me the fire crackles, and the flame lights my living room with its soft orange glow. The sparkle of the Christmas tree seems to have dimmed now that the festivities are over and all the presents have been unwrapped, opened, played with, and put away for the night. All except for one, that is.

The tiny, odd-shaped box sits on the arm of my sofa, with its pretty red ribbon and white wrapping paper, eagerly waiting for someone to open it. It's the last present, and it's addressed to me, from Travis. The presents we bought him still sit under my tree, reminding me that I should've taken them over to him, but for some reason, I didn't.

Seeing him yesterday, and having to tell him that he's my client and nothing else, hurt worse than when Elijah left me, pregnant and alone. I thought I could shield my heart from Travis, but after the gut-wrenching pain I experienced yesterday, I know that's not the case. I barely made it off his steps before I was hyperventilating. I tried to save face in front of the media, but the reporters knew that something had happened inside his home. It's my hope that they left it alone and didn't badger him or assume the worst—that he hurt me—because he didn't. I had no choice but to let the tears flow freely, almost freezing to small icicles as they fell down my face because of the harsh wind and cold temperatures. I deserved it, though, because I know how much pain I was causing him.

Days ago, my Christmas morning looked so different in my eyes. I had every intention of inviting Travis to spend the day with us. Truth be told, I wanted him here on Christmas Eve so he could enjoy the night with us and be here when I pretended to be the jolly man dressed in red as I set Lucy's presents out. I wanted to stand under the mistletoe and share kisses with the man who has slowly worked his way into my heart.

Elijah changed that for me, taking away the little happiness that I was trying to build. I know better than to not take his threats seriously. I've seen him destroy people in court and not bat an eyelash in the process. I wish I could tell Travis that I did this for him, to save him from a man who is willing to hurt whomever I love to get his way. Travis would never understand, though, and he'd try to save us, even though no one can. I was stupid when I fell for Elijah, and unfortunately I'll pay the price until he has no financial control over my life.

Tears fall as I stare at the present and imagine the way Travis would've looked this morning while we watched Lucy open her presents. I could easily see him in a white T-shirt with plaid flannel pants on, barefoot, with his hair messier than normal and his megawatt smile lighting up everything around him.

Instead, my only recollection of him right now is the anger in his eyes and the sour way he excused me from his home. I wanted to tell him that I don't have a choice, but he'd never see it from my point of view, especially since he's going through so much right now. The last thing I want to do is burden him with my baby-daddy drama. I sigh and wipe angrily at my tears, berating myself for wallowing. I don't have any right to feel sorry for myself. Not when I've hurt the one man who needed just a bit of compassion from me.

Leaning forward, I pick up the pretty wrapped box and touch the satin bow through blurry eyes. I should return this to him, unworthy of his affection, but I selfishly want to open it to know what's inside. I want to hurt some more when I see what he's picked out for me. It's twisted and evil, but it's the pain I feel I deserve.

Only, I don't open it. I leave it the way it is and set it on my coffee table before lying down so I can stare at the box while the fire dances behind it and more tears fall.

A loud pounding startles me awake. The fire has since timed out, and very little warmth remains. I try to focus through the darkness, but my eyes are tired and somewhat hard to open. My name is called, and my heart starts racing. Slowly I get up from the couch and make my way to the door, only to jump when the next knock happens.

"Who is it?"

"It's Irvin; open up."

I do as he requests, not even bothering to check the peephole to make sure it's him. "What time is it?" is the first question out of my mouth when it should've been, "What are you doing here?"

"It's after seven," he says, looking at his wrist, even though he's not wearing a watch.

"Come in. Can I get you some coffee?"

"No, thank you." He looks around my apartment, and when his eyes land on me, I feel awkward. I quickly cover my face, wondering what the hell he's seeing.

"Sorry—I was sleeping."

"And crying," he points out.

I nod and excuse myself to the bathroom. As soon as I look in the mirror, I cringe. Not only am I cursed with dark bags, but also my makeup is streaked down my face in dark lines, making me look like something from a horror movie. I cried myself to sleep last night, never bothering to wash my face, not caring because there wasn't anyone here to see me. I freshen up as much as I can and go to check on Lucy, only to remember that my mother took her for the night. I led my mother to believe that Travis would be over later, and she wanted to give us some privacy, when all I really wanted was to be alone.

"Rough night?" Irvin asks when I step back into the room. I nod and head into the kitchen.

"Are you sure you don't want some coffee?"

"No time. I'm due at the courthouse in twenty."

"The day after Christmas? Must be a serious case," I say as I spoon the coffee grounds into the filter.

"You haven't heard? I assumed because you were crying…"

"Heard w-what?"

He runs his hand through his hair and sighs. "Travis was arrested early this morning and is being arraigned at eight."

"For what?" My tongue is thick in my throat. I grip the edge of my countertop, waiting for Irvin to tell me.

"Rape and assault. It seems that he followed Rachel Ward into a restaurant and assaulted her in the bathroom."

But he didn't!

I step back and cover my mouth to hold in my sob. This woman is vile, lying like this. I know for a fact that he didn't do anything to her at the restaurant because I was there, just like I had been at the bar.

"Anyway, I'm here because I want to hold a press conference after his arraignment."

"Okay," I say as my stomach threatens to expel my dinner from last night.

"I'm convinced this is a witch hunt, and the DA is only doing this to boost his reelection bid. If he had evidence to arrest Travis for rape, he would've done so weeks ago. He's stalled repeatedly, and the rape kit has suddenly disappeared."

"How can they arrest him, then?"

Irvin sighs again and shakes his head. "According to the complaint, Travis has been following her for weeks. Showing up where she is, trying to bribe her to make everything go away. When she wouldn't take the money, he beat her up. The DA wanted to arrest him two nights ago but felt after the holiday would be better."

Is that why Travis left us standing outside in front of my apartment, to go look for her? I don't want to believe it, but it's possible. This woman is ruining his life, and at some point, your willpower breaks and you do stupid things.

"I'm coming with you. I'll be ready in ten minutes." I hustle off to my room and try to keep the tears at bay. I have no doubt I'm the last person Travis wants to see, but I have to be there. He has to know that I support him. I know he didn't rape that woman but can't be sure he didn't go out and look for her after we left the restaurant. But why would he? Why would he risk everything to confront her when he could've easily done it at the restaurant?

I slip into a sweaterdress, fleece tights, and boots before putting my hair up into a bun, and quickly do my makeup, dabbing on some lipstick after brushing my teeth.

"I'm ready," I say as I enter the living room. I grab my coat and slip it on before holding the door open for Irvin and following him out. "You know I'm on vacation," I tell him as I pull out my phone and start messaging all the media channels.

"I heard. So is Jeffrey, but he's out of town."

"So that was my mistake, huh?" It's a joke, but even I'm not laughing. I had planned, albeit sort of late, to spend time with Travis and Lucy, exploring Boston and making sure to visit the ice sculptures. I was looking forward to New Year's Eve and watching the fireworks from the top of the hotel during the Boston Rotary dinner and then spending the next day watching football. It's nothing but a fantasy now and something I knew I should've never even allowed myself to dream about.

We take a cab to the courthouse, and by the time we arrive, the news stations are setting up. I speak to each one briefly before entering through the heavy double doors. Not surprisingly, the halls are quiet, making it easy to find Travis.

"All rise," the bailiff says as I slip in. I take a spot behind Irvin and Travis, who is dressed in an orange jumpsuit. Seeing him like this pisses me off. He doesn't deserve this type of treatment.

"Be seated," the judge says. He immediately starts shuffling papers and yawns. "This is the matter of the state of Massachusetts versus Travis Kidd on the counts of rape and assault. How do you plead?"

"Not guilty, Your Honor."

I'm taken aback by the hollowness in his voice. When he turns and makes eye contact with me over his shoulder, I start to smile, but his eyes are vacant. To him, I'm nothing more than someone he pays to make him look good, and I haven't been doing a very good job of that lately.

"The state is asking that Mr. Kidd be held without bail."

"Oh, you've got to be kidding me, Your Honor." Irvin stands. "My client has cooperated with the police from the beginning, even voluntarily submitting his own DNA sample, and still to this day, the state has been unable to produce a report implicating my client. Mr. Kidd is being accused of multiple crimes that he did not commit, and the state is willing to ruin this man's career because of who he is. I'm asking that my client be released on his own recognizance."

"These are some fairly strong charges, Mr. Abbott."

"Yes, sir, they are, but I assure you that Mr. Kidd is innocent. We have a witness that can confirm his whereabouts if this were to go to trial, but wasting the taxpayers' money is not in the best interest of the state. The victim in this case is my client, and not the accuser. She's simply a woman scorned."

My eyes drop to my hands as my life flashes in front of me. This is another mark against me, and one Elijah will happily add to the growing list of reasons he's coming up with to take Lucy away.

"The state is willing to accept three million for bail," the assistant district attorney says.

Travis's head falls, and I desperately want to reach out and tell him it'll be okay, but I know it won't be.

The judge continues to look over the summons, flipping pages back and forth, while we wait for his answer.

"Mr. Kidd, you are being accused of a heinous crime, and you voluntarily provided your DNA?"

"Yes, sir," Travis says after he stands.

"Did you hit this woman on the day in question?"

"I did, but not in the way she's describing."

"How so?" the judge asks.

"As I told the officer this morning, I was coming out of the bathroom and ran into a woman. I didn't know it was her until after she moved her hair out of her face. I immediately stepped back, and she told me she was calling her lawyer."

"You can sit down."

He returns to reading, stopping only to jot notes down.

"I'm going to deny the state's motion to seek bail in this matter. However, Mr. Kidd, you are not free to leave town. And you"—the judge points to the ADA—"better be ready to proceed next week. I want to see everyone back here after the first of the year."

He slams his gavel down, causing me to jump. Irvin and Travis hug, and while I'd love to feel his arms around me, the press is outside waiting, and I'll be damned if the state is getting to them before me.

BREAKING NEWS

Left fielder Travis Kidd has been arrested and charged with rape and aggravated assault. According to the state, Kidd assaulted the victim after he cornered her at her place of employment. The complaint shows that Kidd has been following her around since the rape was reported and even offered her money to "make it go away."

During the arraignment, Kidd pled not guilty and was released without bail. A court date was set for next week where the state will need to present their case against Kidd. Speaking on behalf of Kidd at the press conference after the hearing, his publicist, Saylor Blackwell, indicated that the state is purposely dragging their feet and that their lack of evidence in this case is bothersome. Kidd's attorney, Irvin Abbott, stated that a lawsuit against the state would be forthcoming on his client's behalf.

Our staff reached out to Kidd, but we were unable to get a comment from him.

The BoRe Blogger

CHAPTER 27

Travis

I stand back while Saylor rips into the district attorney's office about their shoddy investigation and the damage that it has done to my career. What she doesn't mention is that my life is in shambles and she's the only one who can fix it, or at least that is what I keep telling myself. She can give me an alibi for that night, telling the judge that I attempted to leave with her and about the threatening comment that was made. I need her to help put this farce behind me. Little does she know that I'm not giving her an opportunity to say no this time. Saylor doesn't get to call the shots anymore.

Hundreds of questions are asked as soon as she finishes her tirade, but the microphone is taken over by Irvin, who echoes everything Saylor said. When it comes down to it, I have a team of people surrounding me who are looking out for my best interests. It's unfortunate that a handful of my teammates don't feel the same way. I guess the joke's on them when I accept the first trade that comes my way. I have never been more excited to get out of Boston than I am now, which is funny because I used to love it here and saw myself retiring in the area.

Saylor stands next to me, poised and confident. She faces forward, keeping her hands in front of her, watching the crowd of reporters take in everything Irvin has to say. I should listen to him, but I can't take my eyes off of Saylor. Memorizing everything about her is high on my priority list because I won't see her ever again after today. I can't continue to pine for a woman who is hell-bent on keeping me at arm's length. And when I thought I finally broke through to her, when she finally felt like I was worth the risk, shit hit the fan.

I sigh heavily, causing her to look my way. She offers me a sweet, and professional, smile before turning her attention back to Irvin. His voice booms over the microphone as more and more onlookers start to gather. The amount of people outweighs the media coverage. I chuckle, thinking about how fucking cold it is outside and yet people are clamoring for any piece of information they can get. Once again, I'll be front-page news, and the story is pure bullshit.

When I opened my door this morning, I thought the officers only wanted to question me. I expected them to show up days earlier and had warned Irvin about my encounter with Rachel Ward. I'm not stupid. I wasn't going to hide this from him, and he told me not to answer any questions unless he was present.

Let me tell you, there is nothing like being cuffed and stuffed while the media is living outside your house. Being slammed up against my door, having my face pushed into the glass and my legs kicked apart, all while cameras are filming, is such a fucking blow to my ego. It would be one thing if I had done any of the shit I'm being accused of, but I haven't. Not that my innocence seems to matter to anyone. I suppose I'm lucky that at least I was somewhat dressed, so I was saved from having my junk displayed all over the news.

As soon as Irvin is done speaking, he's ushering me back into the courthouse. I glance briefly at Saylor, who has stepped back up to the podium. Sly move on her part, because she knows that I need to speak with her. She has to know her time for being silent is over. This situation is out of hand.

We're led to a conference room where Jeffrey sits inside at the small table. He shakes hands with Irvin, and they both motion for me to sit down.

"I cut my vacation short for this shit, Kidd."

"Next time, I'll make sure my legal issues don't fuck with your ability to get laid."

He smirks, knowing all too well that I know what his vacations entail. Jeffrey pushes my contract and a pen over to me and asks me to sign the bottom. My signature allows him to start seeking a trade on my behalf.

"Before you sign, I think we should meet with Stone."

"What for?"

"Let him know you're disgruntled."

I shake my head. "It's going to be easier to let me go than replace multiple members of the team. Besides, it's more than that. After this morning, the way the police treated me and this case, the people of Boston don't trust me. Parents aren't going to encourage their kids to get my autograph. My endorsement deals are going to start dropping. The stores are going to stop carrying my gear. I'm ruined here." I leave out the part where I want to have a relationship with his employee, and she's one of the reasons I'm leaving.

"They already are," he says.

"Are what?" I ask.

Jeffrey slides another sheet of paper my way, a spreadsheet full of numbers. "This is what you earned last year," he says, pointing to one column before moving to the one next to it. "And this is where you currently are with UA pulling their endorsement deal. I'm expecting Nike to follow suit later this afternoon," he says, sighing.

"All because some dumb bitch is lying."

He nods.

"This is why you want me to talk to Stone, isn't it? You don't think you can get me a good deal?"

He shakes his head. "Not after this morning. You'll be a hard sell until you're cleared."

"Which should be next week," Irvin adds.

"Which will be today," I state.

"What do you mean?" Jeffrey asks.

"Travis has a witness who is reluctant to come forward. I'm giving him one more opportunity to try and convince her to do the right thing before I subpoena her to testify."

"Good," Jeffrey says. "Make sure she understands that she has no choice."

"Meaning what?" I ask.

Jeffrey leans forward. "Meaning I can make her life hell if she isn't willing to play ball."

I want to slam his head down on the table and tell him to shut the fuck up, but he doesn't know he's referring to Saylor. She has said she could lose her job for being with me, if our time together ever came to light. That's not my intention. The other factor, the one where she could go to jail—that is where Irvin will have to step in and protect her. I don't want to hurt her, but I'm left without a choice, and it seems that my time is very limited.

Jeffrey and Irvin continue to talk about my contract and my declining endorsement deals while I watch the door, waiting for Saylor to come through. Even though she's made it very clear that we aren't together, seeing her still makes me happy, although I wasn't expecting her to be at my arraignment this morning and she caught me off guard.

I'm sure the look I gave her made sure she knew exactly how I was feeling, because, honestly, this matter could've been cleared up weeks ago if she would have just told her side of the story.

Irvin offers lunch. I decline, but Jeffrey takes him up on his offer. I can't imagine what those two are going to discuss while sitting in a restaurant with liquid courage running through their veins. Irvin is nice enough to have his driver take me home, though. It's the last place I want to be after what went down there this morning, but I have no choice. I'm more alone now than I was after the first accusation.

The media frenzy is in full force when we pull up outside. I'm barely able to get the car door open without bumping into someone. Microphones are thrust into my face while requests for comments are thrown at me, and protesters are pumping their signs up and down, yelling at me. Everything from *rapist* and *pervert* to *creep* is being slung my way, and they're demanding that I be released from the Renegades. Across from them, there are a few die-hard fans screaming obscenities at the protestors.

There's a police presence but they're not concerned with me getting to my door. They're holding back the fans and the protesters from going at each other. Irvin's driver tries to help, but he's jostled by the media and ends up back in his car. I don't blame him. It seems to be the safest place right now.

One officer yells to let me by, and I want to thank him and invite him for a cup of coffee, but he's doing the job he's being paid for. In all likelihood, he doesn't give a shit about me.

When I finally reach my door, I feel something slam into my back. Even before I can turn around, another object smashes into my door. My house is being egged, and all the police are doing is telling people to knock it off.

I feel like turning around, giving them the bird, and telling them that their wish has been granted. Boston will no longer be my home.

As soon as I step inside, I lock the door and close the blinds. Once again, my home is dark and drab. I don't bother trying to clean my suit jacket once I take it off. Instead, I throw it away, not needing an article of clothing to remind me that the town I adopted as my own has turned its back on me.

My phone is ringing with multiple calls. Ethan's and Cooper's names are in my notifications, but I ignore them. I have nothing to say. They should run far away from me so I don't ruin their careers as well.

The one call I do answer is from my father, who sounds drunk.

"Shit's not getting better?" he asks. Not "Hey, son" or "Are you okay?"

"No," I say as I sit down and kick my shoes off. If it weren't for Irvin, I would've been at the press conference in my pajamas. He had enough foresight to stop by my place and grab a suit for me to wear.

"Fly to the Keys; spend the rest of the winter on the yacht."

"I can't leave or I'd be there in a heartbeat. I asked for a trade but my agent doesn't think it'll be feasible. After today, I have a feeling they're going to let me go."

"That's bullshit. You'll sue them."

"I don't know, Dad. Shit's just…"

"Do you want your mother and me to come to Boston?" he asks.

The thought is nice but not what they want to do. While the offer seems genuine, he's a selfish son of a bitch who enjoys his yacht and won't survive one day with the cold weather here. Not that I can blame him.

"Nah, you earned your retirement. Think of it this way. Either I'll see you for spring training or you'll have to pick me up at some port, because I'll be staying with you until I find a new job."

There's some shuffling in the background, and then my mom's voice comes on the line. "Your house is on the news. You should go to the window and wave so I can see you."

"No, I'm not doing that, Ma."

"It would make me happy."

"Not today, Ma. I don't want anyone outside to think I give a shit."

"Well, if I were there..."

Right. If she were here, she'd be on the porch with a cigarette hanging out of her mouth and a rolling pin in her hand, looking like she belonged in a bad Aerosmith video. I know they mean well, but sometimes my parents are better left where no one can see them.

"I know, Ma, but I want you to have fun and relax. Everything will work out."

My parents continue to pass the phone back and forth until I tell them that I need to eat, and by eating, I mean drinking. This new liquid diet that I'm on is super in keeping me so fucking numb that I don't have a clue as to what's going on. It allows me to talk to myself and surprisingly give appropriate answers, and I've even found out that I can sing. Maybe that should be my next career move, the former baseball player who turns into a drunken singer.

Sounds pretty fucking legit if you ask me.

TWENTY-EIGHT

Saylor

As soon as I step away from the podium, I have nowhere else to stand except next to Travis. This is where I should be, but after the other day and the unpleasant look he gave me inside the courtroom this morning, I'm inclined to say that he'd rather I be elsewhere. I try to keep my focus on the reporters, watching their mannerisms and reactions to what Irvin is saying. I knew he had discussed the potential of a lawsuit with Travis and am honestly not surprised they're moving forward. Someone should be held accountable for the injustice that has been brought upon Travis, not to mention how this has disgraced his name.

Paul Boyd signals at me, letting me know he wants to talk. Weeks ago, I promised him a sit-down with Travis, but he's yet to give any interviews. Knowing these reporters, Paul's probably growing anxious and thinks I forgot.

When Irvin walks away from the podium, he guides Travis back into the courthouse, leaving me to answer any lingering questions. Internally, I groan. I'd rather be running down the steps and hailing a cab than answering reporters.

"Go ahead, Paul." I'm sure to single him out.

"Earlier, Mr. Abbott stated that Kidd pled not guilty. Can you confirm if that was on both charges?"

"Yes; Mr. Kidd entered a plea of not guilty on both charges and was released without bail."

"What about the other woman?" another reporter asks.

"I'm sorry?" The question catches me off guard.

"The rumor about Kidd being with another woman that night. Is there any truth to that?"

"I'm not aware. Next question," I say, swallowing hard and pointing to a different reporter. The police would never leak that there's a witness, so that had to come from Abbott and Abbott. Irvin is trying to call me out, even though he doesn't know it's me. He's smart to do it this way. He's hoping that whoever Travis was with that night is watching everything unfold on national television, and Irvin is praying that this will somehow make her feel bad.

I do feel bad—in fact, I feel horrible, and it's eating me up on the inside. Worse than that, though, is that Travis and I aren't speaking, and he doesn't even know why. I thought about telling him about Elijah, but how do I explain the situation? It's more than baby-daddy drama. The threats are something Travis will never understand because he isn't a parent. I have to play Elijah's game in order to protect Travis and Lucy.

"Can you tell us if Travis Kidd was following his victim around?" a woman in the back asks.

"Mr. Kidd has maintained his innocence from day one, so therefore we do not believe there is a victim in his case, other than Mr. Kidd himself. As for him following her around, no, I don't believe he was doing that."

"Excuse me, Ms. Blackwell, but the *victim* has stated in her complaint that, and I quote, 'Mr. Kidd has been following me around town when I have been out with my family numerous times, and finally assaulted me while I was enjoying lunch out.'"

"I'm only aware of the complaint to which the accuser states that Mr. Kidd assaulted her. Next question."

"But," the woman continues, "the victim alleges that he was present at a pizza parlor and ice-skating rink."

My blood turns cold and my tongue thick. Those are places that Travis took Lucy and me on our dates. The skating rink was a turning point for us. There is no way he took us there to spy on this woman.

"Unfortunately, I haven't seen the full complaint and cannot comment. If there are no further questions…" That's my cue that I'm done. I step away from the podium and make my way toward the side steps, away from the reporters.

"Saylor, wait up."

I turn to find Paul chasing after me. I continue to walk, knowing that he'll catch up.

"Hey, Paul."

"Tough crowd."

"Sometimes they don't take no for an answer."

"We never will," he tells me, smiling. I smile back and raise my arm for a cab. "Listen, about that interview…"

"You'll get it, but you'll have to go through Jeffrey. After this morning, I am no longer working on Kidd's profile. Jeffrey will either handle him or assign him to another junior rep."

"Too much to handle?" Paul asks.

I shake my head. "No, there are more qualified people in the office to handle what Travis needs. Have a good day, Paul, and Happy

New Year." I slide into the backseat of the cab, and Paul is kind enough to shut my door. What I don't tell Paul is that Travis has asked for a trade, and I don't handle athletes outside of the Boston area. Jeffrey will turn him over to another rep who doesn't mind traveling.

I send a quick text to my mom, letting her know that I'll be home shortly. All I want to do is curl up on my couch and drown myself in sappy love stories that will cause an onslaught of pitiful feelings. It's my substitution for wine. I also order Chinese takeout, hoping that it arrives by the time I get dropped off.

The cab ride takes longer than normal, the cabbie driving extra slow because it's started to snow. I think about where Travis is going to go and how much I'll miss seeing him. It's funny to think how this whole incident has shaped my December, but it will also be nice to get back in touch with my other clients and make sure they're doing okay. The Boston Rotary dinner will be a huge event for many of them, and I should be there, but knowing that Travis will be means I'm staying home.

We arrive at the same time my food does, making things easy. I pay the cabdriver and holler out to the deliveryman to hold up. No need for him to head to my apartment if I'm standing right here.

"Do you always conduct business on the streets, Saylor?"

"Thank you," I say to the deliveryman as he hands me my food. "Every day, Elijah. It's how I pay my bills." I keep my back to him as I head toward the door, hoping he's passing by. But that wouldn't be my luck.

"I find that mildly disturbing."

"What do you want, Elijah?"

"I've come to visit Lucy."

I roll my eyes and jostle my food in order to press the Up button on the elevator. "Don't you think spending Christmas with her was enough?"

"On the contrary. We've extended our stay in Boston and would love to have Lucy join us for New Year's Eve. She really needs to get to know Renee and the children."

Once again I roll my eyes but know that I can't do anything about it. I know I have to let him see her, but it doesn't mean I have to like it or let him take her places. This needs to be done in baby steps, especially since she's really not fond of him. Not that I can blame her. I must've been totally blinded by the fact that he was my professor to not see that he's a pompous ass.

He follows me in, uninvited, and takes off his coat. "Where's Lucy?"

"At my mother's," I tell him as I pull out a fork and dig into my lo mien. I'm starving and have a headache from the lack of caffeine. I look at the clock and realize that today's events have taken up most of the day. I'm slightly annoyed, but there isn't anything I can do about it.

"And when might I expect her?"

I shrug, pissing him off.

"You know," I say, pointing at him with my fork, "you weren't like this when we were dating."

"Like what?"

"Stuffy, like you have a rod stuck up your ass. You were fun; you made me laugh."

"Maybe you were different and I'm not the one who has changed."

He's right—maybe I was. I know for a fact that I was more willing to give my heart away before I met Elijah. I didn't see the world as a jaded place, but something I wanted to explore. Before I can give him another witty response, Lucy swings the door open and cheerily enters until she sees Elijah. My mom's eyes widen in surprise when she sees him standing there. I shrug and make quick work of my food. After Christmas morning, I had told my mother that I hoped he'd get the hint and leave, but apparently Lucy didn't make it obvious enough that she doesn't like him, because he's still lingering in town. Frankly, the sooner he's gone, the better.

"I'll call you later," I tell my mom as she kisses a very-reluctant-to-stay Lucy goodbye. I don't blame her. If I could leave, I would. As much as I love my apartment, this is the last place I want to be right now. My always-comfortable home feels like a giant eggshell waiting to crack.

"Lucy, would you like to sit and talk?"

I try not to laugh when Elijah asks her this. Five-year-olds rarely want to sit and talk to adults, unless it's about the newest Disney movie coming out or what toy is their newest obsession. On a good day, I can get Lucy to tell me about her day at school, but since she spent her day with my mother, I doubt she has much to say, especially to Elijah.

"I wanna watch TV," she says with the most exaggerated sigh I have ever witnessed. I stuff my mouth full of food to keep from laughing. Sure enough, though, Elijah sits down next to her. I hate giving him credit, but at least it's an effort.

I decide to stay in the kitchen so I can watch them interact with each other. This is the perfect time for Elijah to show me that he can be a father. When Lucy tells Elijah that she's thirsty, he gets up to get her a drink. When she's bored with her current show, he offers to find her something different to watch, even if he briefly stops on CNN to catch the latest headlines. As I look at them, I can't help but miss Travis. I'd much rather have him on my couch than Elijah, and I know Lucy would, too. Knowing that he can never be here again makes me despise Elijah.

As the night continues, I grow more and more tired of staying in the kitchen, but I refuse to join them in the living room. The last thing I want is for Elijah to think he's welcome or for him to feel like I accept what's going on. He can think I'm a coldhearted bitch for all I care—at least he'd know his place in my life.

The knocking on my door has me glancing at the clock and then to Elijah, who is starting to stand. If it were my mother, she'd let herself in after knocking.

I open the door, startled to find a slightly drunk Travis leaning against the doorjamb. I angle my body between the partially closed door and the outside, hoping to keep Elijah's prying eyes away from Travis. When he reaches for me, I have no choice but to step back.

"Why, Saylor?"

"Please don't do this, Travis," I whisper.

"Saylor, who's here?" Elijah says. I close my eyes and shake my head slightly. I can feel Travis's hand as it whizzes by my face. He pushes the door open with a ton of force, slamming it against my wall.

"Who the fuck are you?"

"Travis, please—you're drunk. We can talk about this tomorrow," I implore him as I pull on his arm, trying to get him out of my house.

"Travis!" Lucy yells happily as she flings herself into his waiting arms. He holds her tightly while he glares at Elijah.

"Put my daughter down," Elijah blurts out as he steps toward

Travis. My instinct is to protect Lucy. I reach for her, meeting Travis's gaze. He lets her go, but not very willingly.

"Lucy, please go to your room." I point her in that direction and give her a small shove. I know she wants to see Travis, but now is not a good time. He's been drinking, and I have a feeling nothing good is going to come from the brewing showdown with Elijah.

"So this is the sperm shitter?" Travis asks, pointing at Elijah. I want to laugh at the one-liner but know better.

"Can we talk tomorrow?" I ask him again.

"You heard her—leave. Besides, you have no business being here," Elijah adds.

"Are you fucking him?" Travis blurts out. "Is that why you broke things off with me? Because of this pecker diddler?" He points at Elijah, seething.

"Are you sleeping with *him*?" Elijah decides to throw the same question out. I cover my face and scream into my hands, thankful for the muffled sound.

"What do you care if we're fucking? That's none of your business, unless of course she's letting you into her bed now, too. Are you, Saylor?"

"Travis, please stop," I beg him. "Please just go." When I look at him, there are tears in my eyes. I let them fall, hoping he can grasp the severity of the situation. Elijah brushes past me, grabbing his coat off the chair.

"I warned you, Saylor, and apparently you didn't take me seriously. I'll see you in court."

Elijah doesn't even bother slamming the door for full effect; he calmly walks out and disappears down the hall.

"About fucking time he left," Travis says, stepping closer to me.

When he reaches for my waist, I push him away with all the anger building inside.

"Get the fuck out of my house," I yell, pounding his chest. "Get out! Get out!" I say the words through sobs as I continue to push him toward the door. Without even knowing it, Travis sealed my fate with my ex. Elijah swore he'd leave everything alone if Travis wasn't a part of my life, and I was stupid enough to lie and tell him that Travis meant nothing. That all we had done was kiss, and that was the night at the skating rink. That Travis would never come around to see Lucy.

I lied to protect Lucy. I lied to protect myself. And once again, I'm going to lose everything because of Travis Kidd.

TWENTY-NINE

Travis

Whenever I wake up with a hangover, I often ask myself why I drank so much and promise that I'll never do it again. That promise is something I've been breaking for the past few days, and up until now, I didn't care.

I had hoped the booze would muddy my memory of last night, but it hasn't. Every word she said, every expression she had, every punch to my chest to get me out of her apartment is crystal clear. I fucked up, and I don't even know how. All I know is that the sobs I heard on the other side of Saylor's door last night were enough to sober my stupid ass up.

For hours, I sat against her door, until a resident suggested I leave or they were going to call the police. If I hadn't been arrested earlier, I probably would have encouraged them to dial Boston's Finest. Another man might understand my plight. The woman that I want to be with kicked me out of her house, and while I probably deserved it, I didn't want to leave until she stopped crying. I didn't want to be the one to walk away in her time of need.

But as egos go—and believe me, mine is huge—I couldn't let it get in the way any longer, so I walked my drunk ass back home with my tail between my legs, only to stay up all night while the booze wore off, knowing that I had to live with whatever I'd done to Saylor.

She's the last person in the world who I want to hurt, and she's the one person who can save me. Not only from a life behind bars, but also from myself. When I'm with her, I'm a different person. The cocky son of a bitch who everyone is used to doesn't exist when she's near me, and frankly, that is the man I like, or at least I used to. It's easier being a fucking douche. It's second nature to me and comes with the territory of being named one of the city's most eligible bachelors.

Except when I'm with Saylor, I can be the man who hides in the shadow of that Travis Kidd. I can be the kind of man who doesn't have to have a one-liner available or wink in order to get a phone number. When I'm with her, life outside of baseball starts to have a meaning, a fucking purpose.

This morning, I'm meeting with Ryan Stone. I shouldn't be here without Jeffrey or Irvin, but I am. As far as I'm concerned, unless Saylor has a change of heart, my career is over. I know I can subpoena her to testify, but I'd never be able to live with myself if she lost her job or the judge revoked her probation because of me. No one is ever going to understand my situation, or my decision, and that's okay as long as I do.

Stone has a sweet setup in his office with his floor-to-ceiling wall made up of glass overlooking our snow-covered field.

"It's a great view when the team is down there practicing," Stone says as he walks into his office. I know I've called him away from his vacation, his family time, but this is important.

"I can imagine. I always thought I'd find myself in a front office position after retirement," I say, staring out at the field.

"You'd do very well within any organization," he says. I turn and shrug, keeping my hands buried deep within the pockets of my pants.

"Maybe in another life."

Stone motions for me to sit down across from him, and I do. He appraises me for a minute before leaning back in his chair. He's younger than me and has done a hell of a job with the Renegades.

"I'm asking to be let out of my contract," I tell him. He leans forward as if he didn't hear me correctly. "I'm not asking for a trade, or to be put on waivers. Only to be let out."

"Why?" he asks.

I pick the imaginary lint off my pants. "This case…it's caused a divide among the team and the staff. I don't want to walk the halls of a place where I'm not welcome, and no one is going to pick me up off waivers. I'd rather save face."

"Quitting isn't the answer."

My throat tightens. I've never quit a damn thing in my entire life until now. "No, it's not, but I don't see another choice."

Stone's fingers steeple as he thinks about what I'm asking. Surely I'm not the first player to come forward and ask for this—possibly the only one in his tenure, though.

"Why not retire?" he asks.

I straighten in my seat and clear my throat. "I need to leave Boston. I'm not welcome here anymore, so there isn't a point in staying. Retirement would allow you to keep me on staff, and I can't be here."

He nods and drops his hands. "Let me think about this, Travis. Honestly, I wasn't expecting you to come in here today and quit, and it's a lot to process."

"I understand."

"I do have one concern, though," he states.

"What's that?"

"What happens if I let you go and you're cleared of any wrongdoing? What then?"

I shake my head. "If I had the answer, I'd wait it out, but people have made it clear that I'm no longer welcome in the clubhouse."

"Teammates?"

When I don't answer, he nods. "I'll be in touch, Travis, and until then, please keep us updated on the case. I heard you have a court date next week?"

"Yep. The state has to put up or shut up."

"Huh, let's hope it's the latter." He stands and shakes my hand, clasping it with both of his. I'm fighting back the emotions, not letting them get the best of me. I love playing for the Renegades, but I have to have the full support of everyone involved. Not only a few whom I call friends.

The sun is shining when I step out of the stadium. I thought about cleaning out my locker, but the idea truly rips my gut apart. My life as a baseball player is over, and I can thank myself for that.

A different decision, on any given night, and I'd be walking the streets a free man. If I hadn't talked to Saylor, what would the likelihood be that this other woman would have gotten jealous? Slim to none. I've made so many mistakes recently, and each one seems to come full circle to Saylor.

Hailing a cab, I give the driver her address. I don't know if she'll be at home or not, but I need to see her. Hell, I don't even know if she'll let me in. I wouldn't. I should've never gone over there last night, especially in my inebriated state. Booze and bad attitude do not mix, but I *needed* to see her.

I ask the driver to let me off a block before her building so I can buy her flowers. If anything, they'll brighten her apartment, and she can remember the good times we spent together. Even though our time was limited, every memory is burned into my mind, and it's a time I'll never forget.

Honestly, I want a chance to redeem myself. She saw the good in me once. She can see it again. And if it's her job holding her back, well, we can figure that out together. I want her and Lucy in my life.

With the white and red roses in my hand, I knock on her door.

"Go away, Travis," she says moments later from behind the closed door.

"Please, let me explain and apologize in person, Saylor." Right now I have a lot to make up for, but I also have questions about the guy that she was with last night. Harsh words were exchanged, and tears were shed.

"Please, Saylor," I beg as I adjust my weight from foot to foot. The locks on her door clink as they move, and she opens the door slightly.

"I can't give these to you if you don't open it all the way." I stick the flowers up, blocking my view of her, praying that she'll let me in.

"I don't want your flowers. I want you to leave me alone."

I stick my hand against the door, preventing her from closing it. One small push and it's open, and she's stumbling back. Stepping in, I shut it behind me and lock it for good measure. I don't want that asshole from last night interrupting us.

"Is Lucy home?"

Saylor shakes her head, pulling her robe tighter around her waist. It hasn't gone unnoticed that she won't look at me. I step closer, gauging her reaction. She doesn't move, and that's a relief. Gently, I reach out and caress her cheek until my fingers are under her chin, lifting her face until I can see into her eyes. Her bluish-green orbs are dull and lifeless, and the whites around her eyes are bloodshot.

"What happened?"

"You," she spits out, yanking herself away from me. I stand frozen, watching as tears stream down her face. "I told you that we couldn't be together, and you pushed. You made me feel things for you when you knew I wasn't allowed. You used me and you used my daughter to spy on that woman, putting us in harm's way each and every time we left here. I told you over and over again that we could never have anything more than a professional relationship, but that wasn't good enough for you. You had to parade us in front of your victim so she could see that you chose me that night instead of her."

My mouth hangs open at the verbal attack. I don't have a clue as to what she's referring to, because I would never in my life do anything to harm her or Lucy. "Saylor—"

"Don't," she says, holding up her hand. "Don't tell me you're fucking sorry, Travis," she cries out, using the back of her hand to wipe away her tears. "For a moment, I let my guard down and believed you. I wanted the fucking fairy tale where my knight in shining armor swoops in and saves me from this mediocre existence I'm living, but I knew better and know this is why Jeffrey forbids us from dating the athletes…because they always do something to fuck everything up, and it messes with our minds. It screws up how we represent you, favoring one over the other. I was so stupid to believe that you actually cared for me." She stops and shakes her head.

"I do."

"Then why did you take us to all those places knowing she'd be there? Did you think I wouldn't find out?"

"No fraternization with the clients."

"Yet you went home with him?"

I nod and wish I could blame it on being drunk or unaware, but I can't. And I won't. I went home with him because I was attracted to him as a person, not because he's Travis Kidd from the Boston Renegades. "I did but left in a panic after the text from Jeffrey. Still drunk, I got behind the wheel of my car and ended up crashing into a telephone pole. I was arrested and charged with a DUI. Because it was my first offense, I was given probation. One of the conditions of my probation is that I stay out of bars or where alcohol is served. If it's a work function, I have to get permission from my probation officer."

"Why are you here, Saylor?" he asks, likely growing frustrated with my story.

"Because I need your help. I need someone powerful enough to fight my ex in court, to prevent him from taking my daughter away. He doesn't know about the arrest, at least not yet, and I don't want him to use it against me."

"He must know something. He's claiming that you're an unfit parent."

I look away, unable to maintain eye contact with him. "That's because of Travis."

"He's your client."

I nod, letting the silence speak for itself.

"Are you saying that you and Travis have become intimate again?"

"Yes," I whisper. "But I broke it off when my ex threatened me. Someone caught Travis giving me a kiss while we were ice-skating with my daughter and posted the picture online. Elijah saw it and demanded that I keep Travis away from Lucy because of the rape accusation. He threatened to take her away from me, so I did what I had to do, except Travis got arrested and came over to my house drunk. He and Elijah exchanged words, and now I'm here."

Irvin leans back in his chair and lets out a sigh. He picks up the summons and reads through it before setting it back down.

"Are you going to lose your job if this gets out?"

"Yeah, I will. Jeffrey isn't keen on keeping reps around who break his policy."

"And you know Travis is planning to leave Boston?"

"Yes." My voice breaks.

"You're in quite the pickle," he says. The baseball pun isn't lost on me.

"That's not all." I take a deep breath and exhale slowly. "The witness that is reluctant to come forward for Travis—that's me. I went into the bar that night because my ex had sent me a letter asking about my daughter. I hadn't heard from him since I was pregnant, and out of the blue, I receive a letter from him, asking to see her. I was scared, and when I walked in, Travis was there. He followed me out after some time, and we talked briefly before the woman came out. Travis and I got into a cab together. She yelled that he would pay for this. Before the car pulled away, I got out. I watched Travis leave by himself, and I saw the woman get in her car and leave.

"I was also in the restaurant when Travis ran into her. He wasn't gone for five minutes when he rushed back and told me we had to leave. My daughter was with us as well, and I know Travis would never do anything to put her in harm's way." I wipe away the tears that have fallen and keep my eyes focused on Irvin's desk.

"You're fucking kidding me, right?"

I shake my head.

"For weeks, you've watched him suffer when all you had to do was tell the truth."

"And go to jail?" I ask, making eye contact. "You think I want to go to jail because I had a weakened moment and went into a bar? Do you think I should be behind bars when a man who fucks half the damn city got accused of rape, which shockingly hasn't happened before now?"

"That's unfair." I hear Travis's voice behind me, and when I turn, his face is like stone. His eyes are narrowed to slits and glaring at me. I should tell him I'm sorry, but I'm not. It's the truth. His actions have snowballed, creating a disaster all around him.

I fiddle with my bag as Travis moves into the room. He stands off to the side instead of sitting next to me. I don't blame him. I wouldn't want to sit by me either.

"This is unexpected," Irvin says, and I don't know if he's talking about my revelations or the fact that Travis is here.

"I came here to ask you to help Saylor with her custody issue."

"Seems to be a popular subject today." Irvin laughs at his own joke, which I don't find funny.

"Can I speak with Saylor alone for a minute?" Travis asks. Irvin huffs as he stands but doesn't say anything as he leaves his office, shutting the door behind him.

"I have a proposition for you, Saylor, that I think we'll both find beneficial. You can take the offer or leave it, but either way, I will be moving forward with having you subpoenaed to testify about the night in question. I don't know if it'll be enough to clear me, but it should be enough to cast doubt on the case against me."

Travis sits in the chair next to me and angles mine so that I'm facing him. "I need you to look at me when I say this."

I do as he says, getting lost in his gaze. The hard expression he wore after hearing my harsh words is gone and replaced by the kind man who brought joy to Lucy's and my life for a few weeks. In front of me is Travis Kidd, a man who wants to be loved, and not the cocky baseball player that fans have turned on.

"I'm going to pay for Irvin to fight your ex in court, and I don't care what you have to say about it. The thing is, I love Lucy." We both laugh. What he doesn't know is that growing up, I used to watch the show with my dad, and it was my way of paying homage to him when she was born. "Anyway, I do. She owns my heart, but so does her mother. These past few days I've been lost without you both in my life, and the thought of leaving you behind in Boston is killing me. So I propose that we get married."

My mouth drops open, but he shakes his head, letting me know he's not done. "First off, once Jeffrey finds out about everything, he's going to fire you. Marrying me will give you access to my bank account until you find another job. Two, you can come clean about the night in question, clearing my name. Three, once again, Irvin will be there to help with any legalities that come up from you being in the bar. He'll be at your full disposal, which brings me to four. Lucy loves me, and she can tell the judge that. You know she wants us to be together, and you know she'll choose me over that man who claims to be her father. Will it be an uphill battle? Yep, it will be, but I'm willing to climb the mountain to keep her where she belongs, and that's with you...with us."

I replay each point over and over in my head and still come back to the missing fifth one. "I'd want more. And I don't think you can give that to me."

"Like what?" he asks, pulling my hands into his. I willingly let him hold them, because being held by him is worth the heartache I'll suffer later.

"I want a marriage, Travis. I want a husband who loves and cherishes me. I don't want to wonder where my husband is at night, or if I'm going to find some strange woman roaming around the house with barely any clothes on. I don't want to find random hotel receipts or underwear in your pants pockets when I go to wash your clothes."

Travis leans forward and kisses me softly. "For years, my family was plagued with rumors about my father's infidelity. I saw what it did to my mother, how it affected her day in and day out. I asked her one time why she stayed, and she said because she loved my father more than anything. I never understood what that meant until now. I can promise you, Saylor, that as long as you're my wife, I'll be your husband. My dick will only leave my pants when you say, and if that's never, then so be it." He tilts his head and gives me a cocky smile as my mouth drops open. "I'm serious, Saylor. Marry me? Let me fix all these problems that I seem to have created for you."

"What about Boston, and the team?"

His thumb rubs over his left ring finger. "If you want to stay in Boston, we can, but Florida is nice, especially during the winter. As for the Renegades..." He pauses and shakes his head. "I think I'm done, Saylor. This case...after the arrest, the city has turned on me."

"Jeffrey can fix that for you."

He shrugs. "Maybe, but spring training is nine weeks away, and there's been a lot of damage done." Travis perches on the edge of the chair. "Marry me, Saylor. I know this isn't the proposal you've probably dreamed of, and I'm probably not the man you thought would be asking you, but right now, we can make things better for the both of us by doing this. And after a year or so, you can walk away."

A marriage of convenience isn't unheard of, and having the money to fight Elijah would be a godsend. Lucy does love Travis, and the thought of seeing her happy is worth the sacrifice.

What sacrifice? I ask myself. Travis Kidd wants to marry me and promised to be faithful.

"Okay," I tell him. "I'll marry you."

BOSTON RENEGADES

Travis Kidd can't seem to stay out of the news, and while most of you are on pins and needles about his case and upcoming trial date, we bring you something interesting...

The staff at the BoRe Blogger has had the privilege of covering everything Kidd does, not only on the field but off as well, and honestly, we don't know what to believe.

However, it is being speculated that Kidd and his publicist, Saylor Blackwell, who we know have been getting cozy, have applied for a marriage license.

Now, ladies, before you freak out, we can't confirm. We can only go by the fact that they were both present at the county clerk's office, applying for one.

We reached out to Kidd for a comment, but when asked if the rumors are true, he stated, "Call my publicist."

Of course, when we called Ms. Blackwell, she stated, "I don't comment on my clients' personal relationships, but Mr. Kidd will be present at the New Year's Eve Rotary celebration."

More to come, Renegades fans. We promise!

The BoRe Blogger

THIRTY-ONE

Travis

Within an hour of applying for our marriage license, the news has spread like wildfire, which is something I wanted to avoid. I had thought that by flirting with the clerk, she'd keep our impending nuptials on the down low, but as soon as we left the office, my phone lit up like a Christmas tree with tweets that Travis Kidd is officially off the market. Even as I read those words, I realized I liked the sound of them.

This is probably the craziest, most harebrained idea I have ever come up with, but I'm happy I did. Our marriage may be unconventional and for the purpose of saving both of us, but truth be told, I'm in love with her.

Once we signed the dotted line, we both rattled off text messages to our parents, letting them know before any of the media outlets got wind of what was going on. My father didn't have much to say, but my mother went on and on about how excited she was to finally have a daughter and, most importantly, a granddaughter, and asked if I was planning to adopt Lucy.

Honestly, the thought hadn't crossed my mind. Initially, my intention was to keep her with Saylor and keep this family that I'm creating together for my own good. I'm a better person when they're around. But the idea of Lucy being a Kidd is appealing and something I may have to broach with her father. I know he doesn't like me, but there's a long list of men like that out there who feel the same, so he can take a number and get in line. The simple fact is that his daughter adores me, and his ex is going to be my wife. And let's not forget the fact that I have spent a hell of a lot more time with his daughter than he has. Put us side by side and that girl is running to me each and every time.

Coming up with this idea was not easy. After I left Saylor's apartment, I sat outside her building, contemplating my next step. Going to Irvin was always a priority, but I needed something that would protect the both of us. The only thing I can't prevent is if she's arrested for a probation violation. Everything else I can fix, or at least attempt to.

Finding her in Irvin's office was dumb luck. I went there to tell him what I knew and to beg for his help. I never even had a second thought after I heard her ask why she should go to jail for a guy who has fucked half the city. The comment hurt. But it's the truth. She shouldn't. And neither should I. From the get-go Saylor has backed me and tried to make everyone around us see that I was innocent. Even Irvin started to second-guess me after my arrest. I get it, I do, but it fucking hurts when the man you're paying to keep your ass out of jail starts to wonder if his client is an abusive asshole.

"What'd your mom say?" I ask, taking Saylor's gloved hand in mine as I walk her back to my SUV.

"She sent me a string of emojis." I open the door for her and make sure she's seated before running around to the driver's side.

"Of what? Like, a sad face, tears? I mean, is she excited, apprehensive?" Pressing the ignition button, I make sure Saylor's seat warmer is on and let the car heat up before we head to our next destination.

"Well, there's a champagne bottle, a thumbs-up, a smiley face with hearts, the praying hands, the man and woman with the heart, and…"

"And what?"

Saylor sighs and looks out the window, avoiding eye contact. She looks down at her phone and shakes her head. "And she says, 'Show me the ring' but uses the emoji for that."

"So let's show her," I say, leaning across the console to give her a kiss. "Let's go get your ring."

"I don't need a ring, Travis. It's not like this is a real marriage." Her voice wavers at the end, causing me to slightly move back.

"This is real for me, Saylor. I care about you and want to protect you. Besides, I have a feeling we were well on our way to falling in love before complications arose." I know I should've told her right then that I am in love with her, but I hold back. Saylor seems to be apprehensive. I get it. I sprung this on her as a way to get us both out of our legal troubles.

She doesn't say anything. She doesn't have to. Regardless of how she feels, I'm confident in my feelings toward her. Saylor does, however, reach over and grab my hand, and when I look at her out of the corner of my eye, she's smiling. It may not be directed toward me, but the fact that she's touching me and grinning like someone who's about to get married speaks volumes.

The drive to the jewelers isn't as painful as I thought. I expected to feel a rush of panic, for my palms to start sweating or my heart rate to skyrocket. But even as I get out of the car and help her out, I'm cool as a cucumber.

Inside, the saleswoman behind the counter greets us with a smile. "Can I help you find something?"

"We're looking for engagement rings," Saylor says.

"Actually, wedding sets," I interject, smiling at Saylor. I plan to wear a ring as well so everyone knows that I'm spoken for.

We are directed over to the side where their wedding pieces are. I can't recall a time when I've purchased jewelry for anyone and am floored by the number of rings we can choose from.

"Do you see one you like?" I ask her.

"They're all so pricey."

"That's not what I asked, Saylor." I can see it in her eyes. There's nervousness present in the way she's acting. I can't tell if she's having second thoughts already or if she's worried about the money I'm spending.

"Excuse me, but can you measure her ring finger so we know what size we're looking for?"

"Sure," the woman says. Saylor pulls her glove off and extends her hand, letting the lady measure. "She's a five and a half."

"Great—thanks." I motion for Saylor to follow me to the other side of the room. "I'm doing this all wrong, and I can see the wheels spinning. You're worried about cost and all that shit when it shouldn't fucking matter. I should've been here this morning and had a ring picked out for you, but I'm an impulsive moron and didn't think about this part until I had already asked you. So why don't you go wait in the car and I'll pick out what I want people to see every time you walk into a room, answer a phone, or open a door?"

"Okay."

I hand her the key fob and watch her walk out and climb into my

car. I turn back to the clerk, who is pulling out trays of diamond soli-
taires for me to look at.

"She's beautiful and very lucky."

Shaking my head, I say, "Nah, I'm the lucky one." I look over my
shoulder quickly to make sure she's still in the car. Yeah, I'm that
paranoid that she may change her mind before I can get her back to
the courthouse in three days.

"What's the biggest stone you have?" I don't want anything too
gaudy sitting on her finger, but I want something sizeable. There has
to be no question in anyone's mind that she's my wife and that she's
spoken for. Something small won't do.

The saleswoman returns with another tray. "These are shown in
platinum, but the stones can be changed into a different band if you
wanted gold."

Every ring in the case sparkles, and the decision is hard. "That
one," I say, pointing to a single diamond on a platinum band.

"It's understated, but at three carats it definitely makes a splash."

I hold the ring in my hand even though I don't have a clue as
to what I'm looking at. I should've done some research, but we all
know that's not how I operate. One thing's certain—this isn't the
right ring. "Hmm. I want something square."

"Sure," she says, pulling out another tray. She doesn't need to
know that it's a reference to baseball and that if I'm giving up the
game I love, at least I'll be able to look at a diamond on Saylor's finger
and remember how she came into my life.

"That one." I point to a diamond-shaped solitaire on a platinum
band.

"Four carats." She hands it to me as if I'm going to try it on.

"This is the one I want. What size is it?"

"Six, which is the standard size. We can have it sized, though, to fit her finger." She motions toward the front window of the store. I turn and see Saylor looking my way. I wave, hoping that she can see me.

"How long will that take?"

She goes over to a book and flips through the pages. "It looks like we are about three weeks out."

I shake my head. "That won't do," I tell her. "Can I pay extra to pick it up tomorrow?"

"I'm sorry, but he's on vacation until next week. The holidays and all…" She nods toward the back, where I'm assuming the jeweler works.

"Okay, I'll take it anyway, but I need to add a band for her, and I'll need one as well."

The saleswoman shows me a compilation of bands that would work with the ring for Saylor, as well as points out what is popular for men right now. I finally decide on the last two pieces, and she sets Saylor's rings in one box and mine in another as I pay for them. I thank her for my purchase and exit the store.

"You found one?" Saylor asks as I get back into my SUV. I set the bag down in the middle, letting her eye it for a bit. I know it's mean, but I can't help but laugh.

"I did. I fucking love it. It's going to look hot on your finger."

She tries to hide her eye roll from me, but I catch it. Pulling her face toward me, I search her eyes for any discontent. "Don't do that, Saylor. This will be a good thing. I promise."

"I know, but I can't help but think that you might find someone else."

"Sort of hard to do when I'm not looking. I'll be good to you—I promise." I kiss her once for good measure before starting up the ve-hicle and entering the city traffic. I want to take her back to her place and give her the ring, but the thought of having her ex show up isn't something that is sitting well with me. Instead, we head to my place. Since our news is already out there, it doesn't make sense to hide her from the media that has been camping out at my house this entire time.

When I pull up, the cameras are poised and ready. Saylor looks fearful even though she's been here before. I suppose this time is dif-ferent, though, now that she's not working and this is very much a social call.

"Travis, are the rumors true?" the reporters start asking as soon as I get out. Thankfully they aren't blocking my way to the other side of the car, and I'm able to be a gentleman and help Saylor out.

"Ms. Blackwell, how does this change your working relationship with Travis?"

"Mr. Kidd, is this a publicity move to make you look better in the eyes of the court and the public opinion polls?"

The last question irritates me, but I don't let that show on my face as I lead Saylor into my house. Closing the door blocks out the noise from outside, giving us some peace and quiet. "They'll be gone soon."

"Yeah," she says, standing in the middle of my foyer with her hands pushed deep into her coat pockets.

"Let me take your coat."

"I can't stay long. My mom has dinner plans tonight, so I have to pick up Lucy."

"We," I say, correcting her.

"Excuse me?"

"We have to pick up Lucy. I told you, Saylor, I'm in this with both feet. This isn't going to be some mistake I make or something I regret when I wake up tomorrow. If Lucy needs to be picked up, we do it together."

She shakes her head. "Elijah—he could show up at any time."

"So stay here." I spread my arms out wide. My house is open concept with three bedrooms and more than enough room for both of them.

"I don't know how to explain this to Lucy," she says as she starts to walk around. I place my hands on her shoulders and guide her down the hall and into the guest bedroom.

"This can be Lucy's room, or she can go upstairs. There's another room up there with a private bath."

"Where will I sleep?"

"With me," I say, turning her in my arms. "Before your ex showed up, we were on our way to building a relationship. We may be doing things backwards, but I think that is who we are."

She nods and turns around to look at the room. "I really love my apartment, though."

"Yeah, me too." I sigh as I pull her to my chest. "Remember this will only be temporary unless we decide to stay in Boston."

Saylor heads for the stairs and checks out the third bedroom. After I've given her the grand tour, including a stop in the bedroom I'm hoping to share with her, I bring her back into the living room.

"I should've done this earlier, but sometimes words are more important." I pull the box out of the bag and drop to one knee. "Be unconventional with me, Saylor."

THIRTY-TWO

Saylor

Now that I've said yes, I'm having second thoughts. I suppose every woman at some point in her life dreams of that spur-of-the-moment proposal when the man you've been pining for comes and sweeps you off your feet, or in my case, storms in to try to save the day.

Any woman would be lucky to have someone like Travis Kidd getting down on his knee to propose, but I don't feel that way. I feel confused, lost, and more alone now than I did this morning. I can't explain it, but something in my heart tells me that this is wrong—that marrying Travis isn't going to fix anything but make everything worse.

Yet Travis says he's going to fix things. When he said those words to me this morning, I had no idea what to expect. And now here I am, standing in his house with the most beautiful engagement ring on my finger from this man who has offered me financial security if I marry him. His bank account will be at my disposal to fight against Elijah. That in and of itself should be enough, except I'm in this situation because of him. If only he would've listened to me each time I told him I couldn't be with him, Elijah wouldn't be taking me to task over my parenting skills.

I don't think Travis realizes what he's getting into. His lifestyle is drastically different from mine. I tried to explain to him earlier that I don't want a sham of a marriage where my known playboy of a husband is out gallivanting, picking up random women and making headlines with his philandering ways.

My life is Lucy. Not the parties and late nights that he's used to. I don't know if his word is enough to make me go through with this. I don't know if the feelings I have for him, which are no doubt love, are worth the heartache that I'm going to feel later.

Travis moves about his house with more pep in his step than I've seen in him recently. The sullen demeanor is gone, and the man that I've been accustomed to working with is back. Honestly, it's a nice sight to see, because he has one of the most contagious smiles I've ever come across in years.

"What's so funny?" he asks, catching me off guard. I shake my head, because there is absolutely nothing funny about what I've been thinking. My thumb rolls over the underside of my ring finger. The ring is a half size too big, but Travis said he didn't want to wait three weeks before giving it to me. Truthfully, I'm happy that he didn't. I continue to rub circles around the bottom of my ring. My ring. The one he picked out after he asked me to leave the store. Travis may have done things backward with a proposal, but he did this right.

"Are you okay?" Travis sits down next to me, keeping a healthy distance between us. Even though he's kissed me a few times since he asked me to marry him, I'm trying not to read into anything. I know we're attracted to each other, and we've been together, but to actually wrap my head around being with him every day is a bit much to handle. Not because I don't like him—because I do—but because he's Travis Kidd, and I'm me. And his legion of female fans are going to make it very well known that he could've done so much better.

"Yeah, I'm fine."

He blanches at my statement, and I look at him squarely.

"Look, I may be a novice at this marriage thing, but I do know that when a woman says she's fine, something is wrong."

"How would you know such a thing?" From the years working with him, I know that he's never had a relationship last longer than a week, and honestly, I can't even imagine Travis being the type to care whether his current flavor is okay.

"Cooper. When he took me to Lamaze class, the teacher really drove the proverbial nail home that 'fine' doesn't actually mean fine."

"Sounds like some teacher."

He shrugs and picks up my hand, admiring the ring that is now there. "Are you upset about something?"

I shrug also.

"Talk to me, Saylor. I can't fix it or make anything better if you don't tell me what's bothering you."

"I'm confused, nervous, and telling myself that everything is going to be okay."

"It will be," he says as he turns to face me.

"For you, yes. But for me..." I shake my head. "Coming clean means jail time and a long legal battle."

"Saylor, I know you're scared, and honestly I am, too. Your testimony may not be enough, but I'm hoping it's enough to cast doubt and this case goes away. As for your probation violation, Irvin will take care of that. We can meet with your officer and explain why you were there. I saw you; you didn't take a drink, and I can vouch for you. I've drunk in front of you, and you haven't touched any liquor.

It was a lapse in judgment over a stressful situation. All that matters is that you didn't drink. As for Elijah…" He pauses and takes a deep breath. "I love that little girl, so I'm willing to fight for her. At best, we come out with full custody, and he receives visitation. It'll be a cold day in hell before she goes to live with him. Irvin will have someone there for us."

"Elijah…he has friends. He's already threatened to make sure you go to jail."

If those words faze Travis, he doesn't let it show. "I wouldn't be the first innocent man to go to jail."

"Then what's the point of getting married?" I demand as I sit up and face him. If he's ready to live a life behind bars, why are we going through with this?

"It's the least I can do for fucking things up, Saylor."

I shake my head as tears start to fall. "We don't need to get married. I know this isn't what you want."

Travis cups my cheek. His thumb caresses away some of my tears. "I think we're stronger together, Saylor. And it is what I want." He leans in, only to be stopped by the beeping of my cell phone.

"That's Jeffrey," I tell him, even without looking. His eyebrows rise. "Designated tone," I say, answering his unspoken question. Slowly I pull my phone out of my pocket and swipe to read his message. "Get here now!" The words tumble out of my mouth. I've been summoned before with similar words, but this time it's different. I can feel it in my bones. It's not going to matter that Travis is marrying me so I can save my daughter. The fact of the matter is, I crossed the line, and I'll be punished for it.

"Let's go," Travis says, pulling me off the couch. "I'm going with you whether you like it or not."

"It's my battle," I protest.

"And I caused it."

Travis doesn't wait for me to argue or agree. He has us out of the house, through the reporters who have doubled since we arrived, and into his SUV, all while I'm still trying to formulate a viable response in my head. Maybe this is one of those situations where things are better left unsaid? I'm not so sure. Either way, he's coming with me to my office whether I like it or not.

The look on my assistant's face when I walk in, followed by Travis, tells me all that I need to know. I should've brought a box to pack up my office, because when Jeffrey is done berating me, I'll need to clean it out.

"Wait here," I tell Travis, motioning for him to sit in one of the chairs that line the wall. As much as he wants to protect me from this, he can't. I knew what I was doing when I continued to see Travis outside of work. And I could've stopped, but I chose not to because it felt good to be around him. I knew I was providing him with some normalcy under the circumstances, and he was doing the same for me.

I rap my knuckles on Jeffrey's door before twisting the knob and entering. He looks up from the papers on his desk and leans back in his chair.

"That didn't take you long."

"I was in the area," I say, taking the familiar seat in front of his desk. He smirks, and I can only assume that he's calculated the time difference from my apartment and Travis's house to the office.

"Here are your termination papers." He slides the document that he was reading toward me.

My hand shakes as I reach out to take them. I'm not even going to try and hide the tears that are falling. "I wish you'd let me explain."

"There's nothing to explain, Saylor. I have one rule in this office, and you not only broke it, but also you're doing so in a way that makes me look like I've been duped by my employee for a period of time."

"It's not like that, Jeffrey. We're only friends," I plead. "He's helping me out of a situation with Lucy's father."

Jeffrey stands and places his hands on his desk so he can tower over me. This tactic works, because I find myself shrinking back into my chair, feeling about two feet tall.

"I don't care about what prompted you to seek Kidd's help. The fact of the matter is it's against policy, and I will not stand for my employees dating, fucking, or marrying my clients. It's a rule I've never wavered on, and I'm not about to do it today. You have no idea the embarrassment you've caused my firm. I've been dealing with clients calling and asking if the endorsement deals that Kidd landed over them are because he's fucking his publicist."

"But—"

"There are no *but*s, Saylor. The integrity of my name is on the line because you couldn't keep your damn legs crossed."

"That's not fair," I say weakly.

"Fair? You want to talk about fair? I gave you a job when you had nothing. I taught you everything you know and guided you along the way. I have one rule, Saylor. One! And you couldn't even follow it after I warned you. Sign the fucking papers, get your shit, and get out of here. I'm done."

I haul my ass out of the chair and open his door with a huff. I look back at Jeffrey, who doesn't look the least bit upset, and look at Travis, who is now standing. I shake my head when he comes toward me and I walk over to my office, but not before I hear the intercom come alive with the words, "Travis Kidd would like to see you." A quick glance at Travis earns me a shrug from him before he's disappearing behind Jeffrey's door.

Flipping the switch for my overhead light, I can already see that someone has started packing my personal belongings. I try to log into my computer, but my password has already been changed. I shouldn't be surprised, but I am. I thought I meant more to Jeffrey than a policy, but I guess not. I fucked up, and that's all there is to it.

I sit down at my desk and pore over the termination agreement. The language is standard. I have thirty days to find new health care for Lucy and me. I'll be paid for my vacation time, but that's it.

Loud voices carry down the hall. Part of me wants to press the intercom button so I can hear what's going on, and the other part doesn't care and wants to get out of here. I leave the contract for last and start packing what's left of my office. Mostly pictures, a few awards, and my degree. I hung that proudly on my wall so I could remember how hard I worked to obtain it.

When a door slams, I jump. It's a natural reaction, I think. What's not natural is how Jeffrey's voice continues to carry down the hall, and while I can't make out everything he's saying, it's clear that he's rather upset.

"What'd you do?" I ask when Travis appears in my doorway.

"Fired him."

"What? Why?"

"Because he fired you."

"Travis," I say, shaking my head, "I violated my contract. I deserve to be let go. Jeffrey is great at his job. He doesn't deserve this."

"Well, I think you'll be better."

"Excuse me?" I set my diploma down on what used to be my desk. "What do you mean?"

Travis steps into my office and stalks over to me. With his hands firmly on my hips, he pulls me to him. "Exactly what I said. I think you'll make an even better business manager."

"But I'm not—"

"But you can be. I Googled it before I even asked you to marry me. I hadn't forgotten about your contract with Jeffrey, and I wanted to know your options. You don't need a degree to do this. You only have to know how to negotiate contracts, and I know you can do that. Plus, you have to have your client's best interest in mind, and I think if my wife is my agent and business manager, I'll probably make out pretty well."

I eye him warily, unsure if I'm fully grasping what he's saying. I love that he has confidence in me, but I'm not sure if this is something I can do.

"One client won't pay the bills."

"Cooper Bailey is looking for an agent as well. The one he has is someone his father found for him, and since he and his father aren't speaking, he wants to break free."

"I see."

"And that means you can come to spring training with me, if you wanted," he adds.

A smile spreads across my lips. "As your wife I could go, but as your manager, I have to ask: Are you pulling your resignation off the table? Do I need to call Stone and tell him to forget everything?"

He steps back and shakes his head. If I had to guess, I think his own admission about spring training caught him off guard. I know deep down he doesn't want to quit, and once his name is cleared, the public opinion about him will change. *He* just needs to get his story told.

"I don't know, Saylor. Right now, it feels right to leave. The city, the people—they've turned their backs on me, and that is really hard to swallow."

This time I'm cupping his cheek and caressing the worry lines away. "Let's give it time, Travis."

"Who is saying that?" he asks as his hands slide under my sweater. "My wife or agent?"

My breath catches as I find myself made vulnerable by his question. "Your agent," I reply, unwilling to bring myself to say the other word out loud.

"Well, she would know," he says with a wink.

They both know, Travis…

They both know.

THIRTY-THREE

Travis

After convincing Saylor to take me on as her first client, I made a phone call to Irvin and read him her termination papers. He suggested she quit, which would allow her to represent any of her current clients if they chose to leave Jeffrey. Needless to say, when Saylor handed in her handwritten letter of resignation, he knew her plan. If Saylor decides to only represent me, that'll be enough for her to stick it to him.

I understand where he's coming from and how things look, but there's a reason behind my proposal and our upcoming marriage. Jeffrey could've listened to her instead of saying the shit he did. Honestly, that is what prompted me to fire him. Sitting outside his office and hearing the words he was saying to her really pissed me the fuck off. If anything, he should've been yelling at me, but he'd never do that.

"Are you okay?" I ask after we leave her office. She had tears in her eyes as she packed her things, and while I felt bad for her, I knew this was going to be a good thing. Our marriage is going to start off as one of the rockiest ones in history.

"I feel lost. That's been my job for so long. I don't know what I'm going to do on Monday."

"Well, you could make my breakfast." I laugh, but the look on her face tells me to shut up. "Or not," I say, setting her box in the back of the SUV.

"We need to set some ground rules," she states as she climbs into the front seat. I don't know how I feel about rules. It's been years since I've lived with someone, and the only person who spends any considerable amount of time with me is Ethan Davenport, and that's when we're on the road.

"Okay, I'll play along. Are we talking no underwear on the floor? Make sure the toilet seat is down?" I climb into the driver's seat and start the engine.

"Well, yes, those are definite, but I'm referring to your habit of eating takeout. Lucy seems to think that whenever she doesn't like her breakfast, I can pick up the phone and order her whatever she wants."

"Okay…"

"No, it's not okay, Travis. I don't want her growing up thinking that money grows on trees. Everything that I have has been earned by hard work. She needs to know the value of a dollar."

"And she will, Saylor." I enter into traffic and head toward the police station, where her probation officer is. Irvin is meeting us there in hopes that he can convince her PO to go easy on her. He's hoping for a little community service and not a night behind bars.

"Right now she thinks that you can come over with pancakes whenever she wants."

I sigh and reach for her hand. "I know I have a lot to learn about being a parent. Hell, even being a partner, but I'm going to work at it each and every day. Until you're comfortable letting me make decisions for Lucy, I'll defer everything to you, and I'll work my hardest to make sure the toilet seat is down, that I aim correctly, and that I'm always wearing pants when I get up in the middle of the night to take a leak."

She barks out a laugh, and I smile in return. "See, babe? We got this," I tell her.

"I'm afraid that you'll tire of my nagging rather quickly."

"I probably will. And you'll get pissed at me for the stupid shit I do. We're not perfect, Saylor, and I'm not looking for the perfect wife or partner."

"You're not?"

"Fuck no. I like to cuss, fart, and scratch myself. If you can put up with that, I can put up with your nagging, but…"

"But what?" she asks, biting her lip to keep from laughing.

"But don't be shocked when I call you out on your bitching." I pull into the parking lot and find a spot, shutting off the car. I turn to face her. "Here's the thing, Saylor. We are going to fight, and shit could get ugly, but at the end of the night, we'll make up. And if in the morning you're still pissed at me, I'll have to fuck it right out of you," I say, winking at her.

"Jesus, Travis," she says, covering her face. "And here I thought we'd ease into the sexual part of a marriage."

"Why the fuck would we wait?"

She shrugs. "I thought that after the way I acted…"

"Fuck that noise, Saylor. I want to be with you, all of you, and that includes putting my dick in your 'gina."

"I'm sorry—my what?"

I can't help but laugh. This is the side that I've kept hidden from her the past few weeks for fear she'd never want to be around me. But now she doesn't have a choice since she's about to marry my sorry ass.

"'Gina," I repeat.

"What the hell is that? Did you name my…lady bits?"

"Nah, only shortened it because *vagina* sounds so damn clinical. I could say *pussy*, if you like that better."

Saylor's cheeks turn red, and she moves to face the window. It's a good thing the windows are tinted; otherwise, onlookers might wonder what we're doing in here.

I set my hand down on her leg and move it slowly until it's centered between her thighs. "What's it going to be, Saylor? Are you going to let me into that pussy of yours once we're married?" I whisper into her ear. She nods as my teeth pull down slightly on her earlobe.

I really want to throw her into the backseat and let her ride my hard-on, but the fact that we're in the parking lot of the police station really deters my plans. Besides, knowing that I have so much more to explore when it comes to her is truly a turn-on. I never thought I'd get married, but to make a commitment to someone I've only been with twice, and dry humped once, is a huge achievement for someone like me.

"As much as I want to fuck you silly right now, Irvin is inside waiting for us."

Saylor sighs and nods, but not before leaning her head into mine. This is the first real emotion she's shown me since I proposed. I have initiated everything else when it came to contact between us. I'm hoping that changes very soon, because there's nothing sexier than a woman showing a man what she wants from him.

We walk hand in hand into the police station, which is ironic since the police station, albeit a different location, is really where everything started for us. The day she walked into the interview room to sit with me is the day I realized that she was more than a publicist for me. I can't believe it's taken me two years, and countless women, to figure it out.

"Hi, I'm here to meet with Officer Frey," Saylor tells the desk clerk.

"Have a seat. He's with someone right now."

"I believe he's with my lawyer," she says. The clerk nods and instructs her to go to room 2. I follow, because I'll be damned if I'm letting her do this alone. I know Irvin is here to help, but he's not exactly keen on us getting married, especially without a prenuptial agreement. I explained that, with everything she's going to lose by being with me, the least I could do is make sure she's taken care of for the rest of her life.

Irvin's eyes catch mine as we walk into an interrogation room. Officer Frey stands and shakes my hand, ignoring Saylor.

"This is my…" Saylor sighs as she gets lost on what to call me.

"Fiancé," I tell him.

"Nice to meet you. Please have a seat." The legs of his chair scrape against the linoleum, causing my spine to go rigid. Being in this box brings back memories of when I was arrested. The interrogation was brutal, and it didn't matter how many times I said I didn't do anything to that woman, they came back with the same question, only asked differently, all meant to screw you up and get you to admit you've done something wrong.

"Ms. Blackwell, it seems you're in a bit of a mess."

Saylor nods as her hands twist together.

"You're two years removed from the accident and have already violated your probation. However, I have to say you're doing better than some of my other probationers."

"I know, and I'm sorry," she answers meekly. I want to butt in and explain everything for her, but it's not my place. "I didn't drink," she says. "And I haven't since the day of the accident. You can check my place if you want."

"Why'd you go into the bar in the first place?"

I wish her answer could be because of me. Because she was trying to save me from making a giant-ass mistake, but if she said that, she'd commit perjury when she goes to testify for me.

Saylor takes a deep breath and looks her probation officer square in the face. "I received a letter that really threw me off-balance. The bar was right there, and I walked in. I ordered a drink and held it in my hand. Travis interrupted my thoughts and made me realize that I was making a mistake. I quickly left."

"And you haven't been back since?"

"No."

"Did you drink that night?"

She shakes her head.

"Am I to understand that the only reason you're here today is because you're the key witness to Mr. Kidd's case?"

"Yes."

"With all due respect, Officer Frey, do any of your cases come in here willingly to let you know they've violated their probation?" Irvin makes a very valid point, and it was something I was going to say. "Let's be fair here. My client is here confessing her actions and asking for leniency. She made a mistake and is willing to complete another round of community service."

Just no jail, I plead silently.

Officer Frey taps his pen on the table. The constant echo is annoying and getting on my nerves rather quickly. His face contorts from an expression of anger to concentration and into some odd look that I can only liken to constipation. When he finally sets his pen down, he leafs through the file folder in front of him. I'm assuming it's Saylor's case. I catch brief glimpses of photos of what looks like a car accident. My insides turn, knowing that she was in that mangled mess and drunk because of me. And Jeffrey. I know it's not entirely his fault, but I can blame him. If he hadn't texted her that night, none of this would've happened. For all I know, we could've been together this entire time, and our lives would be different.

"I'm going to assign you thirty hours of community service, which needs to be done by March first."

Saylor's body visibly sighs. "Thank you."

"Ms. Blackwell, I like you. You're one of my few cases that actually follows the rules. Please don't get into any further trouble. Next time I won't be lenient, and you will face jail time."

"Yes, sir. Thank you."

"Let me know when you start your CS hours and where. I'll be watching."

Irvin motions for us to stand and leave, and honestly, I can't get out of there fast enough. As soon as we step out, I pull her into my arms and give her the best fucking hug I can give her.

"Piece of cake," I whisper before adding, "one down, and two to go." My court date is next, but not before we have a chance to get married. When she takes the stand in my defense, she'll be my wife, and she'll tell the truth about that night. Part of me is hoping that Blue, or Rachel Ward, decides to testify. I know that rape victims get to keep their names out of the paper, but something tells me that she'll want everyone to know who exactly is bringing Travis Kidd down.

I wish I could tell her that I'm ready for her and there isn't anything she can say that will hurt me. I know the truth, and so does she. Now Irvin has to make sure the judge realizes it.

THIRTY-FOUR

Saylor

I have thought about my wedding day for as long as I can remember. As a young girl, I dreamed about the horse-drawn carriage and my father walking me down the aisle. My bridesmaids would be dressed in soft-pink dresses with their long hair cascading down their backs in intricate braids with flowers woven throughout. As I got older, the scene changed with the times. And there was this one moment in high school when I met a much older guy who I thought was my soul mate, and I had convinced my best friend that he was going to whisk me off into the sunset to elope in front of Elvis in a Las Vegas wedding chapel. Thankfully, I came to my senses on that last one.

One thing that I'll miss today is my father. I always thought, like most daughters, that my father would be around to walk me down the aisle. A massive heart attack took him from me years before Lucy was born. I told both Travis and my mother that walking down the aisle in the city courtroom can easily be done alone, but both balked at the idea.

When Travis proposed, I knew it was going to be a quickie wedding. Not once did I stop and imagine a massive ceremony with all our friends and family gathering to watch us exchange vows. After I accepted, I knew my wedding would be in front of a judge, and we'd be nothing more than a number being called in a long list of people eager to get married on New Year's Eve.

I should've suspected something was up when Travis was evasive about a date or when my overly eager mother sat down on my couch with a pile of bridal magazines and interrupted my self-induced pity-party movie marathon. By all accounts, I should've been happy. I escaped being brought back in front of a judge by my probation officer, and I was marrying Travis. A true dream come true for any romantic at heart. Yet I couldn't bring myself to be happy about my impending nuptials. Or the fact that Elijah hadn't called or contacted me through his lawyer. I'd like to think he hadn't heard the news, but even I'm not that naïve.

My mother gushed over dresses, asking for my opinion. Even going so far as to ask Lucy what she thought I'd look pretty in. I sat there while the two of them marked page after page, until she abruptly left. I asked my five-year-old what that was all about, and she shrugged before she went back to coloring. I should've known there was a master plan to make me cry on my wedding day.

"You look beautiful," my mother says as she stands behind me with her hands on my shoulders. I stare at myself in the mirror. The woman who stares back is someone I'm not sure I know. My makeup is flawless, and every blemish I have is somehow gone. My hair is down and loosely braided, with tendrils outlining my face, and while they look out of place, they're perfect. And the dress I'm wearing—the off-the-shoulder, cream A-line cut—is one that I never knew I wanted until it was taken out of the bag and I was told it was mine.

"I can't believe all of this is happening"—this being a wedding in a church, with flowers, guests, and a minister, but it seems that my groom-to-be wanted something more than a trip to the courthouse. I imagine he's probably tired of being in that place, and I can't blame him.

"It is, sweetie, and you deserve it," my mother says.

Do I? I keep questioning why all of this is happening to me. Surely he's not in love with me, unless he is and hasn't said anything. Here he is spending his hard-earned money to make sure I have a ceremony that I'll remember...That's love, right?

"I don't know that I do, Mom. We're getting married for all the wrong reasons."

She sits down next to me and hands me a wad of tissues. "Saylor, sometimes the wrong reasons become the right ones. I know that Travis feels responsible for Elijah seeking custody and that he's using marriage as an answer, but I've seen you guys together. I've seen the way he looks at you. That man is smitten, and he's not willing to let you get away from him."

"I keep questioning whether or not he's good for Lucy."

"He is. I saw them together yesterday, and everything between them is natural. I know you don't believe in fate or kismet, but I believe in my heart he is meant to be a part of her life, and a part of yours."

She wipes the tears that have welled in my eyes and rests her forehead against mine. "Saylor, if I had any doubt about you marrying Travis, I would tell you. The anxiety you're feeling—every woman goes through this. The only difference is that they've had time to adjust; you've had a few days. I was the same way with your father when he asked me. I second-guessed my reasons for saying yes, much like you are now, and I can easily tell you that once I said 'I do,' all the self-doubt I had was gone."

"You dated him much longer than I've known Travis."

My mother shrugs slightly, as if to brush off my statement. "It's all relative. Some people meet in Vegas and marry right off, and they're still together."

I turn back to the mirror and stare at the bride I've become. Travis has gone out of his way to make this as memorable as possible. We will have a story to tell, other than saying we married in front of a justice of the peace with my mom as our witness.

I push the vanity stool back, and more of my dress comes into view. When I stepped into the gown earlier, I felt like a princess. I know it's a cliché, but there's a feeling that washes over you when your fairy tale is about to come true, even if it isn't exactly how you imagined.

My hands brush down the front of my dress as I stand. I turn on my heels so I can hear the tulle underneath swish back and forth. The sound brings a smile to my face. It's something I've always wanted to hear. "Okay, I think I'm ready."

"One thing," my mom says as she comes behind me. I feel cool metal against my skin before I can register what she's doing. I bend my neck forward, allowing her to clasp the necklace. "This is your something old and blue," she says as my fingers fiddle with the sapphire. "This belonged to Travis's grandmother, and his mother has asked that you wear it today."

My hand covers my mouth as an "Oh God" slips out. "It's beautiful."

"And perfect for you," she says as she brushes her hands up and down my arms in comfort. "I know you're scared, Saylor, but sometimes being scared means you care, and I know you care about that man who is standing at the altar, waiting for you."

"I do." I love him but have yet to say those words to him out of fear that he may not feel the same way.

"Don't tell me; tell him."

Mom hands me my bouquet of red and champagne-colored roses. It's simple, yet elegant, and matches her corsage. She opens the door to the vestibule where I'm greeted by Lucy and Branch's son, Shaun, who is dressed in a tux. Along with Ainsley Bailey and Daisy Davenport, who are dressed in long red dresses that match the cut of my gown.

"What's going on?" I ask, looking at my mother.

"Travis wanted Ethan to stand up for him today, and when he asked me about your friends, I told him that most of your college friends are living out of state, so he improvised."

"We hope you don't mind," Ainsley says with a smile.

"Shaun is going to walk me down the aisle," Lucy says as if it's a bigger deal than the fact that her mother is getting married.

"Right, well, let's do this," I say, threading my arm through my mother's. "Who is my maid of honor?"

"That'll be me, since Ethan is the best man," Daisy says as she comes forward to straighten my dress. "Travis is a lucky man."

"What if I'm the lucky one?"

Daisy shakes her head. "I've known him for a while now, but something changed in him. Now I know what it is. You're good for him, Saylor, and he needs you."

He needs me. This whole time I've been looking at this marriage from the angle of my needing him. That he's saving me from my impending doom.

"He needs me." I mutter the words that Daisy has spoken, and by the time I'm done, my smile is so big my cheeks hurt. I nod, letting the door attendant know that I'm ready. Once the doors swing open, music starts. I don't know what to expect when I turn the corner and see Travis standing there, waiting for me, but whatever it's going to be will be worth it, because as soon as I take a step toward him, I can't continue to second-guess myself and this marriage. It is what it is, and Travis and I will have to work to make it the best thing for both of us.

Ainsley heads down the aisle, followed by Daisy. Lucy and Shaun go next, and instead of waiting for the music to change, I turn the corner with my mom at my side and watch my daughter throw rose petals onto the aisle.

It takes me a minute or two to meet Travis's gaze, and once I do, a rush of heat washes over me. As the wedding march begins to play, I step forward, trying to look everywhere but at him for fear that my steps will falter. I smile at the guests who are here—some I know and others I can only assume are his family. His parents are easy to spot in the front row, and I mouth a thank-you to his mother as I pass by.

The church goes quiet as my mom and I come to the altar. Travis keeps his eyes on me, causing me to blush, and each time I look at him, the heat within intensifies. Seeing him in a tuxedo is doing things to me.

"Welcome," the minister says as he steps forward. "Today, on the eve of our new year, we are here to celebrate the marriage between Saylor and Travis. I have known Travis since he arrived in Boston and am looking forward to getting to know Saylor and Lucy." I look at Travis questioningly. He smiles and shrugs, keeping his face as calm as possible.

"Love is the most unconventional feeling we'll ever experience. It warms you, it guides you, and it can also cause you immense heartache, but it will always be there to heal. Love brings people together; it blends families and makes us stronger. Love unites us as one.

"And that is why we're here today, to share in the union between our friends, Saylor and Travis, and help them start their path as a blended family with all the love we can give them. Who gives this woman to this man?"

"I do," my mom says. She cups my face with tears in her eyes and smiles. "I love you, Saylor."

"Love you, too."

I take a deep breath and step forward, matching the way Travis is standing. Behind me, Daisy fluffs my dress, and somewhere I can hear the shutter of a camera snapping pictures.

"Travis and Saylor, please join hands," the minister says. I turn and hand my bouquet to Daisy.

"Travis, do you take Saylor to be your wife?"

"I do," he says.

"Saylor, do you take Travis to be your husband?"

I nod and say, "I do."

"Do you promise to choose each other every day?" he asks.

"We do," we both say at the same time.

"Do you promise to treat each other as equals and support each other's goals?"

"We do."

"Do you promise that no matter what you both may face, whether it be a crazy ex, a tabloid scandal, or a trade to the worst baseball team in the league, you're in this together?"

"We do." Only, this time I hesitate briefly, causing Travis and the guys to laugh. I look over his shoulder at Ethan and Cooper, and both refuse to look at me. I'm starting to question who wrote these vows. I suggested we stick to traditional vows because of our situation, but these sound more like Travis has had some input.

"And, Travis, do you promise to be the coolest, most amazing father to Lucy, and when boys start asking her out on dates, do you promise to show them your barbed-wire baseball bat?" I cover my mouth to stifle my giggles.

"Hell yes," he says through laughter. Everyone in the church roars. I knew this wouldn't be serious. Nothing can be when Travis Kidd is in the room.

"The rings, please."

Travis lets go of my hand and turns to Ethan. They exchange words as I watch, realizing that I didn't even consider getting Travis a ring. The thought never crossed my mind that he would want one. The soft tap on my shoulder has me turning around, and Daisy hands me a band.

"Oh, thank you."

"Lucy, can you please step forward?" the minister requests. My eyes go wide as Travis gets down on his knee in front of Lucy.

"Lucy, I would like you to accept this token of my friendship, love, and intent to be not only your friend, but also your stepfather, as well as your protector." I watch as Travis puts a chain around her neck.

"What does the K mean?" she asks.

"K is for Kidd. We may not share the same last name, but you're a Kidd to me."

Daisy hands me a tissue as Lucy wraps her arms around Travis's neck. "I told you that you're good for him," she whispers in my ear. When he stands, he has tears in his eyes, and Lucy is now standing next to him. He reaches for my hand and slowly slides the matching wedding band onto my finger.

"I promise to give you my everything, every single day. With this ring, I thee wed."

"Oh, wow," I say, trying to gain my composure. Of course, our guests aren't making it any easier on me. Every woman in the church is crying, and the men are all clearing their throats, because we all know they're too macho to cry.

Travis holds his hand out, waiting for his ring. The sight makes me chuckle. I grab his calloused hand and slide the ring halfway, stopping only to look at him. "I promise to be the voice of reason, your backbone when you are struggling, and the wife you need, every single day. With this ring, I thee wed."

"By the power vested in me by the Commonwealth of Massachusetts, I now pronounce you husband and wife. Travis, you may kiss your bride."

THIRTY-FIVE

Travis

While kissing Saylor, all I can think is, *Holy nipple sniffer, I am fucking married!* This woman, the one I'm holding with both my hands, is my wife. She's going to kick my ass when I need it, love me when I don't deserve it, and be my constant when I need her the most. She may think I'm doing her a favor, but that is so far from the truth. When I'm with her, it's the only time I feel like I can be me. Saylor is the only woman I've let in, and thankfully she's mine forever now.

"Let me be the first to introduce you to Mr. and Mrs. Travis Kidd," the minister says, effectively pulling me away from Saylor. It's time to cash in my man card, because hearing him introduce us like that really makes me fucking happy.

I grab her hand and raise ours together as everyone starts cheering for us. When the music starts, we step toward the aisle, but not before I reach for Lucy's hand. Together, as a family, we walk to the front of the church, with our impromptu wedding party following behind.

"Pop the cork," Cooper yells as we enter the small eating space that the church has. There's a quick succession of popping champagne corks that echoes over the voices of my friends congratulating us as the guests filter into the room. The moms worked tirelessly to make sure the room was decorated and that we'd have a cake for today. The guys were in charge of the booze. I figured they should get the easiest job. And the wives made sure we'd have food.

"I can't believe you did all of this on such short notice," Saylor says as she leans into me.

My arm wraps around her as I nuzzle her neck. "I wanted today to be special."

"It is—thank you."

Ainsley hands us flutes of champagne, and that prompts me to say something about today. "I want to make a toast." I raise my glass high and wait for everyone to focus on me. "To my wife, daughter, and new mother and to all of our friends and my parents—thank you for being here today with us. I know you're busy with your own families, and it's a holiday, so I appreciate you coming on such short notice."

"Here, here," Ethan yells out as most of us clank our glasses together. As far as a reception goes, this is it. Tonight we have the Rotary gala that we'll be attending, and it marks two years from when Saylor and I hooked up. I've thought about reminding her of the day and the significance, but it's also the day that she wound up in trouble. Honestly, some things are better left unsaid.

I see my parents making their way toward us, both eager to meet Saylor. They flew in early yesterday morning, and my mom has been doing everything she could to make today go off without any complications, along with Norma.

"Beautiful ceremony," my mom says as she kisses me on the cheek.

"Thank you for everything, Mom. Allow me to introduce you to Saylor, my wife." I'm looking at Saylor when I finish my sentence to gauge her reaction. I know she's had cold feet, and I wondered if she would show up today. She's not very good at hiding her feelings from her facial expression.

"Saylor, these are my parents, Terry and Tonya Kidd."

She steps out of my hold and hugs my father first, then my mother. "It's so great to meet you," she says before grabbing my mother by the hands. "And thank you for letting me borrow this exquisite necklace."

"You're welcome, sweetie. I'm just so happy that Travis has finally settled down. I can't wait to be a grandmother."

Saylor's eyes go wide, and I cough to get rid of the frog that has suddenly lodged itself in my throat. Having children isn't something we've talked about, not that we've discussed much of anything about our future, except that she'll play a role in my baseball and financial future. And if I'm lucky, she'll let me into her pants. As of right now, I don't know where we'll live, and while I think that it'll be my house, I don't want to assume anything. But it only makes sense that they move in with me.

"We have Lucy, Ma. That's enough for right now."

"Oh, Travis, she's such a doll."

I laugh. "Wait until you spend time with Lucy. You'll see why it's been so easy to fall in love with them." The *l* word slips out before I can stop myself from saying it. Saylor tenses, but my dad quickly brushes the comment aside.

"When Lucy is ready to drive, her grandfather will be happy to teach her," he says, giving Saylor something else to focus on.

"You'll be the first one we come to, Dad," I say, giving them both another hug. As soon as they're off mingling with others, Norma is ushering us to the cake.

"Gather around," she yells, getting everyone's attention. "It's time for cake."

"Wow, you really thought of everything," Saylor says as she picks up the knife.

"I tried, babe." She smiles up at me, giving me every opportunity to kiss her. I do, first on her nose, then fully on her lips, keeping everything PG. My only hope is that later, after the gala, she'll want to become my wife in every sense of the word.

Daisy guides us on where to cut the cake, and once we've sliced our way through, Daisy is there to finish the process.

"Are you going to smear that all over my face?" I ask Saylor, who is eyeing me wickedly.

"You probably deserve it."

"Probably," I agree. "But I have to wear this tux tonight and I'd rather it not get dirty." I lean in and whisper, "We could always do this again later, if you want. I can smear a little frosting on your…" I let my words trail off and her imagination take over. She doesn't need me to tell her what I want to do to her. I've made myself very clear from the last time we were together. The urges I have toward her are strong and have never wavered.

"Let's do this," she says, moving her piece closer to my mouth as hers drops open. I don't know if we do it at the same time or not, but the moment my tongue touches the cake, I'm biting down softly, conscious that her fingers are in my mouth.

She pulls away and uses her hand to shield her mouth. Our little wedding party is cheering, and Lucy and Shaun are first in line to get a piece of cake.

"I sort of forgot you had to go to the Rotary dinner tonight."

"We," I correct her.

"What?"

"You're going, too."

She shakes her head. "No, I'm not. I don't have anything to wear."

I point at her dress and nod. "You're wearing your dress. Daisy and Ainsley are wearing their dresses as well."

Saylor pulls my head down so she can speak quietly. "I can't go, Travis. I'm not allowed, and I think one probation violation is enough, don't you?"

I kiss her along her cheek until I reach her ear. "I'll never let you fail, Saylor. I already took care of it with Irvin. He has a letter from your PO saying you can go. You'll be safe with me."

<hr />

After our reception, Norma and my mother whisk Lucy and Shaun, along with Bailey's twins, away for the night, giving Branch a break from single fatherhood and giving Cooper and Ainsley a night to themselves. Getting Branch to agree was the hard part, but in the end, he relented. Of course, it helped that if he didn't attend tonight's gala, the Renegades would fine him.

At the hotel where the gala is being held, I rented the honeymoon suite for the night, and while we're upstairs partying the night away, hotel staff will come in and place rose petals all over the room, add champagne and strawberries, and turn on the mood music.

Until then, our suite is the staging ground for the women to freshen up and the men to kick back and drink before we have to head upstairs.

"You're fucking married," Ethan says as he taps the lip of his beer bottle to mine.

"I know."

"And she ain't even pregnant," Cooper adds. We all gave him shit for marrying Ainsley while she was pregnant even though we knew how he felt about her. I've never seen someone become a head case over another person before, but he did. She consumed his thoughts 24/7. I had joked that her pussy was laced with marijuana, because he was so mellow and laid-back, and that's why he was having performance issues on the field. But that wasn't the case. The dude was so in love with her he didn't know how to control his emotions. It almost cost him his career.

"That she's not."

"I think Daisy wants a baby," Ethan adds. "She hasn't come out and said anything, but every time we walk by a baby, she's gushing. I caught her crying the other day while watching some movie."

"Saylor does that. She thinks I don't notice, but I do. These women live for those damn Hallmark movies."

"Man, you guys make me happy to be single," Branch adds. "I don't want to mess around with emotional baggage."

"It's the emotional baggage that gets your dick sucked," Cooper says, smiling.

"Shouldn't you be servicing her?" I ask.

"Tonight will be the first night since before the twins were born. Ainsley got the okay this morning at her appointment."

"Shit, I would've tapped that the second she walked in," I say. Cooper has been on pins and needles since the twins arrived.

"I tried. Cal started crying, her boobs started leaking, and Janie shit her pants so bad she had to be hosed down."

The three of us start to laugh, pissing Cooper off.

"Fuck you," he says. "Wait until you have kids."

"I have one," I add. "She's five, and walked in on me and Saylor already. I fucking hit the floor so fast that it brought back memories from high school. At least with the twins, they don't know what's going on, so if they hear mommy moaning, they're not walking in to find out why."

"Truth," Cooper agrees. "I can't wait to get laid," he says, sighing. We all laugh but have at one point felt his anguish. Saylor and I will have to be creative when it comes time for adult entertainment. I'm sort of thankful that she doesn't have a job, because once we drop Lucy off at school, we can fuck all over the house without interruptions.

"By the way, I fired my agent and hired Saylor to represent me. I'm not saying I want you to switch, but she'll take you on as clients if you want. Oh, and...I asked to be let out of my contract."

"What the fuck?" Branch barks out. "Why?"

I tell them about what happened in the gym a week or so back and the grumblings I heard around the clubhouse. To say they are shocked is an understatement.

"You can't quit," Cooper says. "I'm the fucking captain, and I say no."

"You don't have a choice," I tell him.

"Fuck you, I don't." He stands and goes to the door that is separating us from the women. "Saylor," he yells, knocking loudly.

"What?" she asks as the door flies open.

"Your husband can't quit or get traded."

She eyes me and shakes her head. "Don't worry, Cooper. I'm on it. Travis knows how I feel about him quitting. Seeking a trade, though, if that is what he wants, that is the angle I'll pursue."

"He can't leave Boston," he pleads.

"I know, and he won't." She shuts the door in Cooper's face, and as he walks back toward the couch, he looks victorious.

"You're ass slime," I say to him as he sits down with a smug look on his face.

"You're pissed because I told on you."

"She's not my mother, Cooper."

"No, but she's your wife, partner, and agent," Ethan adds. "Plus, you have a kid to think about now."

"Players with families get traded all the time," I point out. Many kids are uprooted from their schools when their fathers land new contracts or are put on waivers in the middle of the season.

"True, but people love you here," Ethan says.

"Not my teammates."

"Fuck them," Branch blurts out. "They're not speaking for the whole team. What does Ryan say?"

"He doesn't want me to go and asked me to wait until after my hearing next week to make a decision."

"Well, do what he says." Branch finishes off his beer as the women come out of the room, primped and ready to go.

I stand as soon as I see Saylor. She's added a red fur shawl to her dress, making her even prettier than before.

"I can't believe I get to show you off tonight as my wife. That means no hiding from anyone, and if I want to steal a kiss, I can do so without wondering who is going to see."

She nods and meets my gaze. "Will you dance with me?"

"All night long, babe. And when we're done upstairs, we are going to perfect the horizontal tango."

In a matter of seconds, I took a romantic moment and made it crass. Her hand lands on my lapel in a smack. I can't help but laugh as I take her hand and follow the guys out of our suite.

BOSTON RENEGADES

It's official.

Travis Kidd has wed his publicist, Saylor Blackwell, in an intimate ceremony on New Year's Eve. According to sources, Ethan Davenport served as best man while Cooper Bailey was a groomsman.

For the bride, Daisy Davenport stepped in as matron of honor, and Ainsley Bailey rounded out the wedding party as a bridesmaid. Branch Singleton's son, Shaun, escorted Miss Lucy Blackwell down the aisle while she performed her flower girl duties.

The wedding party was later seen at the Rotary Dinner and Gala, still dressed in their wedding attire, giving the guests an opportunity to celebrate with the newlyweds.

There was no word on who designed Ms. Blackwell's dress, but revelers from the gala gushed about how beautiful it was. Congratulations, Travis and Saylor!

The BoRe Blogger

THIRTY-SIX

Saylor

The rooftop terrace provides the most amazing view of the harbor. Everyone gathers around, keeping close for added body heat while we wait for the countdown to the new year. Resolutions are muttered among the onlookers, many seeking a new lifestyle with diets and whatnot, while a few say they're quitting their jobs or going to finally take that family vacation they've wanted.

I don't think I can make just one New Year's resolution. The most obvious is to retain custody of my daughter. That is the highest on my priority list, which leads me to my next one—my need to stop second-guessing my marriage to Travis. Going into today I expected us to say "I do" and head our separate ways for the holiday because he had to be here. He surprised me, though, and has made this one of the most memorable days of my life.

Travis and I huddle together for warmth with the Baileys and Davenports on either side of us while Branch is off talking to a woman he met this evening. It's one of the drawbacks of living on the East Coast during the winter, especially near the harbor, but the fireworks are spectacular and shouldn't be missed if given the opportunity.

All night the guys have played their parts, posing for pictures and signing autographs, even partaking in a few dances with the older women of Boston. The wives, as we were dubbed by a few cleat-chasers, stood back and watched our men dazzle the socks off the city's most elite.

"Do you have a New Year's resolution?" I ask Travis.

"To make you fall in love with me," he answers with a kiss to my cold nose. I imagine I look like Rudolph right about now but can easily say I'm not the only one. His words should make me weak in the knees, but the truth is they scare me. I have already fallen in love, and what happens when he decides that this marriage is no longer beneficial to him? Granted, he's entered into this union without a prenup, something I don't agree with, but it's his money. But even money can't mend a broken heart—only time can, and I've been down that path before.

"I can see the doubt in your eyes, Saylor."

"I know, and I'm sorry. It's just…"

"What?"

"Overwhelming," I tell him. "Today was nothing like I expected. I honestly thought we'd go to the courthouse, get married, and maybe grab a bite to eat before I went home and ate bonbons while I watched the ball drop. But you…I don't know," I say, shaking my head. "It's like you want this to be real, and that's what I want, too. I'm having a hard time grasping it all."

"Grab it all by the horns, baby, and hang on tight, because I promise it's going to be one hell of a ride."

"You make everything sound like a carnival ride."

He laughs and kisses me again. "I have a feeling you're going to give me a run for my money, but it's going to be worth it."

Before I can respond, the crowd starts counting down from ten. Travis and I join in but never take our eyes off each other. It's been years since I've been kissed at the stroke of midnight. Two years ago, Travis and I were in the comfort of his home when he finally kissed me. Tonight, it'll be in front of the entire city.

"Five…four…three…two…one…Happy New Year, Saylor," he says as he holds my face gently with his fingers and moves painstakingly slowly toward me. I lick my lips in preparation for his. The first touch is soft and lingers a bit until I feel him open his mouth and his tongue swipe along my lower lip. I open for him, his tongue sending shivers down my already cold spine. I clutch at the lapels of his jacket, trying to pull him closer as his arm wraps around my shoulders in an attempt to shield me from onlookers.

We both jump away from the kiss as the first boom from the fireworks sounds. He doesn't smile or even wink. The Travis standing before me, the one playing with a tendril of my hair, has a subdued look on his face. Yet his eyes yield an urgency that I haven't seen before.

I reach up on my tippy-toes until my lips are perfectly angled with his ear. "I think I'm ready to call it a night," I tell him, hoping that he understands what I'm saying. I'm going to go for it, put both feet in the water as they say, and be his wife. He deserves the benefit of the doubt, and I think he's done a stand-up job trying to prove himself today.

"Yeah?"

"Yeah." I nod, slipping my hand into his.

"What about the fireworks?" He motions toward the harbor and the lighted sky. Fireworks are my favorite, and maybe he knows this, but I can wait to watch them in July.

"We can make our own."

"Fuck yeah, we will," he says. "Hey, guys, we're out—wedding-night duties are calling."

The guys high-five while my already rosy cheeks turn even redder. I didn't expect him to blurt it out to everyone. I manage to hug Ainsley and Daisy before Travis pulls me away from them and into the celebratory crowd. People try to stop him, but none are successful until we're in the elevator and the gentleman we're riding with proceeds to go on and on about the Chicago Cubs winning the World Series and how the Renegades have once again let him down.

My hand caresses Travis's back while he stands there taking every word from this drunken man. Our only saving grace is that our floor is closer to the top. Travis bids him well as he steps off, and once the doors are closed, Travis flips him off.

"Stupid fucker," he mumbles as he has a stare-down with the closed doors. "Sorry, babe."

"Don't be," I tell him. I've heard it all before, people giving me shit because my clients are underperforming. It's the nature of the beast.

Travis places his arm around me, and I sag against him as we make our way to our room. The few minutes we've been inside has allowed the cold to subside. I still shiver, though, when his fingers brush under my shawl and against my bare arms.

He pulls out the key card to our room and pauses. "I meant what I said today, Saylor. Every word."

"Me too." I squeal as he picks me up, swinging me into his arms. "Travis, let me down."

"Nope," he says, shaking his head. "I'm carrying my bride over the threshold." He manages to open the door without dropping me, and he safely gets me through the doorway without a bump.

"Oh, Travis." My eyes water from the scene before me. Candles are lit throughout our suite, and rose petals line the walkway to our bedroom. He sets me down gently and removes my shawl in the process. "This is beautiful."

"So are you." His lips press against my bare shoulder while his fingers nimbly pull the zipper down on my dress, letting the capped sleeves fall down my arms. I move slightly, allowing my gown to settle on the floor.

"I take that back," he says as he comes around to stand in front of me, his hand never leaving my body. Each touch causes more and more goose bumps to rise. "You're fucking gorgeous and all mine." He picks me up again, this time in a straddle, and carries me through the bedroom and into the bathroom.

"We have a bed, ya know." I point to the wall, but he doesn't say anything. He proceeds to undress and motions for me to do the same.

"Since the first time we were together, I've dreamed of fucking you in the shower, and honestly, I'm afraid that I'm going to wake up in the morning and you'll be gone."

"So our first time as a married couple will be in the shower?" I take off my bra and add it to his pile of clothes.

He nods and slips his fingers into the sides of my panties. "You'll always remember this moment, Saylor, each time you take a shower. We'll have plenty of time to fuck in a bed later."

"Okay," I whisper, placing my hands on his shoulders so he can slip off my underwear and shoes. He leaves me standing in the middle of the bathroom, returning only after he's set the water to the right temperature.

"Come along, wife." He pulls me behind him and opens the door to the shower. "After you," he says, swatting my ass as I walk by. I yelp, and he chuckles deeply. I manage to pull the pins out of my hair before standing underneath the water.

"Fucking fantasy coming true." Travis turns me to face him, but I stay under the showerhead. He bends and laps at the water that is falling off my breasts until he decides he's quenched his thirst and takes one nipple into his mouth while his fingers pinch and massage the other. "Exquisite," he says, switching to the other side.

I'm doing all I can to keep my knees from buckling. Reaching between us, I grab ahold of him, and he gasps. It's the best feeling, knowing that I make Travis Kidd hard. And that he chose me to give his name to. His mouth crashes down on mine, and our tongues tangle for dominance as he backs me up against the shower wall.

"I had this whole foreplay scenario played out in my head, but fuck it. I need to be inside of you now."

"Okay," I say breathlessly as his fingers delve between my legs. When his thumb presses down on my bud, my knees finally give way. His strong arm wraps around my waist, holding me up.

"Do I need a condom, Saylor?"

"I'm on the pill," I tell him.

He steps back, halting the intimacy building between us. "That's not why I'm asking. If you want a baby, I'll plant seeds every fucking day until you're pregnant. I'm asking because I need to know if you trust me."

I look deep into his eyes and see a hint of pain that lingers from the rape accusation. "I trust you, Travis. I trust you with everything."

In one swift motion, we're kissing, and my legs are being wrapped around his waist. He pulls away and sets one hand above me and the other on my hip. "I can't believe you're my fucking wife. How'd I get so lucky?"

His thrusts start out slow and build momentum with each kiss, bite, and pull I add to his body. My response is to open my mouth while my eyes roll back in my head. When I tug on his hair, he groans and bites my shoulder while pushing deeper into my center.

Our bodies move together as the water from the shower coats our skin. He moves us from the wall to the glass door, where he asks me to lock my ankles. My head falls back, and my shoulders move up and down the glass as he buries himself within me.

For every moan I emit, he matches, turning me on even more. I bask in the knowledge that I'm now the only one who will ever hear him like this, to see him come undone from pure pleasure from this day forward. He is mine.

My hips buck, meeting every advance, as Travis grips the top of the glass door, keeping us from falling. The heels of my feet push into his ass, urging him to bring us to the brink as warmth starts to seep through my belly. I reach for him and look into his eyes. I open my mouth to tell him that I'm close, but his lips capture mine as he swallows each cry I have throughout my orgasm.

He holds me in place, pushing in and out of me with a slower pace. Gently, he unhooks my legs and keeps his hands on my waist until I've regained my balance.

Travis shuts off the water and cups my face in his large hand. "Race you."

"To what?" I ask, slightly confused.

"To be the first one to fall in love." He winks, sending my heart into a frenzy.

THIRTY-SEVEN

Travis

"Your Honor, with all due respect, the state needs more time to build the case against Mr. Kidd," the assistant district attorney says, which causes Irvin to mumble under his breath.

"They've had weeks, Your Honor, including an arrest where the police failed to conduct a proper investigation," Irvin says as he stands up.

"The complexity of the case is—"

"The complexity of the case?" Irvin starts to pace the courtroom floor. "My client is being accused of rape and assault. A rape kit was performed on the night in question, and I have yet to see the results. The victim has since accused my client of battering her, but my office has yet to see the pictures of these wounds. Do I need to go on, Your Honor? Because at this point, I think the state is harassing my client."

He's damn right they are. My endorsement deal with Nike is barely hanging on, and I plan to sue the state for the money I've lost with Under Armour.

"It's my understanding that Mr. Kidd has a witness to the night in question?" the judge asks.

"Saylor Blackwell-Kidd," Irvin states. I find myself smiling because this is the first time since we've been married that someone else has called her by her new last name. Granted, it's only been a few days, but still, I do like hearing it.

"And her relation to the defendant?"

"She's his wife," Irvin states.

"And she was there at the time of the incident?"

"Yes, and they started dating shortly thereafter and were married on the thirty-first."

"Very well; bring her in," the judge says, requesting Saylor's presence.

The guard that is stationed at the back of the courtroom opens the door and motions for her to enter. From the moment she steps in, my eyes are on her, taking in every inch of her body that I have had the privilege of getting to know. Repeatedly, I might add. And thanks to her mother and my parents, they've kept Lucy occupied for the past few days so our honeymoon could extend to every room, surface, and available space inside my house. I have no doubt the reporters outside are getting a nice dose of her screaming out my name.

Saylor's dressed in a black skirt that hugs the contour of her hips and a red blouse, likely paying homage to the Renegades. Yesterday, we spent hours listing the pros and cons of staying in Boston and continuing my career. For every con I gave her, she came back with multiple pros, beating me at my own game. On paper, the reasons to stay are perfect, but in my heart, I'm not sure it's going to be enough. She says the fans will come around after today's hearing and subsequent press statement from Irvin. Her faith in me has been unwavering from the start, and I can't thank her enough.

She winks at me as she passes by the table. I watch the sway of her hips as she prepares to take the stand.

"Please raise your right hand," the court bailiff instructs. "Do you solemnly swear that you will tell the truth, the whole truth, and nothing but the truth under pains and penalties of perjury?"

"I do," she says, taking a seat.

"Ms. Blackwell-Kidd, where were you on the night in question?" Irvin asks. Earlier this morning we rehearsed everything he would ask Saylor, even though the judge might find it a bit damaging to me. It's my hope that her testimony is enough to get this case thrown out, and I can move on with my life.

"I was at the bar on Langdon Street."

"Was Mr. Kidd there?"

"He was," she says.

"Was he alone?"

Saylor shakes her head. "No; he was with a woman. They were playing a game of pool."

"Did you observe Mr. Kidd with this woman?"

"I did, briefly."

"Why?" Irvin asks.

She sighs, and by the slight movement of her arm, I'm guessing she's playing with her rings. I caught her staring at them the other day, holding her hand out so the sunlight would hit her diamond perfectly and cast prisms onto the ceiling.

"Because he's my client, and because I had residual feelings for him stemming from an encounter we shared years prior."

"Would you say that you were jealous of this other woman?"

"In a way, yes."

"Please explain," Irvin instructs.

"Well, due to the nature of my previous job, being with Mr. Kidd wasn't possible. I was jealous of the freedom she had with him."

"And what did you do about it?"

"I left the bar."

"Is that the only reason you left?"

Saylor looks down at her hands and takes a deep breath. This is the part of the testimony she wanted to avoid, but Irvin told us that she'd look more credible if he was asking her the tough questions and leaving nothing for the ADA to discredit her on.

"I'm on probation and not allowed in bars."

"But you were, on this night in question."

"Yes, I was."

She looks at me, and I offer her the most genuine smile I can. When we're done here, I'm going to take her home and fuck the memories of today away. I know how hard this has been on her, how much stress she has endured. I also know I haven't made it easy, and she questioned my motives when I asked her to marry me. Each day, I'm finding new ways to prove to her that I want to be bound to her.

"What happened after you left the bar?"

"Travis...Mr. Kidd followed me out."

"Was this the first time he spoke to you?"

Saylor shakes her head again. "No; he came up to me earlier when I first arrived."

"What did he say to you?"

"He asked me why I was at the bar. I assure you, our exchange was anything but pleasant."

"And when he followed you outside?"

"He asked me if I needed a ride home."

"Did you take him up on the offer?" Irvin asks her.

"No, I did not. I hailed a cab. I needed to get out of there because the woman that he had been with inside was starting to throw a fit."

"What happened next?"

Saylor sighs again before saying, "When the taxi pulled up, I got in but wasn't fast enough. Travis followed me. I opted to get out, and before he could react, the cab was pulling away."

"What else do you remember from that night?"

"The woman," she says. "She threatened him. Said, 'Fuck you, Travis Kidd. You'll pay for this.'"

"Did you see Travis return to the bar?"

"No, I didn't. I watched the woman get into a car and leave. Then I walked toward the direction of the taxi, but I never saw it double back."

"Thank you. No further questions." I look over at the ADA, and he looks frustrated. Part of me had hoped that he would bring Rachel Ward in to provide testimony, but Irvin said it would be a long shot.

"Does the state want to cross-examine?" the judge asks. The ADA rises but shakes his head.

"The state is moving to drop all charges against Travis Kidd," he says as he flips the top of his file folder closed. He looks pissed, but I don't fucking care.

"Smart move by the state," the judge says. He turns to face me. "Mr. Kidd, you are free to go. Good luck next season. I'll be rooting for ya!" The slam of the gavel has me up and out of my seat, racing toward Saylor. She's in my arms with my lips pressed to hers in no time.

"I'm fucking free," I say in between kisses.

"Yes, you are. Now let's go tell everyone else." She takes my hand

and leads me out of the courtroom and into a small conference room where she and Irvin start talking strategy. I pull out my phone and text the guys, along with my parents and Norma, to turn on the news.

"You two kids have fun with the press. I'm going to go file our case against the state, and one against Rachel Ward as well for falsifying accusations. She could've ruined your career," Irvin says as he pats me on the shoulder.

I want to tell him to stop, but the words don't come out before he's out of the room. Saylor slides her hand into mine and squeezes.

"He's right, ya know," Saylor says. "What the DA did is wrong. He didn't have a case against you, and he let it drag on for far too long. We have a lot of damage control to take care of, so if Irvin can recoup your lost expenses, it's for the best."

I kiss her hard, not wanting to let go of her. "This is why you're my agent."

"And publicist."

"And wife," I point out.

"And sex slave?"

That is where I draw the line. "You can't be a sex slave if you're begging for it, babe." I swat her on the ass as she walks out the door and back into the hallway. Once we get outside, the reporters are lining up. She called ahead and told them to be ready.

"Today, we finally have some answers," she says into the microphone. "Mr. Kidd has been cleared of any and all wrongdoing. I repeat: He will not face any changes stemming from the false rape and assault claims brought by the state. I'll take questions now," she says.

I thought I would speak today, but she's saving my story for ESPN, in a promised deal that she made.

"Is it true that you were a key witness?" a reporter asks.

"I was a witness," Saylor answers.

"What about the rumors that Kidd is being traded?"

"Those are unfounded. Kidd and the Renegades have been in constant contact since the night in question, and his position with the team is safe." This is where she and I differ.

Saylor points to another reporter, who asks, "When will we see pictures from your wedding?"

I butt in and say, "Soon," causing her to push me out of the way.

"Will Kidd seek damages from the state?"

"Yes, he will," she says. "These untruths have hurt my client financially. He's lost endorsement deals that will be hard to get back. If a proper investigation had been done by the state prior to accusing and questioning my client, we would not be here right now."

She looks back at me and smiles.

"If there are no further questions, I want to thank you for all the support you have shown Travis. He loves the city of Boston and is determined to bring home another pennant for you all. Your support of him means a great deal. Thank you."

Saylor steps away from the microphone and motions for me to walk toward the security guard who is stationed outside. He's about to take us back into the courthouse when someone yells out Saylor's name.

"Hey, Paul, I haven't forgotten," she tells the reporter from ESPN.

"When can I have a sit-down?" he asks. Saylor pulls out her phone and thumbs through her calendar while I stand next to her as if I'm invisible. I want to jump up and down, waving my arms like a spastic monkey, to get his attention, but he's focused on my wife.

"We have some personal stuff to take care of, so give me a couple weeks. I'll want this edited and broadcast right before he leaves for spring training."

"Shouldn't be a problem. I'll wait for your call."

I grab ahold of her arm and pull her to me. "What if I don't go?"

"What if you do?" she counters. "What if next week you're at the park with Lucy and children ask for your autograph?"

I look at her questioningly, wondering why she would ask that. "I won't sign them, not when I'm with her."

"Bad example; you know what I mean. Give this time to blow over."

"And what if this doesn't?"

She shrugs. "We'll cross that bridge when we get there. But for now, you're a Renegade. I've already spoken to Stone and told him that any offers made by you or Jeffrey are off the table. If he wants to get rid of you, it's on him."

"You did?" I question.

"I'm your manager. Of course I did."

BOSTON RENEGADES

Travis Kidd appeared in court today, only to have all charges dropped! Every Renegade fan couldn't be happier for him.

Unbeknownst to the state, the defense had a witness that cast doubt on the story the state had been told by the victim in the case, and with no rape kit available, the case against our left fielder was weak.

The surprise witness was none other than Saylor Blackwell-Kidd, who is not only his publicist but also his wife and newly hired agent. We really hope Travis is paying her well!

In today's press conference, Blackwell-Kidd indicated that her client will be seeking damages from the state, and according to sources at the courthouse, those papers were filed today along with a motion to reveal the identity of the victim so that charges may be brought against her for falsifying testimony.

We're happy to report that this will be the last blog post on this matter.

Case closed! Now bring on spring training!

The BoRe Blogger

THIRTY-EIGHT

Saylor

In the few weeks since Travis and I have been married, our lives have been crazy. I've tried to stay busy by signing new clients to my roster, one of whom is Cooper Bailey. It's not a bad start, even if it's incredibly stressful. Having to sell myself has been a challenge but one that I'm welcoming with open arms.

And it is still my focus to get Travis to reconsider leaving Boston, although I've told him that Lucy and I support any decision he makes. My mother has also given him her blessing if we were to move to Florida. It seems she and my mother-in-law have hit it off, and my mom has been invited to stay on the Kidds' yacht anytime she wants.

Travis and I still haven't moved in together or moved out of my apartment. It makes sense that we move to his place, but until my custody trial is over, I'm not leaving. The last thing I want is for Elijah to say I've uprooted Lucy or find some other convoluted way to use a new home against me. Travis doesn't seem to mind, though, even if we are a bit cramped. Other than to grab his clothes and his daily living essentials, he hasn't left my side, which, for the most part, is fabulous because I love spending time with him, but it makes it hard to work. If he retires from baseball, he'll need another job or I'll have to maintain an office away from him in order to get my work done.

"Your view is amazing," I tell Ryan Stone. I'm looking out over Lowery Field from his office. The crystal-clear day is a sure sign that spring is coming early, and with the sun shining down on the field, it truly makes this view unbelievable.

"Definitely a perk of the job."

"I can see that. Was this office always like this?" I turn away from the window and take a seat at the small conference table in his office.

"No; funny enough I joked about it when they were in the process of luring me away from the Yankees. There were these standard windows that didn't let enough light in. The office felt stuffy and drab. I wanted something different. I wanted my office to feel warm and inviting. When I walked in on my first day, the wall and windows were gone and nothing but this glass was there. I think I spent my first week staring out at the field."

"Do you find it hard to focus when they're practicing?"

"Always," he tells me. "I love this team, the city, and the fans. The early day games, like on Patriots' Day, make it hard to work, and I often find myself cutting out so I can watch the game."

"Well, I'm sure you know why I'm here."

"I do. Jeffrey was kind enough to let us know that he is no longer representing Travis. He assumed you would be taking over but wasn't very forthcoming with information."

"I imagined not. We didn't exactly part on the best of terms, but nonetheless, I represent not only Travis but Cooper as well."

Ryan jots a note down on his pad of paper and smiles at me when he's done. "This is probably a good thing for Cooper. He needs someone in his corner who cares about him and not the bottom line."

"That's what he said, too," I say, laughing. "Anyway, I'm here because of Travis and his situation. As you are aware, all charges have been dropped, and the state has issued a public apology."

"I was very happy to hear that. Travis has maintained his innocence from day one, especially with me. He was very forthcoming."

"But he is still pondering retirement."

Ryan sighs and drops his pen so he can rub his hand over his face. "*That* I was hoping would change."

"Honestly, me too. And I'm trying. He only had the support of a few players, and others publicly bashed him in the media as well as in person. Travis feels like he's let everyone down, and his biggest fear is being disliked by his teammates and booed by the fans."

"Understandable. Does he have any public appearances scheduled?"

"Yes; as a matter of fact, he'll be at the Children's Hospital tomorrow, and he's organized a Valentine's Day toy drive that will take place outside Faneuil Hall Marketplace, where he'll sign autographs and pose for pictures with each toy donation."

"No kissing booth?"

I can't help but smile because not only was that a brilliant idea, but also knowing that he will never kiss another woman again makes my heart skip a beat. "Unfortunately that is something I can't approve." Ryan laughs right along with me. "However, I could set one up for Branch. The publicity is very good."

"Please do. I think the fans would love it."

"A joint effort on Valentine's Day," I tell him as I write the idea down in my notes. "Back to Travis. How long does he have to decide?"

"If he doesn't report to spring training, he'll be fined daily until we can come to a settlement on the remaining term of his contract. If he announces his retirement beforehand, you know he won't be allowed to play for another team until his contract with the Renegades has expired."

I make sure to write everything down as he said it, not that I won't remember the details from our conversation, though. I know deep in my heart that Travis isn't ready to give up on baseball yet, and I doubt the city of Boston is ready to give up on him either.

"Thank you, Ryan, for meeting with me today." I stand and shake his hand.

"I have a feeling you're going to be a good thing for Travis. I look forward to doing a lot of business with you and hope to see you in Florida when I'm there at the end of February."

"Me too."

No sooner do I step out of Ryan's office than my phone starts to ring with Travis's self-chosen ringtone of Aloe Blacc's "The Man." Each time I hear it, I can't keep the smile off my face. "Your timing is perfect. I just walked out of Ryan's office."

"You need to get over to Lucy's school. I came to pick her up, and Elijah is here, demanding that she be released to him."

"What?" I start to walk a little faster, but it's not an easy thing to do when you're wearing heeled boots.

"Irvin is on his way, and the police are here," Travis tells me.

"Where's Lucy?"

"Inside the classroom with an aide. Other parents are lingering, and I swear to God, Saylor, they're taking sides. People are making comments about me, calling me a rapist. I just want to get my daughter so I can take her ice-skating like I fucking promised her this morning. I want out of this goddamn city, Saylor."

"I know, Travis." I can hear the desperation in his voice and fear that this is the tipping point. It might be too late to ask for a trade after the meeting I had with Ryan, but it might be my only shot at making him happy. He loves the game, and I can't see him giving it up so easily. "These parents…they must be friends with the DA or something. Everyone knows you've been cleared."

"Except they're going to believe what they want."

Negative public perception is hard to overcome. It's why publicists work so hard to keep their clients in the limelight doing good deeds. All it takes is one person to destroy someone's career, and in this case, it seems to be Rachel Ward. I caught Travis looking her up one night. As soon as I saw her picture on his phone, I recognized her immediately and asked him to let the courts decide her punishment. Thing is, though, it takes them seconds to arrest someone on suspicion, but it seems like it takes months to arrest the person who made false claims. That is, if they arrest them at all.

"I'll be there as soon as I can," I tell Travis, wishing like hell that I wasn't on the other side of town.

"I'm not letting him take her," he says right before he ends our call.

"I know you won't," I mumble into my phone as I hurry across the Brookline overpass so I can hail a cab. One stops immediately, and I tell him I'll double his fare if he would be so kind as to break the speed limit for me.

I keep my phone in my hand, waiting for Travis to call back or text me an update. And even though I know he won't let anything happen to Lucy, I'm not sure he won't do anything to Elijah.

"Elijah…" I mutter his name. What the fuck is he thinking, showing up at her school like this? I haven't heard from him since he threatened me, aside from being served, and our court date is still a few days away. So what's he doing?

The size of the melee of parents and onlookers gathered in front of Lucy's school is ridiculous, and they're spilling out into the streets, preventing the cab from getting any closer. I toss the driver a wad of money before getting out.

My adrenaline spikes as I try to force my way through the crowd. Even as I tell them that I need to get through to save my daughter, very few people move aside. I'm finding it hard to grasp why there are so many people lingering around what is a domestic incident. This many people is never a good thing, especially when half are supporting Travis while the other half are slinging disparaging comments about him.

When I finally break through, I'm stopped by a police officer, and only after I show him my identification does he let me through.

"What are you doing?" I yell at Elijah as I come through the wrought iron gate of the school.

"I'm here to pick up Lucy," he says, as if this is an everyday occurrence. The man behind him looks at me smugly.

I shake my head, trying to comprehend everything. "On what authority, Elijah? You're not even listed on her school forms. Her teacher, the principal…no one knows you, and neither does she. You have no right being here."

"I'm her father," he roars, and points to the building. "Not that rapist you married, which, let's get real, Saylor—the only reason you married him is because of his money."

I shouldn't be shocked, but I am and can't prevent my mouth

from dropping open. Of course, the other parents lurking around start murmuring, and I hear the words *slump-buster* and *gold digger*.

"First of all, Travis is not a rapist, and if you make that accusation again, my client will file a lawsuit so fast your head will spin." I look to my left to find Irvin standing next to me. "Second, no one is disputing that you're the sperm donor to Lucy Blackwell, but I'd use the term *father* very loosely."

"Who the fuck are you?" Elijah yells out as Irvin approaches him.

"Watch your language, sir. There are children around," the principal says. I stifle a laugh knowing that Elijah is about to blow a gasket.

"I represent Lucy Blackwell in her bid to terminate your parental rights."

"Excuse me?" Elijah says. Irvin hands an envelope to Elijah, who doesn't even reach for it, but the man behind him does. "She's seven. She has no rights."

"She's five, almost six. And you would know that if you were truly a father to her," Irvin points out. "And she has every right." Irvin takes my arm and guides me into the school and down the hall toward Lucy's classroom.

"What's going on?" I ask, stopping before we reach her classroom.

"It's simple. A few days ago, I received a call from Lucy asking if she could divorce Elijah."

"A divorce?" I stand there, shaking my head. "Where did she hear something like this?"

Irvin smiles. "She's resourceful. She told me that she had watched a movie at her grandmother's about a little girl who divorces her parents, and she wanted to do that. When I asked her to explain, she said that Elijah is trying to take her away, and she doesn't want him to."

"Oh...how'd she get your number?"

"You know, I didn't ask. I figured you had it written down or she went through one of your phones."

I nod, pretending to understand, and make a mental note to lock our phones. There are things on there that no one needs to see.

"So now what?" I ask as we start walking toward the classroom. When we get to the doorway and look in, Travis is sitting in one of the beanbag chairs with Lucy in his arms, and they're reading to each other.

"Now we wait. It's tough because she is five and a judge could say that you sway her. However, her claims will be taken seriously."

Both Lucy and Travis look up when they hear us talking. Their smiles instantly lighten the gloom I was feeling.

"Look at him," Irvin says. "How can anyone say he's not good for her?"

I shake my head, wondering the same thing. It's hard to think that I almost kept him from her.

THIRTY-NINE

Travis

My housekeeper scurries to help Lucy pick up the remaining toys from the living room while the camera crew finishes installing their lighting system. Today, I will finally sit down with Paul Boyd and talk about what happened in December. I wish I could say this has been a long time coming, but the truth is, we're only a month and a half removed from the day I was cleared of all charges.

And still to this day, I'm holding fast to the idea that I'm going to retire. Each night, I lie in bed with Saylor asleep on my chest, wondering if I'm making the right decision. I don't know if there will ever be an answer, but I pray that I'm not making a mistake.

The public opinion poll on me is still divided. Some feel that I need to be removed from the Renegades, that the organization didn't take action when they needed to, while some can't wait for the season to start and are expecting me to take my spot in left field. Saylor, and those who are around me, want me to stay and play, and honestly, part of me does, too. But I'm not sure my ego can take the brutality that the fans can dish out. And I don't want Lucy to hear that either. The last thing she needs to hear are people bad-mouthing me in the stands. That is something she won't understand.

After this interview with Boyd, I only have days to decide. I'll either be in Florida on vacation or stretching in the outfield with my teammates.

Since I've been cleared, only Bryce Mackenzie has apologized for his actions. The others have stayed away, and truthfully, I'm okay with that. They broke the unspoken code that we share among ourselves as a team: You always have each other's backs. I would've had theirs, regardless. It makes it hard to go back to a team that can't support you.

My biggest proponent is standing in the kitchen, going over the questions that Paul plans to ask while Lucy plays in her recently painted pink bedroom. When Saylor and I showed her my house and where her room would be, she asked if it could be pink. Apparently, she's wanted this color for a while, but due to Saylor renting her apartment, they were unable to change the wall color. So, of course, I said yes and promptly took her to the paint store, where she picked out the most hideous shade I had ever seen. After a long debate, she finally relented and let me choose the color, as long as it was pink. I have to say that it didn't turn out half bad.

"Wanna play dolls?" she asks after she spots me leaning against her doorjamb. She holds up one of her dolls in anticipation that I'll join her.

"I can't. I have to do an interview in a few minutes."

"Oh." Her face falls as she fiddles with the doll in her hands.

"Don't be like that. This is work, remember?" I walk in and take a seat next to her. This is where Saylor often finds me when she comes home from work, sitting on Lucy's floor either dressed like a princess or doing whatever Lucy wishes. I spend as much time as I can with her so she knows how important she is to me. If I do decide to go back to baseball, our time will be limited, and I don't want her to think that I don't care about her.

"Yeah, but I wanna play."

"We can after," I tell her. "It shouldn't take very long. Besides, you have to let Mommy brush your hair so you look pretty for the camera."

Her frown turns into an instant smile. It wasn't my idea to put Lucy on television, but Saylor said it would help change the public opinion about me if they see me as a family man. I told her that exploiting Lucy isn't the way to go about that, and she promised me that isn't what we're doing. Saylor pointed out that I'm often with Lucy in public and that she was at my fund-raiser on Valentine's Day, so having her participate today is a treat for the viewers who already love me.

"Will the man ask me questions?" she asks as she climbs into my lap.

I pretend to think, but the truth is that he won't. "He might ask you who your favorite baseball player is."

"That's easy. Cooper," she says, shrugging with her hands in the air.

"Cooper? What about me?"

Lucy shakes her head. "Cooper has the babies."

"Ah, yes. I can't compete with the babies." In fact, no man can. We had a party once Saylor and Lucy moved in and invited everyone. The Baileys brought Cal and Janie over, and every female in my house went crazy. I was sort of hoping that Saylor would get baby fever, but she's yet to bring up having children. Which, I suppose, is all for the best since we're newly married, neither of us have said we love each other, and she's launched a new career.

"The babies are so cute." Lucy scrunches her nose, making her face squishy.

"What are you two talking about?" Saylor asks as she comes into the room.

"Babies," I say, winking.

"Oh." Saylor seems taken aback by my comment, lessening any hope I had that she might be ready. It's okay, because we have time. The practice is fun, though, and we practice a lot.

"Is it time?" I ask, and she nods. I scoot Lucy off my lap and give her a kiss on the nose. "Wish me luck."

Saylor kisses me quickly, much to Lucy's delight. The catcalling she's learned from Ethan Davenport is bar none. My stepdaughter makes a construction worker sound tame. I give her a sideways glance, which causes a fit of giggles.

"Remind me to teach Davenport's future kids some bad habits."

"You'll do no such thing." Saylor pushes me out of Lucy's room and back down the hall. She knows I'm dreading this interview, mostly because I want everything to be done and in the past. And the only reason I'm doing this is because she set it up months ago.

I sigh and step into my living room, which has been made into a makeshift studio, and take a seat in one of the chairs they provide. People descend on me immediately, fixing my hair, adding makeup, and attaching a microphone to my shirt.

"Hey, Travis."

"Paul," I say, giving him a nod.

As soon as everyone is out of the way, he starts by speaking into the camera, telling the viewers what he's doing and that he's in my home, giving them a rare look at my private life. Saylor cautioned me on picking my nose during the taping, though, stating that other cameras will be angled on me throughout the interview.

Paul finishes his introduction and looks at me. "Travis, thank you for allowing us to be in your home."

"You're welcome."

"A lot has changed for you these past few months. One of the biggest is that you married your publicist, shocking everyone and adding to the speculation that your marriage is nothing more than a business deal meant to protect your assets, especially without a prenuptial agreement in place."

I bite the inside of my cheek and remember that Saylor approved his questions, so she has to know this is on the list. Rubbing my hands down the front of my pants, I look at Paul and give him a half smile. "Honestly, Paul, I've had a crush on Saylor for a while. I was always doing stupid shit that she'd have to come rescue me from in hopes that she'd give me the time of day."

"It seems you finally won her over."

"Only after I begged, and let me tell you, there was a lot of pleading on my part. She's a tough nut to crack."

"Spring training starts in a few days, and there have been rumors that you're retiring. When will you make the decision whether to hang up your cleats and call it quits?"

"It'll be a reporting-day decision for me, Paul. I love baseball and the city of Boston, but right now I'm not sure my heart is in it."

"And that's because of what happened in December?"

I nod.

"You were accused of rape and spent a lot of time defending yourself for something you didn't do. How has that changed you?"

"It…uh…it was a wake-up call. I really had to open my eyes and face my actions, and it made me realize I wanted more out of my life."

"More being...?"

"A family." And as if right on cue, Lucy comes walking in. She's supposed to sit in the chair next to me but climbs up onto my lap and nestles into my neck.

"She's a shy one?" Paul asks through laughter.

"Not really," I tell him and everyone who is going to watch. "She doesn't understand the fan part of my life, and if people have seen me out with her, they know that I won't sign autographs or take pictures. My time with her is very important to me, and Lucy gets a little jealous."

"That's 'cause you're my daddy," she whispers into my ear. I can't help the ear-to-ear grin that spreads across my face. Lucy's smile matches mine.

"It seems that you have some news to share?" Paul hedges.

"Do you want to tell everyone?" I ask Lucy.

She nods and looks at Paul. "Travis is my really real daddy now."

Paul looks at me questioningly, and I know he's waiting for me.

"I guess the cat's out of the bag now," I say, adjusting us both in the chair. "Anyone who reads the papers or watches the news knows that there was an incident at her school not too long ago, which prompted legal action by Saylor and me. Yesterday afternoon, we attended a hearing in family court where I heard one of the best sentences in my life."

"Which was?"

"You have a daughter." I can barely say the words without getting choked up. Aside from Saylor saying, "I do," or hearing, "the Boston Renegades have just won the World Series," those words said by the judge are my favorite.

"That's amazing," Paul says.

"It is." I look at Lucy and can't believe how lucky I am. Her father signed off on my request immediately, making the process move quickly through the courts. I thought we would have to wait months, if not a year or longer, considering the rape accusation, but Irvin presented a strong case for me, and Lucy's desire to have me as her father helped tremendously.

"Did you ever see yourself as a family man?"

I shake my head. "Not until I met Saylor and she showed me what it was like to have an unconditional love that loved you no matter who you are or what it is that you do with your life."

"If you decide to report for spring training, will your family go with you?"

Saylor sits down near me, far enough away that she's out of camera, but I can still see her. I look over at her and wink. "Yes, they will. We have discussed the possibility and decided that we'd all go together."

"What do you want people to take away from this interview, Travis?"

"That I'm innocent and have been wrongly accused of a crime that I didn't commit. That no matter what you may think goes on in my private life, my family and my team come first and I would never do anything to jeopardize that. Baseball has been my life, and I've adopted Boston as my hometown. I'd like to keep it that way."

"Is that your way of saying you'll be at spring training?" Paul leans forward, hopeful that I'll give him the answer. Hell, I won't know what I'm doing until I wake up that day.

"We'll see. I will definitely be in Florida, because we're going to Disney World—"

"With the babies," Lucy says, sitting up for the first time.

"The babies?"

She nods. "Babies Cal and Janie. They're sooo cute," she says.

"Lucy is talking about Cooper Bailey's twins," I add for clarity.

"And what about Travis—do you want him to play baseball?" Paul asks Lucy.

Lucy looks at me from over her shoulder and nods. "Yes."

"Travis, I'm afraid the women in your life have spoken."

I try to hide my smile, but I can't. "Whether I'll have cleats on is left to be seen, Paul."

With that, my interview is over. We shake hands, and he promises to get this edited and on the air as soon as possible. Saylor takes care of the remaining logistics while I head to Lucy's room to play dress-up. It's a tough job, but someone's gotta do it.

EPILOGUE

Saylor

"I'm in heaven!"

"He's a slice I'd like to eat."

"Too bad he's married."

"Not once he meets me."

"Those pants are so tight."

This is the conversation going on behind me and the WAGs of the Renegades. It's taking everything in me not to turn around and tell them all to shut the hell up. But this is part of the lifestyle. We take it and deal with it on our own, never letting the guys know what goes on in the stands.

They have me questioning my sanity, though, because I've always thought heaven to be white fluffy clouds, harps playing, and men in togas with wings on their backs and halos on their heads floating around without a care in the world.

According to these ladies, heaven is sitting on plastic seats in the sweltering Florida sun, watching grown men grope themselves, spit, and play in the dirt while wearing tight pants.

The tight pants I can agree with, as long as they're not skinny jeans or spandex. I'm talking about baseball pants. I'm talking about my-husband-bent-over-and-showing-me-his-ass-while-he-ties-his-shoes baseball pants.

This is my first ever spring training, and up until a few weeks ago, I didn't know if I was going to experience this as a wife or an agent. Travis waited until the night before to make his decision after he met with the team, Wes Wilson, and Ryan Stone. For hours, I paced the hotel room, waiting for him to come back and share the news with me. And when he finally did, I was elated. I knew deep in my heart that he wasn't ready to give up on baseball, and the fans of Boston aren't ready to give up on him.

In a couple of weeks, we're heading back north to begin our life as a baseball family. Travis and I have discussed his schedule, and we think it'd be best that Lucy stay home during the weeknight games due to how late they run. We are both prepared for the fight we'll have on our hands when we have to tell Lucy she can't go until the weekend. Travis is also going to be the one to take Lucy to school every day. Prior to leaving for Florida, he was the one to pick her up. He told me that he doesn't want to not be involved in her education and felt that it was important that her teachers see us, no matter what. I'm all for sleeping in if he wants to do the morning run.

My in-laws walk down the row in front of me, waving wildly. I stand and hug them both before they sit down. It's been a pleasure being in Florida and getting to know them. They absolutely dote on Lucy, and although Travis said that his family life was strained while growing up, his parents have been nothing but accommodating and accepting. My mom arrives next with her hands full of popcorn and water. She's been having a blast down here, and I have a feeling she's going to move into the house that Travis recently purchased.

Being in Boston without my mother will be difficult, and I'll miss her terribly, but moving will be good for her. She's retired and only stayed there to help me out. Now that I'm running my own business, my time can be flexible—plus, Travis will be around. And it's not like we won't visit. I fully intend to come down as much as possible, especially when the Renegades are playing.

"Did we miss anything?" Terry asks.

"Only the women behind us objectifying the men," Daisy says. Both my mother and Tonya turn and look through the gaps between us.

"Hussies," Tonya says, causing us all to laugh.

"Ignore them, Tonya. We know where Travis sleeps at night," my mother says, much to my surprise.

"Mother!"

She shrugs and doesn't turn around to look at me. Ainsley and Daisy start laughing, and I'm speechless. Maybe it's not such a good idea for the two moms to hang out with each other after all.

After the national anthem is played, the guys run out onto the field. Travis and Ethan come over to the fence where Lucy, Shaun, and Shea, Ethan's niece, are standing and give them high fives. A lot of the families have made it to Florida for spring training this year.

"Saylor?"

I look at Travis after he calls my name. He tosses a ball into the stands, caught easily by his father, who hands it to me.

"Thanks," I say, holding it in the air.

"Read it," he yells.

I turn the ball over in my hands until I come across his handwriting. *I love you, Saylor*, it says in his scrawl.

"That's so sweet," Ainsley says.

It is sweet. She has no idea. By the time I look up, Travis is in left field warming up, and I can't tell him that I feel the same way. I've actually been in love with him for a while but too scared to tell him. I didn't want to pressure him into saying it back if he wasn't ready.

Throughout the game, I look at the ball when I can't see him, and each time, my heart beats a little faster. In between innings, he's signing autographs for the kids who wait at the fence, something we hoped that Lucy would understand was part of his job—that right now he was Travis the baseball player, but at home, he was all hers.

When the game ends, everyone makes their way to their cars. I had asked my in-laws to take Lucy for the night, and my mom snickered while Tonya asked if she'd be getting another grandbaby soon. I wanted to be angry with both of them, but since Tonya had asked for another, and not her first one, I couldn't be mad. There's no doubt in my mind that the Kidds love Lucy as if she's their own blood.

I sit on the hood of our rented Chevy Camaro. It's not a practical family car, but it's a convertible and sexy as hell. A group of the guys walk out together, and when Travis sees me, he pauses.

"I'll catch you guys in the morning," he tells them.

"Practice safe sex, Kidd. Those slump-busters will get you every time," Branch yells out, laughing right along with the other guys.

"Shut the hell up, douche donkey." I join in on the laughter. I've grown to love his one-liners.

"Hey, babe," he says as he pulls my legs around his waist. He leans in and kisses me, not caring that his teammates are catcalling and telling us to get a room.

"Hey," I reply breathlessly. "Good game."

"Thanks." His hands slide up my legs until they're firmly under my shorts. "You know, this is the perfect height for me to fuck you."

"Not here," I tell him.

"Are you telling me that you'll let me find a deserted road so I can fuck you on this car?"

I nod, appeasing his request. When it comes to Travis, I'm willing to do anything he asks. "I do have one condition, though."

"Anything," he says eagerly.

"Say it again."

"Say what?" he asks with a look of confusion.

"Tell me what that ball said today. I want to hear you say it."

Travis removes one of his hands from my leg and cups my cheek. His thumb caresses my lower lip, and he stares into my eyes. "I love you, Saylor."

My breathing hitches as I hear the words. The impact is profound and life altering. I kiss the pad of his thumb and let the tears fall willingly. "I love you, Travis."

"Yeah?"

"Yeah."

"Holy fucking meat sniffer. You fucking love me."

"I do, and I have. I've been afraid to tell you out of fear that you didn't feel the same."

He kisses me deeply, and when he pulls away, he rests his forehead against mine. "That night in the bar...that's when I knew I was in love with you. I used to think that night was a mistake, but now I know it was meant to be. We were meant to weather that storm together to make us stronger. I fucking love you and Lucy so much that it hurts sometimes."

I return his kiss, caressing his stubble as my lips stay sealed to his. I have no doubt that if we could make it through that nightmare, everything else will be a cakewalk.

"You're our world, Travis."

"And that's what I'll always be."

"Come on—we have some baby-making practice to get done." I shimmy off the hood of the car and climb in *Dukes of Hazzard* style, leaving Travis speechless.

"What?" he asks as he stands there with his mouth hanging open.

"You heard me—come on. Practice makes perfect, right?"

"Oh, babe, you know me. I'm a fucking perfectionist."

That's what I'm counting on. I know that if we're going to get pregnant, it has to be now, because asking him to miss time during the season would be selfish. If it happens before we go back to Boston, then I'll be happy, and if not, we'll have a year of marriage under our belts and start trying next year.

Either way, heading off into the night sky with the roof down and the wind in our hair is a pretty good way to start off our night.

Ethan Davenport is Boston's rising baseball star. When he meets Daisy Robinson, a beautiful fan with encyclopedic baseball knowledge, Ethan thinks she can take his game to another level—if he can avoid the curveball that's coming his way...

An excerpt from

THIRD BASE

follows.

ONE

"Why do you read that shit?"

Steve Bainbridge, center fielder for my team, the Boston Renegades, throws a ball at me, causing me to drop my phone so I can
catch it. I'd rather replace a cracked screen on my phone than take a
ball to the face. Having a busted lip or a black eye isn't my idea of a
good time. He picks it up before I can and scrolls through the blog
post I had been reading. The BoRe Blogger hates me and I can't figure out why.

"Well, at least you're not being called out for retirement three
weeks into the season." Bainbridge hands me my phone and sighs.
This is my second season in the league and he's been a mentor to me.
Toward the end of last season, I had a lot going for me until I messed
up one night. Bainbridge was there to help get my ass out of hot water before our general manager, Ryan Stone, could kick me off the
team. The incident in question? I bought some drinks for a minor
who was celebrating her birthday. She was in the bar. Apparently
she had snuck in, but because I'm a Major League baseball player,

the district attorney thought he'd try to make an example out of me. Thankfully, the Renegades have a stellar legal team and I was able to get away with a few hours of community service.

Hard lesson learned. In fact, I've had to learn a few over the past year—for instance, tweeting out my address isn't the smartest thing to do. Women of all ages show up wearing next to nothing, and when your mom answers the door…Let's just say there are things even she shouldn't see.

"Are you done at the end of the season?" We prepare our whole lives for moments like this without even realizing it. Like when your best friend moves away, or the seniors on your team graduate. It's really no different when someone retires or gets traded. Retirement is harder to deal with because guys usually move back to their hometown or their wife's hometown and you don't see them as often. At least with a trade, the next time you play that team, you can hang out.

"My wife…she gave me an ultimatum. I quit or she walks with the kids."

"Oh."

"Nothing for you to worry about, kid," he says as he walks down the stairs and through the dugout, disappearing down the tunnel. Just a handful of the guys on the team have wives. It's a low statistic, according to the BoRe Blogger, citing the fact that our general manager is rebuilding a team with young talent that can last a few years. I think our GM wants to win and is doing everything he can to make sure it happens. It has nothing to do with age or marital status.

I pick up my glove and one of the loose balls sitting by my feet and toss the ball into the stands. We have two home games before we hit the road for six away and then back home for three before we get a day off. It's the start of the season and I'm already looking forward to a day off.

Before each home game, a young fan, along with his or her family, is chosen to be our guest for the game. Not only do they gain early access to the ballpark for a tour, but if a few of us are here early, we'll also come out and throw the ball around for a little while so they can watch. The fan becomes our honorary bat boy or girl for the game, going home with a ton of selfies with the players, autographs, and souvenirs.

Tonight's fan is a girl with pigtails and a thousand-watt smile. Her Renegades hat sits on top of her head, barely hanging on. Her face lights up when she catches the ball easily in her glove and she waves at me before turning to her parents with excitement. Being good to your fans is something my college coach instilled in me after every single game. It didn't matter what test we had in the morning, what the weather was, how tired we were, or whether we got our asses beat—we'd stay to sign autographs and take pictures until the last fan left. Our boss, Ryan, feels the same way. He says fans make or break you, and he's right. That's why the BoRe Blogger gets under my skin so much. I don't know who he is, but I'd like to meet him to find out what his beef is with me.

Reporters line the wall outside our clubhouse, waiting for an interview. The media is allowed in the clubhouse until batting practice begins. Cal Diamond, our manager, has a list of guys who will talk each day, even though the media tries to get audio clips from everyone. I've yet to be chosen. I try not to let it bother me, but it does. I know I'm young and say stupid shit sometimes, but I don't do it to be harmful to the team. My mouth just works faster than my brain. It's something my agent says I need to work on. Stone says he's looking for someone to come in and give us all some media training. In the meantime, I usually visit the trainer or go into our lounge before batting practice, which is off-limits to the media.

They call my name. I wave and smile like I've been instructed to do and enter the clubhouse. It's chaos in here, but it's expected on game day. The Renegades are high energy, unlike some of the other teams out there. I've heard rumors that some clubhouses are quiet zones, the "Zen" zone. We tried that once last year, and most of us fell asleep before the game started. The idea was quickly nixed, and since then the clubhouse has been a mecca for craziness.

On any given day, this room is filled with towel snapping, raunchy jokes, and guys running around bare-assed with only their jockstraps on. The one rule we have in here: no women, no wives, no girl-friends, etc....Not because we walk around naked, but because we're disgusting and our antics will give a bad impression. We want the women to remember us for what we do on the field, not the shit in here. Besides, the wives have a pretty stellar lounge that they can hang in until the game starts.

I change quickly, slipping on my long-sleeved jacket before heading back onto the field for warm-ups. It's still downright cold in Boston. There are a few cheers as we start coming out of the dugout as season ticket holders arrive early. Kids line every available space in hope of getting a high five or snagging a fly ball from batting practice. After a while, you start to recognize the same faces. I look for one in particular that I've been looking at since the midway point of last season. She usually sits parallel to third base, behind the enemy. When I look over in between plays, I swear she's staring at me. I can't always tell, though, because she wears her Renegades hat low and I can't see her eyes.

She's always in a black-and-white BoRe baseball shirt with her long hair pulled back. I've noticed that she changes the color from blond to brown depending on the season, but it's always long. She's always in the same seat for every home game, which leads me to believe she's a season ticket holder, even though, by all accounts, she seems too young to be able to afford tickets this close to the field. It also hasn't escaped my notice that the seat next to her is always empty. It should also be noted that I look for her each time I walk out of the dugout and walk to home plate, or when I finish warming up between innings. There's just something about her that keeps me interested, even though I don't know her name or anything about her.

What I *do* know and like is how she's at every home game, wearing her Renegades gear. I really like that she's a baseball fan, but more important, that she never brings a guy with her, leading me to believe she's single. I also like that she's a mystery—I know finding out who she is wouldn't be hard. I could send an usher to get her or ask the office who the seats belong to. One of these days I'll hit up the usher, because asking the front office seems like a bad idea. I don't want the ladies teasing me, and even though they're nice and motherly, they'll tease the crap out of me for showing interest in someone.

As soon as I step out onto the track, I'm looking in her direction. Her seat is still empty, but it's early. We have two hours before the first pitch. I won't start to worry yet. I've grown accustomed to having her there, even though I know in the back of my mind I'm making up most of the subtle looks I get from her.

"Looking for your girlfriend?" Travis Kidd, our left fielder, slaps me on my ass as he walks by. He turns and makes a lewd gesture with his hand and mouth. I throw a ball at his head, but he dodges it easily and starts laughing as he walks toward center field for warm-ups.

Each game, we meet out in center field to stretch for fifteen minutes as a team before breaking off for individual warm-ups. By *team*, I mean mostly starters and a few of the pitchers who will be working tonight. The rest of the guys linger in the clubhouse until it's time to work on individual stuff.

"I don't know what you're talking about," I say as I catch up with him. He puts his arm around me and makes stupid eyes at me.

"I see you looking at her, grabbing your meat diddler in between batters."

"There are *thousands* of people in the stands. I could be looking at anyone. Besides, every time I look back, you're touching your schlong dangler, so don't even think about giving me any shit."

He shrugs. "I see her looking at you, too."

"Really?" I ask, pausing midstride.

"Nope, but you just affirmed my suspicions that you're into her."

I shake my head and push him away. He stumbles a few steps before righting himself. "Ask her out," he says, in his infinite wisdom.

"Nah, it'll just be more fuel for the BoRe Blogger, and Stone is already annoyed with me. He doesn't need a reason to trade me."

Kidd bellows out a laugh, bending over and holding his stomach. I'm not sure why it's so funny—the thought of me being traded—but you don't see me laughing.

"Dude, even if you started dating the fan, Stone isn't going to trade you." He puts his arm around me and turns me toward the stands. "More than half the people in the stands are wearing your jersey. You're his young rising star, and aside from screwing up last year, which really wasn't your fault, you're the golden ticket."

Growing up, I knew I wanted to play baseball. I didn't care who drafted me, but I knew that once I had a team, that's where I wanted to stay. I worked my ass off in high school, earning a Division One scholarship to Oregon State. My junior year, we won the national championship, and from then on, I knew nothing was out of my reach.

"I want to be the next Derek Jeter." I imagine legions of fans standing and cheering for me as I tip my hat to them in thanks.

"No, you don't. You want to be Ethan Davenport. Be you, no one else."

He slaps me on the shoulder with his glove, leaving me to look out over the stadium. People file in as the smell of hot dogs and popcorn moves through the air. Their laughter mixes with the music, creating a happy ambience. Without even thinking, my eyes travel over to where I'll spend half the night. I'm out too far to see, but everything tells me that the first seat in row C, section sixty-five is occupied.

It's game night at Lowery Field and the Boston Renegades are about to take on the Baltimore Orioles.

ABOUT THE AUTHOR

Heidi McLaughlin is a *New York Times* and *USA Today* bestselling author. Originally from the Pacific Northwest, she now lives in picturesque Vermont with her husband and two daughters. Renting space in their home is an overhyper beagle/Jack Russell, Buttercup; a West Highland/mini schnauzer, JiLL; and her brother, Racicot. When she isn't writing stories, Heidi can be found sitting courtside at her daughters' basketball games.